MURDER AT THE CROWN AND ANCHOR

CLEOPATRA FOX MYSTERY, BOOK 6

C.J. ARCHER

WWW.CJARCHER.COM

CHAPTER 1

LONDON, MAY 1900

There is nothing more anxiety-inducing than waiting for a scolding you know is coming. It's like waiting for the other shoe to drop, where the shoe is made of iron and the floor of glass.

It had been a week since I'd seen Jonathon Hartly leave Uncle Ronald's office on the fourth floor of the hotel. While I couldn't be certain Jonathon told him that I'd continued to associate with Harry Armitage after being ordered not to, I suspected he was vindictive enough to do it. He'd been indignant after I rejected his advances and resentful that Harry had been the one to save Floyd from financial ruin when he could not.

No doubt Jonathon left out the business about the gambling house from his account to my uncle.

That was the only silver lining in the grim cloud about to burst over my head. Floyd may have dreadful taste in friends but he was my cousin, and I liked him. I didn't want him landing in further hot water with his autocratic father.

It was almost a relief when the summons finally came a week to the day after Jonathon called on Uncle Ronald. Relief was quickly replaced by a sense of foreboding as I presented myself at his office on a wet spring morning. I focused on the dense gray bank of clouds through the window and willed him to get on with it.

It seemed to take an age before he finally slotted his pen into the stand and set aside a list of names he'd been compiling. "Close the door, Cleopatra."

I'd left it open in the hope it would encourage Uncle Ronald to keep his voice down. I went to shut it, but it was pushed open wider from the other side. Floyd stepped inside, frowning at me.

"I saw you through the gap." He looked past me to his father. "What's the matter?" He wouldn't ordinarily intrude on a private conversation between Uncle Ronald and me, which meant he knew what this was about, or suspected, and wanted to help me if I needed defending.

I stepped aside to let him in.

Instead of sending him on his way, Uncle Ronald invited us both to sit. He clasped his hands on top of the desk and regarded me with a directness I expected from him. He was not the sort of man who beat about the bush.

"It has come to my attention that you have been in the company of Armitage, Cleopatra."

"Who says that?" Floyd asked. He had not seen Jonathon leave this very room a week ago, nor had I mentioned it, but he knew his friend's feelings towards Harry. And for me.

Uncle Ronald didn't even look at his son. "Well? Is it true?"

"I've seen Harry from time to time," I said. "He wanted my assistance with an investigation." It wasn't quite the truth, but it was close enough. "Before you forbid me from seeing him, again, I want to point out that Harry and I are merely friends. Anything more than that is impossible. Harry is a good person, trustworthy, and we work well together. Since he requires assistance with his work occasionally, and I require mental stimulation and a productive way to occupy my time, we share his case load. I'm discreet and careful. I don't put myself, my reputation, or that of the hotel and our family in any danger. Surely you can't object to that?"

I'd been thinking of what to say for an entire week, and now that the moment had arrived, it spilled out of me. My explanation had been far more eloquent in my head, but at least I managed to get the message across without letting my emotions overwhelm me, as they sometimes did when I was angry. I remained composed, not an easy thing to do under Uncle Ronald's steely stare.

The ticking clock was loud in the silence that followed. In a way, it was good that he took his time to choose his words carefully. Perhaps, like me, he was determined to keep his temper in check and have a calm conversation. "I'm glad you understand the impossibility of it," he finally said. "But does he?"

"Pardon?"

"You said, anything more than friendship is impossible. Does he realize that?"

"Yes, of course. He—"

"Armitage is a good man!" Floyd's outburst made my nerves jangle. "He gave years of loyal service to this hotel and to our family, only to be treated abominably by you."

Uncle Ronald's clasped thumbs switched positions. It was the only movement he made for several heartbeats before he finally turned to look at Floyd. "Armitage lied to me for years. He's fortunate I didn't dismiss his uncle for being complicit."

"You did, but you came to your senses in Hobart's case. You should come to your senses with Armitage, too. The hotel was better when he was assistant manager. He was an asset. The guests miss him."

"Peter just needs a little more time to settle into

the role," I felt compelled to say. I needn't have bothered. Both ignored me.

"What message would it convey to the staff if I let Armitage back?" Uncle Ronald ground out. "I'll tell you what it says. It says that I'm weak, that anyone can lie to me and get away with it. It says that I'm not a man of my word. It says that I allow a common thief into my business—into my *home*—and allow him near my family!" He grew redder with every sentence, and his moustache ends dampened with spittle.

I could throttle Floyd. His defense of Harry may have been well meaning, but he'd turned an otherwise civilized conversation into a shouting match. I may have known my uncle only a few months, but I knew how to handle him better than his own son.

Then it suddenly occurred to me. Their argument wasn't about me. It wasn't even about Harry. It was about father and son. Floyd had grown up, but his father still treated him like a child. Uncle Ronald didn't want to relinquish responsibility, not even a little, and Floyd thought he was ready for more. It was an age-old story that either ended in disaster or success, depending on how it was handled.

I was inclined to leave them to it, but since my friendship with Harry was the catalyst for their tug-of-war, I felt some responsibility to defuse the tension. "You have every right to refuse anyone entry into your hotel, Uncle."

Floyd narrowed his eyes at me but remained quiet. He seemed to realize I was working up to something.

"I do," Uncle Ronald agreed.

"But Floyd's right in that Harry is quite harmless, and his ten years of exemplary service for the hotel proves it. So," I added, speaking loudly to be heard over my uncle's blustery protest. "So, I think there's no harm in me helping him with his investigations when required. We'll maintain a respectable, professional relationship. We're hardly even friends, really, and there is no danger of a misunderstanding between us. I am very content as a spinster, and Harry is courting someone."

That knocked the wind out of my uncle's sails. He looked as though he was getting ready to protest again, but suddenly sat back, deflated. "He is?"

"Her name is Miss Morris. I've met her. She's charming and beautiful, and they're both quite besotted."

The latter may or may not be true, but the former was my honest opinion. Miss Morris *was* charming and beautiful. She was also intelligent and tall. She was perfect for Harry, and unless he was blind and stupid, he ought to be in love with her.

It was a given that she was already in love with him. Few women didn't fall under his spell upon first meeting him. And when he gave a woman his full attention…

I shoved the thought of our kiss aside. Now wasn't the time to think about that heady moment when we'd kissed in St James's Park. I needed to give *this* moment my full attention or Uncle Ronald could make my life difficult. I wouldn't put it past him to assign a chaperone to accompany me whenever I left the hotel.

Uncle Ronald's face settled into its usual soft folds as his temper dissipated. "You should have mentioned Miss Morris earlier."

I bit my tongue so as not to tell him that I'd been about to when Floyd interrupted. "If Harry requires my help with another investigation—and it's by no means certain that he ever will again—it won't interfere with my social responsibilities. I'll attend every party, dinner and picnic Aunt Lilian wishes me to attend. I'll dance with whomever you wish, and I'll be the most amiable companion for Flossy. When my aunt isn't feeling well, I'll be glad to be Flossy's chaperone. I'll be sure she only talks to gentlemen of good breeding."

Uncle Ronald seemed pleased, even relieved, when I mentioned taking over chaperoning duties from my aunt. With her health not improving, and the whirlwind of the social season leaving her more tired and fraught than ever, a back-up plan was needed. At twenty-three, I was old enough.

He grunted as he came to a conclusion. "Miss Morris won't like it if Armitage asks you to assist him."

It was a good point but I remained silent. I couldn't speak for her.

He stroked his moustache and chin in thought. "Very well. You may work with him if he asks, and as long as it doesn't interfere with your social engagements." He waggled a finger at me. "Be sure he pays you fairly for your time."

"I already do."

He smiled. "Good girl. I expect nothing less from my niece."

I refrained from reminding him that I was only his niece by marriage and that any traits we had in common were purely coincidental. I didn't dare rock the boat now that he'd given his permission for me to work with Harry.

Uncle Ronald dismissed us with a flick of his wrist. I stood, relief making me feel lighter.

Thank you, Miss Morris.

There was a brief knock on the door and Uncle Ronald bade Mr. Hobart to enter. The hotel manager must have just come from his morning meeting with the senior staff. They held one every morning to discuss the day's arrivals, departures and important events. Once a week, he also held a meeting with all the staff, including the maids, porters and footmen. He was a hands-on manager, and they respected him for it.

Mr. Hobart smiled at Floyd and me. We exchanged pleasantries before he approached the desk and handed Uncle Ronald a piece of paper.

"More potential guests for the dinner, sir. Did you have any luck with the first batch?" He indicated the list my uncle had been notating upon our arrival.

Uncle Ronald stroked his moustache as he looked over the new list. "Not a great deal, no. Most declined. I haven't heard from the others." He tossed the piece of paper onto the desk with a click of his tongue. "Blast it. We need them, Hobart. If they don't come, nobody will care and the restaurant will be an utter failure. I can't afford it to fail. Is that understood?"

Mr. Hobart swallowed. "Yes, sir."

"Then get them to come!"

"I'll do my best, sir."

Uncle Ronald muttered something into his moustache that nobody heard. It was probably just as well. He'd slumped into one of his morose moods. When there was a problem with the hotel, he tended to get angry and sort it out, or become glum if he didn't know how.

Of all things that could have happened next, the most unexpected one did. Floyd stepped forward.

"Is this a guest list for the restaurant's opening night?"

"Not the *official* opening," Mr. Hobart clarified. "We want to have a private dinner for select honored guests, serving the most delicious and exotic courses that's ever been served in a London restaurant. It will be a spectacle for the senses."

"It'll be expensive," my uncle muttered.

Mr. Hobart powered on. "It'll be free for the guests, of course. The idea is to have it mentioned in all the newspapers. The more important the guests, the more the journalists will clamor to report on it. The resulting publicity will have everyone flocking to dine at the Mayfair Hotel's new restaurant."

"Can I look at the list?" Floyd asked.

Uncle Ronald didn't move so Mr. Hobart scooped up both lists and handed them to Floyd. "This group is our first choice. The second group will be invited if the first decline." He sighed. "Alas, it's looking as though we'll need a third tier."

Uncle Ronald swore under his breath. "I don't understand it. Why are they not interested?"

"They already have their preferred dining establishments," Mr. Hobart said in the voice I'd heard him use to placate irritated guests. "The Savoy, Claridges, the Carlton—"

"Yes, yes."

Floyd handed the lists back to Mr. Hobart. "It doesn't matter. These people aren't going to garner interest from the press."

"Why not?" Mr. Hobart asked.

"They're not fashionable enough."

Uncle Ronald bristled. "The Duchess of Manchester isn't fashionable? She's one of the prince's friends! She's a celebrated beauty!"

"*Was.* She's getting on a bit, nowadays. But I'd leave her on the list."

"Would you now."

"She's still influential. Lady de Grey is also worth inviting. She knows a lot of artists and actors." Floyd pointed to another name halfway down the list. "But he no longer has the prince's favor." He pointed to several more names. "Hartington is old and Cumberland has lost his marbles. Strathconnen became a bore after he married, and the Honorable Susan Malvern hasn't been seen in society for more than a year. Do you want me to go on?"

His father snatched the lists off him. "You would have us fill the most exclusive dining venue with rabble-rousers and singers, no doubt."

"Only the rabble-rousers of impeccable pedigree, and singers if they happen to be the companion of someone important. I can think of a few who fit the bill. Any more than three or four and the society ladies won't come."

I wondered if his own mistress was among them. Apparently she was an actress.

"We need to get into the papers for all the *right* reasons, Floyd. Not because we're providing the latest scandal."

"That's precisely what we do want! To make it into the newspapers these days, you have to provide them with something of interest. Dull old dignitaries that no one is interested in won't make the *Middling Morning Herald* let alone *The Times*." He indicated the lists in his father's hand. "You have two politicians on there, for goodness' sake."

His father sniffed. "You've said your piece, now if you don't mind, I'm busy. Hobart, how are the preparations proceeding for the restaurant? Now that the structural work is complete, I expect you to be creating the right sort of ambience with lighting, decorations and what-not."

Mr. Hobart cleared his throat. "I didn't realize you wanted a detailed update on the restaurant this morning, sir."

"What did you expect? A tea party? The dinner is five days away and all I've got is an empty shell. Of course I want an update on the restaurant. I want to know what it'll look like in case any of these guests decide to show." He picked up one of the lists only to screw it into a ball and toss it into the waste basket near his feet.

Mr. Hobart swallowed heavily. "I've appointed

Mr. Chapman to work with a designer. As steward, he knows what diners want. He also has some exciting ideas and an eye for detail. Shall I fetch him?"

"Yes!"

Mr. Hobart retreated from the office as if he'd been pushed out by my uncle's bellow. Floyd followed, but I hung back. Considering Uncle Ronald's black mood, what I was about to say was risky, but I wanted to do it for Floyd's sake. Besides, it helped knowing that my uncle's temper was a result of anxiety over the opening of the restaurant, and I was going to suggest a way to alleviate some of it.

"You should let Floyd help you," I said.

"So he can make a mess of things like he usually does?"

I winced and hoped Floyd wasn't outside listening. "He may not be the most responsible person, but he's got some fine qualities. Qualities that marry well with what you need right now."

He didn't dismiss me, which meant I had his attention.

I took it as a sign to go on. "I remember the New Year's Eve ball when you wanted Floyd's friends to attend. They were young and popular and just what the ball needed, you said."

"That was a party. The guests for the opening night dinner must represent the type of diner we want in our restaurant. Quality."

"The people you want will follow the fashionable set, and *they* will go where they'll be seen. For that, you need the attention of the press. I know Mr. Hobart and Mr. Chapman will make the restaurant shine, and Mrs. Poole will serve the most exciting menu London has ever seen. But without the press clamoring to write about it, it'll come to naught. I think Floyd knows how to get the press interested better than Mr. Hobart or Mr. Chapman, or even you, Uncle. If I've learned one thing since arriving in London, it's that being fashionable means belonging to a particular group who are young. Floyd has contacts amongst that set. He knows what interests them. He knows what sort of experience will entice them to come."

Uncle Ronald gave a flicker of his eyelashes before dismissing me with a nod directed at the door. I left, but as I closed the door behind me, I saw him crumple up the second guest list and throw it into the waste basket.

I released a breath and turned away from the door to see Floyd and Mr. Hobart watching me. They'd been out of earshot, thank goodness. Their twin expressions of concern made me smile.

"Everything will be all right," I assured them.

"All right for you, you mean," Floyd muttered. "He's letting you investigate with Armitage again."

Mr. Hobart beamed. "Marvelous! No more

sneaking around. Not that they did," he quickly added for Floyd's benefit.

"My father's right, though. Miss Morris won't like it if Armitage asks you to investigate with him, Cleo. Women don't like other women seeing their man when they're not around. Trust me, I learned that the hard way." He frowned. "There is a Miss Morris, isn't there?"

I laughed. "I didn't make her up."

"She exists," Mr. Hobart said. "I've met her. Lovely young woman and quite beautiful."

I schooled my features, determined not to let him see how much I loathed the idea of Harry besotted with a beautiful and lovely young woman, one he'd already introduced to his family. I had no right to be jealous. This feeling would pass, in time. Until then, I would try not to think about him with her.

What I needed was an investigation to distract me. One where Harry wasn't involved.

Floyd rocked back on his heels, looking smug. While he liked Harry, he worried there was something more between us, despite my assurances that we were merely friends. For some reason, he didn't believe me, and he didn't want me to be with someone he thought beneath me. The presence of Miss Morris pleased him. It seemed to please everyone.

"So that's the end of that," he said. "No more

investigating for you, Cleo. Armitage's girl will see to it."

I kept my mouth shut. Like my uncle, he seemed to think the only investigating I did was at Harry's request. But I undertook my own investigations. Now all I needed to do was find one.

As it happened, one fell in my lap.

Mr. Hobart withdrew a torn newspaper article from his jacket pocket and sighed. He passed it to Floyd. "I was going to show your father this obituary before we got sidetracked. I thought he'd want to know."

Floyd read the three lengthy paragraphs about the deceased man named Tobias Plumtree. "I remember him. He used to stay here when he was in London before he married. He often dined at our table. Father liked him but I never cared for him much. He never had time for me." He handed the article back. "It doesn't say how he died."

"That's because it was by his own hand, if one believes the official verdict."

"You don't think it was suicide?" I asked.

Mr. Hobart stared down at the picture. "He didn't seem like the type, from what I remember of him. Harry tends to agree. While he doesn't remember him well from Plumtree's stays here, he told me at dinner last night that he came across him in his current investigation."

"What investigation?"

"I can't tell you, Miss Fox, sorry. Harry wouldn't even tell me."

"I wonder if it has something to do with Mr. Massie," Floyd mused.

Mr. Hobart looked up. "The Salt King?"

"Massie approached me a few days ago at our club and asked me what I thought of Armitage, whether he was reliable, discreet, that sort of thing. He'd seen his agency's name in the newspaper some time ago, I believe, and was considering hiring him, although he didn't say why. I told him he was an excellent assistant manager and the most upstanding chap. I assured him he'd put the same energy and discretion into his new investigative venture as he had in his work here."

"Thank you, sir. That's very kind of you to give such a glowing report of my nephew." Mr. Hobart seemed overwhelmed by Floyd's support. If he knew what Floyd owed Harry, he wouldn't be so surprised. Giving a glowing report was the least Floyd could do. "Harry gave me no specifics about his investigation. All he would say was that he met Mr. Plumtree again recently, and that he didn't think he would take his own life. My brother also expressed doubts, something to do with the manner of death."

Mr. Hobart's brother was Harry's adopted father, Mr. Stephen Hobart, a detective inspector at Scotland Yard until recently. He'd been forced into early retirement by superiors who didn't like that he brought those in the highest levels of society to justice. If he doubted suicide was the cause of death then that was enough for me to doubt it too.

I headed for the lift and pressed the button to alert the operator. Floyd and Mr. Hobart followed and waited with me.

"I know that look," Floyd said. "You're going to speak to Armitage, aren't you?"

"I'm going to pay a call on a friend I haven't seen for several days. If we happen to discuss his current investigation, then so be it."

He scowled. "This is your fault, Hobart. I don't know why you told her about Armitage's doubts over Plumtree's demise. You know what she's like."

Mr. Hobart smiled his benign smile. "I'm afraid I have no idea what you're referring to, sir."

CHAPTER 2

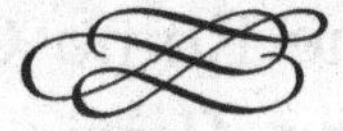

My determination to conduct my next investigation alone to distract me from Harry and Miss Morris was not off to a good start. I could see no way around this meeting, however. To discover more about Tobias Plumtree and the doubts surrounding his apparent suicide, I had to speak to Harry. Hopefully after this initial conversation, I wouldn't need to consult him again. His own investigation didn't directly involve Plumtree, and he would have no interest in investigating Plumtree's death if it turned out to be murder. There was no paying client. Harry couldn't afford to take on another investigation where he received no compensation.

I could, to a point, but it would be beneficial if a grateful relative offered me financial reward for proving he didn't end his own life. It was a slim hope, but one I held onto. Even without payment, an investigation gave me something to do for the next little while. There was only so much shopping with Flossy I could bear.

I didn't stop at the Roma Café when I reached Broadwick Street, Soho. Persistent rain meant I had to keep my umbrella up all the way to the door, and I couldn't juggle it along with two coffee cups and the door handle. I pushed open the door, lowered the umbrella and held it away from my skirt as I ascended the stairs to Harry's office. I opened his door without knocking.

He'd been in the process of throwing his coat on, preparing to leave. He paused for a mere moment, took in my presence with barely a flicker of surprise, and continued to put on his coat. "That didn't take long."

His collar wasn't sitting smoothly, but I resisted the urge to fix it. Getting that close to him wasn't a good idea given the way my pulse quickened at the mere sight of him after several days apart. "What didn't?"

"For my uncle to inform you of the suspicions surrounding Tobias Plumtree's death, and for you to assume he was murdered and take on the investigation, despite nobody asking you to."

"Am I that predictable?"

He gave my umbrella a pointed look. "You're dripping on my floor."

I slotted the umbrella into the cast iron holder then took a seat. "It is murder, isn't it? If it's not suicide, what else can it be?"

Harry removed his coat and sat on the other side of the desk. Wherever he was heading off to, it mustn't be urgent or he would have sent me on my way. He seemed quite content to stay and chat about Mr. Plumtree. "Most people would assume an accident. But not you, Cleo."

"*Could* it have been an accident?"

"No."

"There you are then."

One corner of his lips tilted in amusement. "The official verdict is that he hanged himself. Unofficially, I had doubts which I voiced to my father last night over dinner. He agreed, but for a different reason. Plumtree was a short man, and the stool on which he supposedly stood before kicking away was too low. Even if he stood on his toes, the noose couldn't have reached his neck."

"Your father is familiar with the case?"

"Apparently the lead investigator is not up to snuff, and his second asked my father for advice. Unfortunately, he was unable to re-open the investigation without the lead's consent and a verdict of suicide has been recorded. My father wouldn't have even mentioned it to me except that I voiced my opinion to him after seeing the obituary."

"And he hoped you would look into it?"

"I told him I'd try but I'm busy with my own case and can't take on another where I won't get paid. Uncle Alfred must have decided to tell you about it. It makes sense to involve you since Plumtree was a frequent guest at the Mayfair before he married and some of the staff might remember him."

Mr. Hobart seemed to think I didn't need to be paid. While Harry knew I wanted to become financially independent from my family, he wouldn't have told anyone without my consent. It was quite possible Mr. Hobart thought I was wealthy in my own right. Many people did.

My maternal grandparents had been rich. My mother and her sister, Aunt Lilian, were their only heirs. But they'd cut my mother out of an inheritance when she defied them and married my father, a mathematics professor. My aunt inherited everything, most of which went to renovating Uncle Ronald's mansion home to turn it into the Mayfair Hotel.

I suddenly became aware that Harry had been staring at me for several seconds. When he realized I noticed, he looked away and focused on the window. "It's still raining," he said.

"Dreadful weather we've been having."

"Hopefully it won't last."

The conversation was as dreary as the weather. Unfortunately I failed to improve it with my next comment. "You look well."

"As do you."

"Miss Morris must agree with you."

He made a sound in his throat, part cough, part choke.

"Tell me what you know about Tobias Plumtree," I said quickly. "Why don't you think he took his own life?"

"He was self-centered and arrogant. He treated his staff poorly and those he considered beneath him with contempt. Including me."

"The obituary said his company experienced some problems recently but didn't go into detail."

"That's one of the reasons the verdict of suicide was reached. Gooding and Plumtree is a shipping firm. They suffered a substantial loss when one of their ships went down in January, losing some of the crew and all of its cargo."

"How awful."

"The business is strong enough that it didn't ruin it."

"Did he feel a sense of responsibility for the loss of life? Could he have killed himself out of remorse?"

"The man I met didn't seem capable of empathy. When I brought up the tragedy, he was dismissive."

"Why did you need to talk about the ship sinking with him?"

He crossed his arms. "I was wondering when you'd ask about my investigation. I can't tell you, Cleo. It's confidential."

"Come now, Harry, you can confide in me. You know I'm discreet. Mr. Massie will never know I'm assisting you."

It took him a moment to work out how I knew his client's name. "Floyd," he said flatly.

"He told me he spoke to Mr. Massie about you, but he didn't know why the Salt King needed your services."

"Massie wants total confidentiality. Details of my investigation are given only to those who need to know. Currently that consists of me and me alone." He rose to put on his coat.

I stood too. "Currently? That sounds as though you may need my assistance at some point."

He drew my umbrella out of the holder and handed it to me, but he did not let go. Our hands were close but not touching. "You're reading too much into my words, as usual."

"Then you shouldn't say anything that is open to interpretation."

He tugged ever so slightly on the umbrella, drawing me closer. We stood toe to toe, my nose reaching the height of his chest. My blood quickened. My skin tightened in anticipation of his touch. I tilted my head back to regard him properly. The heat in his hooded gaze thrilled me and worried me at the same time. I wasn't sure what to do. Stand on my toes and kiss him? Or step away?

He made the decision for us both. With a sharp intake of breath, his fingers brushed mine before he released the umbrella. He plucked his hat off the stand and turned to the door. "My father will want to speak to you. I'm having afternoon tea with my parents at three-thirty. You should come."

It wasn't the most enthusiastic invitation, but I accepted before I knew what I was saying.

Harry opened the door and indicated I should walk ahead of him. At the base of the stairs, before we stepped outside into the rain, he said, "If it does turn out to be murder, you will be careful, won't you? Don't confront the killer alone. I'm always available to help."

"I promised my uncle I'll be careful, and I plan to keep that promise."

His brows shot up his forehead. "He has given his permission for you to investigate?"

"And his permission for me to investigate with you."

His jaw dropped and his eyes widened. "Why the change of heart?"

I almost told him that his relationship with Miss Morris had given Uncle Ronald the assurance he needed that Harry wasn't interested in me romantically, but I stopped myself. I didn't want him to know there was a condition attached to the agreement. "I can be quite convincing when I want to be," was all I said, adding a wink for good measure.

He chuckled as he held the front door open. I put up my umbrella and stepped out. Harry flipped up his coat collar, put on his hat, and rushed ahead, skipping over puddles with ease.

* * *

I HURRIED BACK to the hotel with the umbrella pulled as close to my hat as possible to avoid getting wet further. My efforts were thwarted when an omnibus sporting a large advertisement for Colman's Mustard barreled through a puddle as I approached the hotel. I received a drenching and a teasing from both Frank the doorman, and Goliath, one of the porters.

"Didn't you leave in a light blue dress, Miss?" Frank said as he tried to contain a grin. "Now it's more of a muddy color." Grinning wasn't Frank's natural state. He was a crusty old scowler, but he seemed to take delight in my predicament. At least my filthy, wet condition was good for something.

Goliath sniffed the air above my head. "You smell like the gutter, Miss Fox. No offense."

"Saying 'no offense' doesn't lessen the blow, Goliath." I joined them under the porch roof and lowered my umbrella. "Do either of you remember a guest by the name of Tobias Plumtree? He used to stay here a few years ago but stopped after buying a house in the city upon his marriage."

Goliath shook his head, but Frank knew the name. "He had a nice growler that his coachman kept in perfect nick."

"What can you tell me about Mr. Plumtree?"

"He was rude. Never so much as a please or thank you. Toss-pot."

A carriage arrived and Frank put on a welcoming smile, raised his umbrella, and stepped forward to open the door and greet the gentleman and lady inside. He was accustomed to faking amiability when required. None of the guests ever knew how cantankerous he truly was.

I left them to their work and headed inside, depositing my wet umbrella in the holder on my way past. The foyer was busy. Given the weather, some guests had elected to stay indoors. All of the burgundy leather armchairs were occupied and several groups stood about, talking. A woman read aloud from a slim guidebook in an American accent while her two younger charges listened in. The girls couldn't have been more than fifteen or sixteen and hung on the older woman's every word as she read out that Bond and Regent Streets were the best for shopping.

I spotted Mr. Hobart conversing with two men

dressed in the loose, colorful shirts traditionally worn in Western Africa, while Peter nodded along as a pinch-lipped woman complained about the wallpaper in her room being too bright. I wasn't sure how he was going to solve that one. The wallpaper couldn't be changed and the hotel was full. The social season had begun and there was hardly a room to be found in any of the city's luxury hotels. The upper class had descended on London like a plague of locusts. New friendships would be forged in the coming weeks, and old ones renewed. Betrothals would be made and affairs begun—or ended. It was the season where entertainment of any description could be had, for a price, and excess was expected. Gossip would spread like a disease, fueled by scandal.

I'd had a taste of it during my last investigation, both as an observer and its victim. Being labeled a bluestocking hadn't bothered me, although it upset my cousin, albeit briefly. Any lingering nastiness about my education had soon been forgotten when more salacious tidbits about more important people were unearthed. It remained to be seen if anyone still cared enough to snub me.

Instead of waiting with the small gathering at the lift, I took the stairs to the fourth floor. I changed into dry clothes then went in search of Harmony. I found her on the third floor, pushing her cart between rooms. She parked it alongside a door and knocked. When no one answered, she un-locked it with her key and collected a bottle of fur-niture polish and a cloth from the cart. She spotted me approaching before she entered.

"What are you doing here?" She glanced around to make sure nobody saw us. While it wasn't for-bidden, we both knew my family and the guests would frown upon a maid and a member of the Bainbridge family talking familiarly.

"I have a new case."

She jerked her head, indicating we should talk inside. I grabbed another cloth from the cart and followed her. She closed the door, something she never did when cleaning a room.

"What sort of case?" she asked as she set the bottle of polish on the table. This room was smaller than my suite. The bedroom and sitting room were all bundled into one space, but at least it had an en suite bathroom. Not all of the rooms did.

I told her about Tobias Plumtree's demise and how Harry and his father didn't think he killed himself. She stopped polishing the chair leg and straightened at the mention of Harry. She made no snide comments, however. Once upon a time, she would have scolded me for seeing him. Nowadays she believed me when I said I'd never encourage Harry.

She'd also expressed her disinterest in giving her life over to a husband's control, but it hadn't stopped her flirting with Victor, one of the hotel's cooks. As far as I knew, it hadn't gone beyond flirting and walking home to the residence hall together in the evenings.

"Do you remember Mr. Plumtree?" I asked.

She shook her head. "He must have stayed here before my time. I'll ask the maids who've been here longer and get Victor to ask the cooks."

I smiled. "The cooks wouldn't have had anything to do with a guest."

"They might remember his meal preferences," she said huffily.

"Which would assist with the investigation how?"

"I don't know yet, do I?" She pointed at the table I'd been polishing. "You need to go in an anti-clockwise direction now."

"Why?"

"Because going in the same direction all the time wears the grain away in a lopsided pattern."

I did as she suggested, even though I suspected she'd made it up to change the subject. "If you want to speak to Victor you don't need to invent an excuse."

That was met with total silence.

I finished the table and helped Harmony change the sheets on the bed.

"You don't have to help," she said as she re-tucked my side to her more exacting standard. "I do this every day on my own."

"Actually, I have another question to ask."

"Go on."

I stuffed the pillow inside the pillow slip and shook it into place. "I'm going to afternoon tea at Harry's parents' place. His mother doesn't like me."

"Can you blame her? You had her son dismissed from his excellent position here as assistant manager. I'd hate you, too, if I was his mother."

"I didn't have him dismissed. Not on purpose anyway." I threw the pillow at her.

She caught it deftly. "You want my advice on how to win her over?"

"Yes."

"I don't think I'm the best person to ask. I don't care if people don't like me. You do care." She hugged the pillow to her chest as she studied me. "I wouldn't wear that if I was you."

I looked down at the dress I'd changed into. It was sage green with applique flowers of cream on the skirt and a cream lace panel at my décolletage. I'd pinned a black ribbon around my waist and another at my throat. Although my aunt insisted I no longer needed to wear mourning, I wanted some black on my daytime outfits for a little longer. "What's wrong with it?"

"The Hobarts are humble people. You dress like a toff these days."

I sighed. It was true. I'd arrived in London in December with little more than the black dress I'd been wearing in mourning for my grandmother. Ever since, my aunt had kept the city's dressmakers busy making me new outfits suitable for the niece of the owner of the Mayfair Hotel. Uncle Ronald had paid for them all, and not begrudged a penny of it. He was generous with his money, as long as the spending of it served a purpose. Beautiful ball gowns and day dresses were precisely what I needed if I was going to represent the Bainbridge family, and therefore the Mayfair Hotel.

I sighed. "You're right. I'll change into something plainer before I go."

"If Mrs. Hobart is the sort to find fault in anything you do—"

"She is."

"Then you should wear black. She'll think it inappropriate to be seen in lighter colors only six months after your grandmother's passing."

"True, and I don't want to do anything that would make her think poorly of me."

She smiled as she settled the pillow onto the bed. "A person would think you were trying to impress her."

"Then a person would be wrong. I have no reason to impress Mrs. Hobart. It's as you said, I just want to be liked by everyone."

"If you say so." She threw the second pillow at

me. I wasn't ready and it hit me in the face. She giggled.

"Now you're just asking for trouble."

I picked up the pillow, but instead of throwing it back at her, I chased her around the room until she managed to snatch up a pillow of her own and defend herself. After a vigorous pillow fight that ended in giggles and gasps for air, we finished cleaning the room together then parted ways in the corridor.

* * *

THE HOME of Harry's parents was a comfortable family abode in Ealing, within walking distance of the railway station. Fortunately the rain stopped just before I left the hotel so I remained dry and didn't drip all over Mrs. Hobart's clean floor. Thankfully Harry was already there when I arrived. It would have been awkward if he was late.

It was somewhat awkward anyway. Mrs. Hobart's stiff greeting at the door left me with no doubt about her feelings towards me. We exchanged excessively polite greetings before she got in her first comment about Miss Morris, although Miss Morris's name was never actually mentioned.

"Harry has been *very* well of late," she said as she directed me towards the sitting room. "He's been so settled, so happy this past week."

"I'm pleased to hear it."

"Not that we've seen much of him, his father and me. He's been much too busy to call on us every day like he used to."

"That's a shame."

"Oh no, not at all! Not when the reason for his busy-ness is making him happy."

She indicated I should enter the sitting room ahead of her. Harry and his father stood. D.I. Hobart—I couldn't get used to calling him Mister after knowing him as Detective Inspector since our first encounter—greeted me with more amiability and familiarity than his wife. We'd worked together on a few occasions so it was understandable, but his welcome was in stark contrast to Mrs. Hobart's.

Harry's greeting was somewhat odd, too. "I haven't seen that dress in a while. Has something happened?"

I smoothed my hand over my waist and down my black skirt. "Nobody has died," I assured him. "Nobody I know, that is. I just thought it…more appropriate than what I had on earlier."

He frowned. Then his gaze slowly moved to his mother as she headed off towards the kitchen. He didn't quite smile, but his features lifted in amusement. "You'll have to try harder than that," he said under his breath.

"Care to offer any hints as to what I should do?"

With another barely perceptible movement of

his features, the amusement was replaced by earnestness. "Just be yourself."

"That's no help at all."

D.I. Hobart tracked his wife's retreat with the subtle gaze of a man used to hiding it, then suddenly sat forward. Her departure was his signal to begin talking about the only thing that mattered to him at that moment. The death of Mr. Plumtree.

"Did Harry tell you about the stool?" he asked.

"Father," Harry chided. "Don't you want to know how Cleo's family is?"

"Yes, yes, of course, but your mother will be back in a moment and she won't want to hear all the gruesome details of the case. Let's get them out of the way first. So, the stool. It was too low. If Plumtree stood on it to hang himself, he would need to jump into the noose."

"Then we can rule out hanging as the cause of death," I said.

D.I. Hobart shook his head. "It *was* the cause of death, but it wasn't suicide. Hanging as a method for murder is not only incredibly rare, it's also very difficult. There were no other marks on the victim, no evidence of a struggle, so he must have been incapacitated beforehand. Plumtree wasn't a large man, but he still would have been heavy. A single murderer would have been strong, or there was more than one. A woman on her own, for example, couldn't have done it."

"Do we know how he was incapacitated?" I asked.

"He reeked of alcohol, so my former colleague told me. There were also two empty bottles of wine in the room and he had no companions that night, according to witnesses at the inn."

"Inn? He didn't die at home?"

"The Crown and Anchor, down by the Royal Docks. He'd rented a room for the night and ordered the bottles. The innkeeper took them up, but saw nobody with Plumtree, although he admits he didn't go into the room."

Why did a wealthy man with a London house take a room at a dockside inn?

Mrs. Hobart returned, carrying a tray. "Try these iced butter biscuits, Miss Fox. They were a favorite of a particular friend of Harry's the other day when she joined us for afternoon tea." She gave Harry a secret little smile, even though it was no secret who she was referring to.

I selected a biscuit and took a bite. "They're delicious."

"She ate two. I don't know how she has such a slim figure."

Harry shot his mother a glare but she didn't seem to notice.

"It's a mystery," D.I. Hobart muttered absently.

I made sure to select a second biscuit when I finished my first and praise Mrs. Hobart again for their taste while she poured the tea.

"Speaking of mysteries," D.I. Hobart went on, "some witnesses have said Plumtree was acting nervously in the days before his death. He was worried, kept looking over his shoulder, locking his door when he usually didn't, that sort of thing."

I accepted the teacup and saucer from Mrs. Hobart. "What triggered his nervousness?"

D.I. Hobart couldn't answer that.

"It must have been premeditated," Harry said. "It's unlikely the murderer found a length of rope lying around the room. He must have brought it with him. Given the chosen method was hanging, the murderer clearly wanted the police to think Plumtree killed himself. But anyone who knew him would know he wasn't remorseful over the loss of life resulting from the ship sinking."

"So the murderer wasn't close to him," I went on, "but was close enough to know about the sinking."

D.I. Hobart set down his teacup. "You're jumping to conclusions without enough evidence."

He was right, and I didn't want to fall into that trap again.

"Tell me some facts about him," I said. "I understand he married a much younger woman."

"His widow is in her mid-twenties. They have a young son."

"Does she inherit the business?" Mrs. Hobart asked, proving she was interested. The wife of a former Scotland Yard detective must be used to discussing cases with him, and this one was no exception. "That's a strong motive for murder, particularly if he was unkind to her."

"I don't know, but I can find out."

"It will only be half the business," Harry pointed out. "His partner, Gooding, controls the other half."

He said it with such assurance that I wondered if Mr. Gooding was part of Harry's investigation for Mr. Massie. It was possible the man known as the Salt King used Gooding and Plumtree's company to ship his salt around the world. Perhaps he had cargo on the ship that sank and employed Harry to find out why it sank and whether it could happen again.

"What about other family members?" I asked. "Is there anyone else who could lay claim to an inheritance?"

D.I. Hobart accepted another biscuit as his wife passed around the plate. "I don't know. Plumtree's background is largely unknown. If this was deemed a murder case by Scotland Yard, someone would be digging into it, but nobody is." He shook his head at the biscuit. "Shame." He popped the morsel into his mouth.

"He's a self-made man," Harry said, proving he

knew more about Mr. Plumtree than he'd originally let on. "He came up from the slums here in London."

"Whereabouts?"

"I don't know. Plumtree wasn't directly part of my investigation."

"No, but Gooding was," I said, thinking out loud. "And if Gooding was but not Plumtree, then your investigation isn't about the business or you'd be investigating both. So it's a private matter, relating to Gooding alone."

Harry's lips twisted. "Nice deduction, Cleo. Care to be more specific?"

"Not yet, but I *will* find out why the Salt King hired you."

"I don't doubt it," he said softly.

Mrs. Hobart thrust the plate of biscuits at me. "Your family are friends with the Massies, I suppose."

I had an inkling as to where her line of questioning was going, but I pretended ignorance. "I've met his daughter."

"Your friends are very different to Harry's. Their paths would never cross socially."

Harry sprang off the sofa and picked up the teapot. "More tea, Cleo?"

I rose. "I should go. Thank you for the tea and biscuits, Mrs. Hobart. I could have eaten the entire plate, but I must watch my waistline."

Her lips flattened as her gaze dropped to my waist. "Hmmm."

D.I. Hobart stood. "Where will you start your investigation?"

"At the Crown and Anchor."

"Then you'll need the address." He fished into his jacket pocket and removed a notepad. He flipped the pages until he found the one he wanted and tore it out. He handed it to me. "This is the address of the inn, as well as Plumtree's home address—you should speak to the widow—and the office of Gooding and Plumtree."

"You can't go alone to the Crown and Anchor," Harry said. "I'll accompany you."

Mrs. Hobart's lips flattened further.

"I'll be perfectly fine at a pub during the day, Harry. I've visited them as part of our investigations before."

"Not ones at the docks. You'll stand out like a mermaid on a rock."

"I'll wear this dress."

"And yet you'll still attract attention. I'm going with you. I insist."

His mother stamped her hand on her hip. "But you can't! You're busy."

"I can spare half a day."

She clicked her tongue. "Harry, think of...your particular friend. She won't like it."

"She'll understand."

Mrs. Hobart opened her mouth to protest again but closed it when her husband rested his hand on her lower back. "I think it's a good idea for Harry to go. The inns near the docks are not suitable for ladies."

"Then perhaps she shouldn't go at all." Mrs. Hobart pulled away and gathered up the teacups and saucers with China-rattling vigor.

Harry escorted me to the front door. "Sorry about that," he said with a shake of his head.

"Don't be. She clearly likes Miss Morris and hopes that you… She hopes to see her again." I cleared my throat. "Shall we meet at your office tomorrow morning?"

"Ten o'clock, sharp. Can you manage an early start after a late night tonight?"

"How did you know I was in for a late night?"

He grinned. "You're not the only good detective in London."

I rolled my eyes. "You guessed, didn't you, and I just confirmed it. Considering it's the height of the season, it was quite an easy guess that I'd be going somewhere. A truly good detective would know *where* I was going tonight."

"The opera."

I stared at him. How had he known that?

He gave me a smug look. He wasn't going to tell me.

"Harry!" Mrs. Hobart called from behind him. "Come and help with the dishes."

I wanted to tell him to reassure his mother that he liked Miss Morris very much, and ours was simply a professional relationship. But I simply gave him a wave and trotted down the front steps.

CHAPTER 3

I found Harmony in the staff parlor. She wasn't alone. Victor sat on one chair with his feet on another opposite. Harmony stood beside him, her skirt and a lock of loose hair in motion as if she'd just moved suddenly. Her eyes were wide, her lips red and full.

She heaved out a deep breath. "It's only you." She sat and fixed her hair.

Victor sported a small smile and similarly red lips. The scar on his cheek stood stark white amidst his blush. "Afternoon, Miss Fox. How's the investigation coming along?"

"It's early days yet. I'm going to the Crown and Anchor at the Royal Docks tomorrow. Do you know it?"

I'd directed the question to Victor but both nodded. "It's a rough place," he said. "Want me to accompany you before my shift?"

"Harry's coming with me."

Harmony finished tucking the last errant curl into a hairpin. "Make sure he doesn't claim this investigation as his own. It's yours. Pay him for his time, but don't give him half."

"I'll be paying him nothing unless a client comes out of the woodwork. Did you ask the maids if anyone remembers Mr. Plumtree?"

"Some did. They didn't like him. He either ignored them or was rude and demanding. He insisted on everything being perfect. One of the maids dropped a crumpled piece of paper when she was emptying his rubbish basket and he complained to the housekeeper who scolded the maid. Apparently he told her that he was paying for a clean room and he expected it to be spotless."

"It's a similar story with the cooks," Victor said, crossing one ankle over the other on the chair. As if she'd just noticed his feet there, Harmony slapped his legs. He put his feet down. "Apparently Plumtree sent back meals regularly."

"Why?" I asked.

"Different reasons. The sauce was too thick or too runny. There wasn't enough food on his plate, or there was too much spice in the curry." He nodded at Harmony. "Like the maids, he often said he was paying for things to be done perfectly and expected his meals to be made the way he liked them."

"He was fussy," I said.

"He was spoiled," Harmony countered.

But I wasn't so sure. I'd met gentlemen born into money and spoiled from a young age. Most behaved perfectly in the hotel. They knew that treating the staff well ensured they'd be treated well in return. They also liked the food the hotel cooked with its European flair and small but numerous servings. Mr. Plumtree sounded like a plain eater. It fitted with what I knew about his past.

"He made his own fortune," I told them. "But his background is shrouded in mystery." I told them what else I'd learned from Mr. Hobart and Harry. It amounted to very little.

Goliath and Frank entered so I repeated everything for their benefit. Both offered to accompany me to the inn to inspect the scene of the crime and speak to witnesses.

"I can take you when my shift finishes at four," Goliath said.

"Four's too late for Miss Fox," Frank grumbled. "I'm working a half day tomorrow. I'm free from two."

Everyone stared at Frank. We weren't used to him offering to do anything for anyone, particularly in his time off. He must be enjoying being involved in my investigations more than he was letting on.

"What?" he snapped. "I'll have a pint while Miss Fox works."

"There's no need for anyone to accompany me," I said. "I'm going with Harry at ten."

I left them to their afternoon tea break and returned to my suite. Thirty minutes later, Harmony joined me. As I ran the bath, she perched on the edge and tipped half a bottle of oil into the water. It smelled lovely, a combination of different flowers and some other scents I couldn't name.

"What's in it?" I asked.

She sniffed the bottle. "I don't know. I bought it off a woman who says she makes them from flowers she gets at Covent Garden."

I eyed the bathwater dubiously where traces of the oil floated on the surface. "Are you sure I won't come out covered in a rash?"

She rolled up her sleeve and dipped her hand and forearm in. After a few seconds, she pulled it out and inspected the skin. She showed me her unmarked arm. "You'll be fine." She sniffed her arm. "And you'll smell lovely. The woman assures me the scent will last for hours, unlike the perfumes you buy at Harrods."

I turned off the tap and signaled for her to turn around while I undressed and climbed in.

She turned but didn't leave. "You could have accepted the offer from Victor, Frank or Goliath to accompany you to the Crown and Anchor instead of going with Mr. Armitage."

I sank below the water, up to my chin, and breathed in the scent of the oil. "None are available until the afternoon."

"Is that really why you're going with Mr. Armitage? Or does it have more to do with you liking him?"

"He's courting Miss Morris now."

"That doesn't mean you stop liking him immediately." She half-turned her head, presenting me with her profile. "Or he you."

"I can assure you his attention is entirely focused on Miss Morris."

She inspected a spot on her chin in the reflection of the bathroom mirror. "I wonder if he's kissed her yet."

The thought made my stomach sink. "It's none of our business if he has."

"I wonder if he liked it more than he liked kissing you."

"Harmony!" I picked up the sponge and scrubbed my legs only to stop and glare at her back. "You haven't told Victor about it, have you?"

"Of course not. It's none of his business."

I breathed a sigh of relief. Harmony might like to tease me, but she was a good friend. She wouldn't tell my secret unless I gave permission.

* * *

I DIDN'T WEAR a trace of black on my evening gown. It was a golden silk with a swathe of delicate chiffon across the top of the low-cut bodice and another at my waist. According to Harmony, the vines embroidered into the skirt gave the illusion I was taller, but I didn't feel tall. Indeed, I felt somewhat ordinary beside Flossy. She was all curves and strawberry blonde curls arranged expertly by Harmony. My own hair was a dull brown by comparison. When I commented as much before we left the hotel, my cousin assured me my striking green eyes and full lips saved me from being ordinary. I accepted her compliment gratefully and followed her outside, attempting to copy the way she swayed her hips when she walked.

A night at the Royal Opera House was an opportunity for the ladies to dress in their finest gowns and wear as many jewels as possible. Throats, wrists and hair glittered with gemstones. I wore a gold and diamond hair ornament I'd borrowed from Aunt Lilian. She wore emeralds, while Flossy's necklace of rubies suited her pink dress.

Arriving well before the performance began was considered gauche, so we didn't have an opportunity to mingle with other members of the audience until the interval. Floyd and I remained in our seats. My uncle spotted someone he wanted to speak to across the aisle and insisted my aunt accompany him, while Flossy turned to talk to a friend behind us.

"Don't look up," Floyd said quietly to me. "Jonathon is in one of the boxes."

I kept my eyes on the closed stage curtain ahead. "Have you spoken to him lately?"

"Yes, and I've told him what I think of him tattling to Father about you and Armitage. If it helps, he's remorseful."

"It doesn't help. I'm surprised he admitted it."

"He didn't. My father told me a few days ago. I tried to give Armitage as a good a reference as possible without going overboard, but I'm not sure I did a very good job. I was caught off-guard."

I squeezed his arm. "I think it helped." It would seem Miss Morris wasn't the only reason Uncle Ronald gave his permission for me to investigate with Harry. "Thank you, Floyd. You're a dear."

"I didn't do it for you, Cleo. I did it for Armitage. I owe him. But don't think Father's permission gives you license to see Armitage whenever you wish."

I let go of him. "I don't think it's any of your business how often I see Harry or why."

He looked around, checking for eavesdroppers, then bent closer. "Armitage might be a good man, but he's not for you."

I sighed. "How many times must I say it? We are

merely friends who investigate together from time to time. We are not, nor will we ever be, romantically linked."

He grunted. "You forget that I've seen the two of you together. My father hasn't, not really. Let's keep it that way, for everyone's sake."

I crossed my arms, even though I knew it was an unladylike pose. "When did you become so insufferable?"

"It's my prerogative as your cousin." He nudged me with his elbow and winked, probably thinking that would negate his obnoxious behavior. "Don't be petulant. It doesn't suit you."

I lowered my arms. "I suppose you hope I'll change my mind about being a spinster and decide to marry someone like Jonathon."

"Lord, no." He glanced up. I followed his gaze to his friend, seated in one of the private boxes. I blinked twice as I realized he sat with Mr. and Mrs. Massie and their son and daughter. "Not only did he treat you poorly, despite claiming to be in love with you, but he's proven to be a poor friend to me of late."

I tore my gaze away from the box to look at Floyd. He sighed heavily as he turned towards the stage. "What do you mean?"

He checked his watch. As if on cue, the lights dimmed and people began to filter back to their seats. Floyd returned his watch to its pocket. "Someone was following me."

I gasped. "Not Dutch!"

Dutch was the gambler Floyd owed money to. Harry had beaten Dutch and wiped Floyd's slate clean. I'd been concerned all week that Floyd would relapse into old habits, but he'd stayed home most nights instead of going out.

"Shh." He glanced around then lowered his voice. "No, not him, thank God. I'm only followed sometimes, usually when I'm with a...particular friend of the female kind." He must be referring to his mistress. "When I realized I was being followed, I asked Jonathon to help me catch the fellow in the act and question him. He refused. He said he didn't do that sort of thing, which is nonsense, since lording it over others is precisely what he enjoys doing." He huffed out a breath through his nose. "I confronted the man on my own."

"You should have asked Harry."

A small dent formed between his brows. "He's done enough for me."

"So who was he and why was he following you?"

"He's a journalist from *The Illustrated Courier* by the name of Paisley, or something like that. He was probably looking for some salacious gossip to print in his rag, although he admitted nothing."

"I see. And he thought you'd provide this gossip with your female friend."

The orchestra began playing and the audience hushed. I waited for Floyd to say something further about the journalist. When he didn't, I prompted him.

Without taking his gaze off the rising curtain, he silenced me with a finger to his lips. "Her solo is immediately after the interval," he whispered.

"Whose?" I whispered back.

He was too distracted by the beautiful mezzo soprano on the stage to answer me. I recognized her from a recent magazine article as well as an advertisement for corsets. At least, I thought it was the same woman. With the stage lighting and a heavily made-up face, I couldn't be entirely sure if it was Miss Aldridge. If it was her, then her star was rising. She might not be the lead in tonight's opera, but she garnered a lot of publicity. It would seem Floyd's mistress wasn't an actress, after all, but the dark-haired songbird on the stage.

"Speaking of inappropriate paramours," I muttered.

After the opera, we mingled with others in the foyer. My uncle seemed to want to talk to everyone, but my aunt no longer joined him. She put on a smile and brave face, but I could tell she had a headache and was tired. Her tonic had worn off and she wanted to go home to bed, but she dutifully waited for her husband. Usually he noticed when she was ready to leave a party, but he seemed keen to continue to speak to friends. It wasn't until Floyd pointed out that they were all names from Uncle's guest list that I realized why he was making such an effort.

Although he returned to us sporting a smile some time later, it was strained. "Damnation," he muttered. "None of them can come."

"I'm sorry," I said and meant it. The special dinner in the new restaurant deserved to be a success. Knowing Mrs. Poole, the food would be spectacular. But without the right people attending, who would care?

Uncle Ronald didn't seem to hear me. He watched Floyd. My cousin stood with a group of friends, laughing. One of the men clapped him on the shoulder. A beautiful woman joined them and he kissed the back of her hand. She smiled and beckoned two more friends to join them. Jonathon wasn't among the group.

When it was time to leave, Floyd told us to go on ahead, he'd make his own way home later. No doubt he would wait for one particular performer to emerge after changing out of her costume.

We left him with his friends, still chatting and laughing. He looked happy. I was very glad to see it, after the difficulties he'd had with Dutch.

Flossy took my arm as we exited the building.

She nodded at Jonathon, up ahead with the Massie family. "He hasn't got a hope with her."

"Hyacinthe Massie? Why not?"

"I heard she's quite besotted with Jeremy Gooding."

I turned sharply to her. "Is he related to Mr. Gooding of Gooding and Plumtree?"

"He's the son."

I smiled to myself. I would enjoy wiping the smug smile off Harry's face tomorrow. "Do you know the Goodings?"

"Not at all. There's no Mrs. or Miss Gooding, and Mr. Gooding and Jeremy don't socialize much. They keep to themselves. I've never actually met Jeremy but Hyacinthe claims he's handsome and kind. She becomes quite dreamy when she talks about him."

We watched as Jonathon climbed into the carriage behind the Massies. As the footman closed the door, Jonathon's gaze connected with mine. I quickly looked away.

"Floyd should tell Jonathon that Hyacinthe's heart is otherwise engaged," Flossy said.

"You and I both know that a woman's heart has nothing to do with marriage."

She sighed in agreement. "I suppose there may be an objection on the part of their parents, but I don't see why. Both the Massies and Goodings are wealthy families."

"There may be something we're not aware of. Something that Mr. Massie wants to find out before he hands over his daughter to Jeremy." Something Harry had been hired to uncover.

"Oh? Do you think so?"

"It's just a theory. Anyway, perhaps Mr. Massie isn't interested in marrying his daughter to a wealthy man. Perhaps he wants to marry her to a title, or to the heir of one."

"Lady Hyacinthe Cremorne does sound very grand." She wrinkled her nose as their carriage drove off and ours took its place at the head of the queue. "But not grand enough, if you ask me. I wouldn't marry Jonathon if his father was a duke." She tossed her head, making her curls dance at her temple. "Any man who calls me fat isn't worth it."

I took her hand and squeezed. "Quite right."

My aunt closed her eyes on the way home, so I kept my voice low so as not to disturb her. "Mr. Hobart told me about the fellow who died recently, the one who used to stay at the hotel years ago. How very sad." I didn't address my comment to anyone in particular, but I watched my uncle closely for his reaction. He simply gave a nod and continued to look out the window at the passing lights in the buildings and those illuminating the advertising boards. "Did you ask Mr. Hobart to send flowers to his family?" I prompted.

"Hobart doesn't need me to tell him what to

do," Uncle Ronald said before becoming silent again.

I would have to try harder if I wanted to learn something about the victim. "What was Mr. Plumtree like?"

Uncle Ronald shrugged. "Intelligent, driven. He didn't suffer fools. I was surprised to hear how he died. I didn't think he was the sort."

When I asked him to clarify, he simply shook his head and fell silent again. I gave up and settled back until we reached the hotel.

We weren't the only ones returning after the opera. Several guests had also been there, and some lingered in the foyer before retiring. My uncle excused himself and adjourned to the billiards room with a group of gentlemen while others withdrew pipes from pockets as they headed to the smoking room.

I spotted Miss Hessing, one of our long-term American guests, standing with her mother and her gaggle of cronies. I was about to join her, but my aunt held me back.

"Nobody liked him," she said as she watched Flossy approach Miss Hessing. It took me a moment to realize she was talking about Mr. Plumtree. It seemed she'd been listening in the carriage, after all. "Or, rather, the gentlemen liked him, but not the ladies."

"Why not?"

"He was one of those men who doesn't like women much. You know the sort. They think we're all silly and incapable of talking about anything except clothes and gossip. He had no time for me. As Ronald said, he had no time for anyone he thought lesser than himself, which was everyone who wasn't the owner of a successful business, as far as I could tell. He was worse when he'd had too much to drink."

"You saw him drunk?"

"Just once or twice. He didn't hold his liquor well, from what I could see."

"Did he become morose, sad?"

"Just more horrid."

That fit with the theory that he wouldn't hang himself even after imbibing too much wine. The more I learned about him, the more I agreed with Harry—Mr. Plumtree was incapable of empathy for others. He wouldn't have felt remorse over the loss of his ship's crew.

I was more certain than ever that he'd been murdered.

CHAPTER 4

The narrow lanes and dead-end courts in the eastern end of Canning Town formed a maze for the unsuspecting tourist who found themselves disembarking at either Victoria or Albert Dock. Not that many passenger vessels landed at the Royal Docks. It was mostly used for cargo. Without Harry as my guide, I would have been quite lost. I wondered if he'd lived on these streets during his stint as a homeless urchin, or whether his familiarity was simply a result of being born and bred in London.

We avoided the docks altogether and plunged into the shadowy network of streets behind them. Houses were tightly packed like cargo in a ship's hold, with little in the way of aesthetics to recommend them. There were boarding houses and hotels with signs in the window advertising rooms for rent, no references necessary and payment up-front. The carved words above the door of a charity school demanded students "Come in and learn your duty to God."

The workhouse in the next street was equally unappealing. It was quiet, however, with its residents out looking for work. If itinerant work was to be had anywhere in London, it was at the docks where an able-bodied man could do a few hours hard labor to earn a little money.

Afterwards, he could spend it all at inns like the Crown and Anchor. The sign swinging out the front showed a crown hooked by one of the anchor's arms. The crown had probably once been painted a bright yellow but was now a brownish color with black smudges.

I expected the pub to be empty, given it was only ten-thirty in the morning, but there were three patrons nursing tankards at the bar and another asleep in a corner booth. A heavyset woman stood behind the bar, yawning as she dried tankards, and a solid fellow was casting his eye over a ledger, pencil tucked behind his ear. All except the sleeping man looked around upon our entrance.

"You two lost?" the barman asked in a Scottish accent.

Harry handed him a business card. "We're private detectives. We've been hired to look into the death of Tobias Plumtree at this establishment."

"Why?" the woman asked. "He offed himself."

"Some people have doubts about the verdict."

The man read the card, turned it over, and handed it back. "Are these the same people who hired you?"

"That's confidential," I said before Harry could. "And this is not Mr. Armitage's case. It's mine. Are you the publican?"

The man wiped his hand on his apron and extended it for me to shake. A faded tattoo of an anchor covered the back. "Bull. I run this establishment."

"Only for a few more weeks, until he retires," the woman added with a smile that revealed missing teeth.

Bull offered his hand to Harry. "Nice to meet you, Mr. Armitage, Miss...?"

"Fox," I said. "It's a pleasure to meet you, too, Mr. Bull."

"Just Bull. No mister." The moniker suited him well with his thick neck and hulking frame. "Don't see too many lasses like you around these parts, Miss Fox."

The woman snorted. She didn't wear a wedding ring so I doubted she was Bull's wife. When he noticed me looking at her, he introduced her as Nancy.

"Don't mind her," he said quietly to me. "She's not used to pretty lasses on her patch."

I'd worn a plain dress as Harry suggested, but it clearly wasn't plain enough for a Canning Town pub. I felt quite conspicuous next to the ruddy-cheeked Nancy with her stained apron and hastily styled hair. To be honest, I'd not known quite what to expect. My life had been sheltered in Cambridge. I'd attended lectures and society meetings for educated ladies, with the occasional visit to a teashop with friends. Since coming to London, I'd lived in Mayfair, and my investigations had only taken me into the East End a few times. Every time, Harry accompanied me. He used to want to go without me, but he knew better than to insist I stay home, nowadays.

The publican was amiable and happy to answer our questions, but unfortunately neither he nor Nancy could tell us much more than we already knew. Nancy had shown Mr. Plumtree up to his room on the evening of his death. He'd ordered two bottles of wine which made them think he was expecting someone, although he never mentioned visitors and they saw no one enter his room.

"Did he come here often?" I asked.

"Regular enough." Bull gave Nancy a questioning look. "Every few weeks?"

"He used to," she said. "I hadn't seen him in months. Not since last year, I reckon."

"Did he usually stay the night when he did come?"

"Aye," Bull said. The glance he exchanged with Nancy made me think there was something he wasn't telling me.

"Was he always alone when he stayed overnight?" I pressed.

"Sometimes he had a...visitor. But she never stayed all night."

"She?"

Nancy sucked air through a gap in her teeth. "I don't reckon we need to spell it out to you, Miss."

I felt my face heat which made Nancy chuckle into her double chins.

"If he was expecting a...female caller that night, why wasn't he discovered until the morning? Didn't she come across his body?"

"Like I said, no one else entered his room," Bull said.

"Are you sure?" Harry asked. "If you were busy down here, you might not have seen her pass."

"No one went upstairs. I'd have noticed."

"Me too," Nancy agreed. "We know everyone who comes and goes, and there were no whores here that night. So don't you go thinking ill of us." She set down the tankard with a thud and thrust her hands on her hips. "This ain't that kind of 'stablishment and I ain't no abbess."

I'd never heard the term, but I gathered it was slang for brothel madam.

"We don't stop 'em coming if they have a prior arrangement with a guest," Bull clarified. "And there were some here that night, but not for him. Nancy just didn't want you thinking this is that kind of a pub."

Harry apologized. "We don't like asking these questions, but we have to make sure to leave no stone unturned."

Nancy swallowed his apology hook, line and sinker if her smile and nod were anything to go by.

"What time did you take the bottles of wine up to him?" I asked.

Bull shrugged. "Eleven, maybe. I don't know. I don't keep a close eye on the clock."

"And he was definitely alone? You saw no one inside?"

"There could have been someone in there, I suppose. He didn't open the door very wide, just wide enough for me to pass the bottles through, one at a time."

It seemed odd that he wouldn't open the door wider. It was very likely someone else was inside when Bull delivered the bottles. "But you didn't see anyone go upstairs?"

Both shook their heads. "We don't have a chance to scratch ourselves most evenings, mind," Nancy clarified. "It's just the two of us, and we're always run off our feet. It was real busy that night. Remember, Bull? They were lining up where you're standing now, Mr. Armitage, four or five deep."

Meaning they could have missed someone going upstairs, and that person could have been in Plumtree's room when Bull delivered the bottles.

"How was he when you delivered the wine?" I asked. "Agitated? Worried? Sober?"

"Definitely sober." Bull shrugged. "I didn't notice anything different about him."

"He means he was an arse, as usual," Nancy added. "I know you ain't supposed to speak ill of the dead, but Plumtree was a right turd. He'd come in here, demand to be served immediately, and not speak to a soul unless it was to order another drink. Heaven help me if I was slow bringing him his beer. He'd give me an earful, he would. Not loud enough to be heard by anyone else, mind. He was careful never to cause a scene. But there were times I wanted to see him dangling from the end of a noose."

"Nancy!" Bull cried.

She shrugged. "He was an arse, and I ain't sad he's gone. Maybe that's why he was killed. Maybe he treated the wrong person like he was better than them. Lots of folk around here take offense to someone like him. Someone who used to be one of us but forgot where he came from after he made his fortune."

Bull rolled his eyes. "He wasn't that bad, Nance. Anyway, I ain't convinced he didn't off himself." He thrust his chin at Harry. "Are you sure he didn't?"

Harry gave nothing away with his blank expression. "How was Plumtree on the night of his death? Did he seem worried?"

Nancy frowned in thought. "Now that you mention it, he did. When I showed him up to the room, he kept looking over his shoulder. Could be that he expected someone to follow."

"Can we look at the room now?" I asked.

"Everything's been put to rights again," Bull said. "You won't find anything to help your investigation in there."

"We just want to have a look around. Sometimes seeing the crime scene helps put things into perspective."

Bull indicated the ledger. "I've got to get these books sorted, and Nancy's busy, too."

"You can just give us the key and tell us which room it is."

Nancy sucked air through the gap in her teeth. "He wants a few coppers."

I'd assumed Bull had been generous in answering our questions out of a genuine desire to help. But like most people who could ill afford to be generous, he didn't give something away for nothing. I slipped him a few coins and gave another to

Nancy. She bit it before slipping it into the crevice between her breasts.

Bull opened a cabinet behind the counter and removed a key hanging from a hook. "Follow me."

We crossed the flagstone floor, past the man sleeping in the corner booth, and headed up the creaking flight of stairs. We stopped outside one of the rooms and Bull unlocked the door.

The room was small and simple but functional. A bed that would have been a squeeze for two was pushed up against the wall beneath the window. I threw open the brown and yellow striped curtains to let in some light and coughed as dust billowed from them. A large shallow bowl sat on the small table with a jug inside it. Both were empty. There was no rug on the floor and the boards creaked in more places than I could count. The only decoration in the room were the two crowned kings' heads on the mantelpiece above the narrow cast iron fireplace. The shiny brass of one crown was in stark contrast to the dull unpolished one.

Harry pulled the stool that had been tucked beneath the table into the middle of the room. He removed a sheet of paper from his pocket and read the numbers he'd jotted down. "Plumtree was about your height, Cleo. The noose was at the end of three feet of rope."

"The police measured it even though they thought it was suicide?" I asked.

"My father asked his former colleague to check." He put out his hand to me.

I took his hand and stepped onto the stool. It was the sort of low stool a shoeshine boy might use, but it wobbled. One leg was shorter than the other. Harry put his other hand to my hip to steady me. Once steadied, he quickly let go.

He cleared his throat and indicated the beam above my head, stretching from one side of the room to the other just below the apex of the A-frame ceiling. I'd expected an old inn to have low ceilings but renovations must have removed a small attic that had once occupied the roof cavity above the bedchamber, joining the two spaces together and raising the bedchamber's ceiling height. Three feet of rope would leave the noose dangling above my forehead. The only way Mr. Plumtree could hang himself without help would be to stand on something higher, but the stool was the only thing the police had found within the vicinity. It had been tipped over as if kicked aside.

Harry assisted me off the stool then tucked it back under the table. According to the police, the table and the bed were too far from the rope to have been used by Mr. Plumtree to hang himself.

I thanked Bull. "We've seen everything we need to see."

He locked the room again and led the way back downstairs. He picked up Harry's business card which he'd left on the bar and held it up between two fingers. "I'll contact you if we think of anything relevant."

I asked to see the card and borrow a pencil. "Actually, please contact me at the Mayfair Hotel." I wrote the address on the back of the card. "Mr. Armitage was simply my escort for the day."

Nancy gave an approving nod. "I ain't never seen a man be an assistant to a woman before."

"I'm not her assistant," Harry pointed out.

"You are today," I said.

Nancy chuckled. "Good for you, Miss Fox."

Harry and I left the inn and walked back to the main thoroughfare to catch an omnibus. "Where to next?" he asked.

"I'm going to call on the widow. I don't require an escort for that."

He fell silent as we walked. I felt a little guilty for not including him. We'd worked closely together on previous investigations. But that had been out of necessity and when Harry had few other clients. He had a paying client now, and no time to investigate a potential murder where there was no assurance of payment at the end.

"You must have a great deal to do for Mr. Massie," I told him. "Finding out what sort of man Jeremy Gooding is and whether he's worthy of Hyacinthe Massie will keep you busy."

He smiled. "You worked it out much faster than I thought you would."

"I saw the Massie family at the opera last night. Flossy informed me where Hyacinthe's affections lay and I made an assumption."

He huffed a laugh.

"What's so amusing?"

"Your lot never seem to go to the opera to actually watch the opera."

"I'll ignore the comment about 'my lot' and point out that we were very interested in the singing, as it happens. Floyd even shushed me so he could hear the mezzo soprano's solo."

He huffed another laugh.

"You knew Floyd's mistress was a singer, not an actress, didn't you?"

"His previous one was an actress. The singer is new." He was remarkably well informed considering he didn't work at the hotel anymore. "Don't worry. It's not serious."

"He seemed besotted when she came on stage."

"Your cousin is always besotted in the early days of a new relationship. It wears off. He knows his duty." He said it with a hint of bitterness that had me regarding him with a narrowed gaze.

"You know my family better than me."

"I've known them a lot longer than you." He stopped and indicated an approaching omnibus. "If you want to call on Mrs. Plumtree, you need to catch this one. Since I've been roundly told I'm not wanted, I'll leave you here."

"It's not that you're not wanted, it's just that you're not required. You also have a client to please —a *paying* client. He must come first."

"But your investigation is more interesting."

I smiled as the driver pulled the horses to a stop. "I'll keep you informed, if you like."

He put his hand out to assist me up the steps. "Thank you. And if you require another escort, I'll be happy to accompany you."

I accepted his assistance. Instead of letting me go when I was safely on board, he held my hand tighter.

"Even if you just want to discuss theories, you can stop at my office any time. I'll always be available for…" He cleared his throat. "…to discuss a case."

The conductor leaned out of the window. "Sir, are you coming on board?"

Harry let me go and stepped back. I took my seat quickly before the omnibus moved off and watched through the window as Harry headed in the other direction. Had he been about to say he'd always be available for me? Or was my imagination running away?

* * *

KITTY PLUMTREE LIVED in a handsome red brick house not far from Hampstead Heath. It was a lovely leafy area to raise a young child but was quite a distance from the office of Gooding and Plumtree Shipping Company in Moorgate.

"He always told me when he wouldn't be home of an evening," she said. She sat in the middle of a long sofa, a doll-like figure in black holding a black lace handkerchief to her nose. Despite her small size, she seemed to want to make herself even smaller by tucking her arms to her sides, keeping her head bowed and her shoulders slumped forward. Even her voice was small. I had to listen closely to hear her.

"And how often did he work late and not come home?" I asked.

"It used to be once every few weeks, but he hasn't stayed elsewhere for a number of months." That fit with what Bull and Nancy had told us about Mr. Plumtree's visits to the inn.

"Did you know he stayed at the Crown and Anchor in Canning Town on the nights he didn't come home?"

She lowered the handkerchief to her lap. "They told me that's where he was found."

"Did you know, Mrs. Plumtree?"

"He never mentioned it."

"You never asked?"

She shook her head vigorously. "Oh no."

"Does it surprise you to discover he regularly frequented a dockside tavern a few miles from his office instead of something closer and more befitting a wealthy businessman?"

She teased the handkerchief between her fingers. "I… I don't know. I suppose. Miss Fox, forgive me, but…I don't understand. Are these questions necessary?"

I'd already explained that I was following up on her husband's death for an anonymous client and she'd accepted the explanation without question. But now, she seemed to regret accommodating my request. If I wanted her honest answers, I would have to be honest in return. To a point.

"Mrs. Plumtree, you need to prepare yourself. You see, there's reason to believe your husband didn't die by his own hand."

For the first time since joining me in the drawing room, she came alive. Her responses and manner had been somewhat automatic up until that moment, but now she seemed genuinely interested. "Is that what Scotland Yard think?"

"No."

"Who hired you?"

"I'm not at liberty to say." It wasn't a lie, but it was a wide berth to avoid the truth. I felt a little guilty for not being honest but I told myself it was necessary at this point in the investigation. Later, if I was sure I could trust her, I would confide in her.

For now, I needed to protect D.I. Hobart and his former colleague who was still employed by the Yard.

"I know this is difficult," I went on. "But are you up to answering a few more questions?"

She bowed her head again and took a moment to respond. "Yes. I want to get to the bottom of this. The police verdict of suicide doesn't ring true. I hope you come to a different conclusion, for my son's sake."

"Why did you think it was the wrong conclusion?"

She lifted a shoulder in a shrug. "Tobias was... incapable of guilt. Nothing he did could upset him enough to take his own life. Not even..." She touched the handkerchief to her nose.

"Not even the sinking of his company's ship and the loss of life?"

She gave a small nod. "He says it wasn't his fault, that he can't be held accountable."

"Is that what he told you?"

"I overheard him saying it to Mr. Gooding, his business partner. There was an incident at their office one day, shortly after the tragedy. That evening, Mr. Gooding came here to discuss it with Tobias. I heard their raised voices."

"What incident?"

"Apparently a fellow went to their office and caused a scene. He blamed my husband and Mr.

Gooding for the loss of his brother's life. His brother was one of the crew on board the *Elsie May*. My husband threatened to have him arrested if he didn't leave the premises. Mr. Gooding wasn't there at the time. He learned about it later. When he did, he came here to speak to Tobias. I heard him telling Tobias in no uncertain terms that he'd treated the poor man terribly and that wasn't the way he wanted to conduct their business. He said they were a family-owned business and family was important."

"And how did your husband respond to that?"

She teased out the handkerchief before bunching it up in her fist again. "He doesn't like being told what to do."

"Had he argued with Mr. Gooding before?"

"I don't know. They never conducted business here. That time was an exception."

"Mr. Plumtree never discussed his working relationship with Mr. Gooding with you?"

"Oh no, Miss Fox. We never talked about his work." She blinked large dark eyes at me as her fingers busily twisted the handkerchief. She looked so young, even though she was a few years older than me. Young, naïve and completely overwhelmed by the situation she'd been thrust into.

I pressed on with my questions. "Why did the man, the one whose brother died, blame the ship owners and not the captain for its sinking?"

"I don't know."

"How did your husband seem after Mr. Gooding left? Was he angry?"

"I didn't see him. He fell asleep in his study."

"Does he often do that?"

"Sometimes. If he has too much to drink, he's very difficult to wake."

An unconscious man would be easier to maneuver into position to make it appear he hanged himself. After two bottles of wine, Mr. Plumtree would certainly be unconscious if he had a tendency to fall asleep when drunk.

"It's not very often," she added quickly. "When he does fall asleep, Lowell just leaves him there."

Lowell was the butler who'd shown me into the drawing room. He peered down his nose at both Mrs. Plumtree and me, and not offered to bring in tea. I suspected he was hovering outside the door now, listening.

"Was there anything different about your husband in the days or weeks leading up to his death?" I asked.

She picked at a thread that had come loose from the hem of her handkerchief.

"Mrs. Plumtree?" I prompted. "It would really help if you could tell me your husband's state of mind before he died."

She gave a small nod. "He was worried. It was very unlike him."

"What was he worried about?"

"I'm afraid I don't know. He didn't confide in me."

The butler suddenly appeared at the door. Lowell was tall and straight like a pole, with a thin face and crowded teeth. A deep vertical crease cut through each cheek. "If I may, Mrs. Plumtree." It was not posed as a question, nor did he wait for her to give consent before he spoke to me. "Mr. Plumtree told me he thought someone was following him."

"Oh," Mrs. Plumtree murmured.

"He was quite concerned and pressed upon me the need to ensure the doors and windows were secured at all times. No one was to be allowed into the house unless I knew them."

"Thank you, Lowell," I said. This man was better informed than his mistress. I needed to keep him on side. "Did he say who was following him? Or give a description?"

"I'm afraid not."

"Could it have been the grieving brother of one of the *Elsie May's* crewmen?"

"No, miss, I don't think so. Mr. Plumtree's nervousness was more recent than that incident. Besides, when I informed Mr. Plumtree of the brother showing up downstairs, he was unconcerned."

"The brother was here?"

Mrs. Plumtree gasped. She pressed the handkerchief to her chest and stared at Lowell. She hadn't been told, but she wasn't about to admonish the butler for keeping the information from her. Even now, with her husband gone, she was not prepared to give Lowell orders.

The butler nodded. "As I said, it was some time ago, after the ship sank. I sent the fellow on his way. He lingered outside for a good thirty minutes, then left. He didn't return."

"Do you know his name?"

He shook his head. "He just mentioned that his brother had been a sailor on the ill-fated voyage. I can give you a description though. He was early twenties, short hair, stocky build with a muscular face and broad nose."

I noted it down in my notebook. "You say Mr. Plumtree's nervousness was more recent. How recent?"

"It was last Thursday when he asked me not to let in any strangers."

"That's very precise."

"I am a precise man, and attentive to my master's needs and whims. I remember because Thursday is the maid's half-day."

I noted the day down. "Mrs. Plumtree, may I look in Mr. Plumtree's study?"

She quickly shook her head. "I'm not allowed in there."

"It's your house, Mrs. Plumtree," I said gently.

"No one can stop you going anywhere you wish to go now."

She shot a glance at the butler. "It's locked."

"I have the key," Lowell said. "This way, Miss Fox."

Mrs. Plumtree hesitated before following us out of the drawing room and up the stairs. Lowell unlocked the study door and invited me to enter. Mrs. Plumtree remained on the threshold. She looked around, taking in the room as if she'd never seen it before. The furniture was sturdy, masculine, and the desk large. It was tidy, and I wondered if Lowell had been in or if it was the way Mr. Plumtree kept it. The bookshelves were almost devoid of books, and instead filled with knickknacks—small statues of dogs and horses, a globe, a clock, and a miniature train set. The paintings were also of dogs and horses.

I searched the room for clues, although I wasn't entirely sure what I was looking for. Last Thursday was the twenty-third, but I found nothing relating to that date in the desk drawers or anywhere else. The only thing of interest were two letters addressed from Mrs. Plumtree to her father in which she informed him of her husband's cruelty towards her. There was no doubt in my mind that she told the truth. While she didn't go into detail in the letters, it was clear she was afraid of him. The last line begged her father to help her, although she didn't say in what form she hoped help would arrive.

I bit the inside of my lip, wishing I didn't have to confront her. She still hovered on the threshold, unwilling to fully enter the room she'd been banned from by her husband. She clutched her handkerchief at her throat, but it was dry, as were her eyes. There were no signs of tears on her face, and yet she didn't seem happy to be rid of him either. I wasn't quite sure what to make of her reaction to her husband's death yet. It was possible some or all of what I was seeing was an act.

I had to confront her. As his widow, she was the prime suspect.

CHAPTER 5

Ipassed the letters to Mrs. Plumtree while the butler looked on with a disapproving scowl. I wasn't sure if he disapproved of me reading them or Mrs. Plumtree discovering that her husband intercepted them. I was quite sure Lowell knew he had. Indeed, he was probably the one who handed them to Mr. Plumtree.

The widow pressed the handkerchief to her mouth to smother her gasp. "These are my letters!"

I remained silent.

"He took them! Tobias took them and didn't send them on! I wondered why I received no response from my father. Now I know." She glanced at Lowell, but didn't ask him if he'd been involved.

The butler stared straight ahead, unmoving.

I pointed to some key lines in the letters. "You

state that your husband was cruel to you, that he bullied you and you were scared. You ask your father for help. Were you seeking a divorce?"

"I—I don't know. I wasn't sure what to do. I wanted my father's advice."

"It doesn't matter now," I pointed out.

"No," she whispered. "It doesn't."

"Mrs. Plumtree, can you see how this looks?"

For the first time since meeting her, tears welled in her eyes. "I didn't kill him, Miss Fox. I would never... He was the father of my son. He might have been cruel, but I couldn't...I'm not capable of..." She let the sentence drift away.

I shifted my stance, not liking this at all. "I'm sorry but I have to ask...where were you on the night of your husband's death?"

"Here, of course, asleep."

"Oh? You know the time of his death?" I had not been told it, or even if a coroner had noted a time. It was my understanding that no medical time of death had been given.

"I just assumed it was in the middle of the night, after everyone has gone to bed. Wouldn't the people at the inn have heard something if it happened early?"

I gave her a reassuring smile. "You're probably right."

She folded her arms and hugged herself. "Can we get out of here now?"

I followed her into the corridor. "Again, I apologize for my next question, but I have to ask it. I've been informed that your husband…met women of ill-repute at the Crown and Anchor. Were you aware of that?"

She shook her head, but she seemed more upset about being in the study than learning her husband met with whores.

Lowell locked the door and pocketed the key. He waited for instructions, but his mistress didn't seem to know what to say to him.

"One last question, then Lowell can see me out," I said. "Do you know who inherits your husband's business interests?"

"His solicitor called here yesterday. Our son George inherits everything when he comes of age. That's several years away. He's only two, so I'm his legal guardian until then."

"Does that mean you're responsible for making decisions about Gooding and Plumtree on your son's behalf?"

"Goodness, no. I wouldn't know where to begin. Mr. Gooding will take care of all that. He's a good man. He'll do what's right for the business and for my George."

I thanked her for her time and told her to contact me at the hotel if she thought of anything further.

I followed the butler down the stairs and waited

until we were out of earshot to speak. "She's going to need some guidance until she finds her feet."

"Her father will come to London soon."

At least it was someone who'd have her best interests at heart—and those of her son.

Lowell opened the front door, but I didn't exit. I glanced up the staircase to make sure we weren't overheard by Mrs. Plumtree or other servants. "Tell me, Lowell, why are you helping me?"

He seemed surprised by the question. "It's my duty, Miss Fox."

"To Mrs. Plumtree? It's just that you don't seem to like her very much."

"My duty to Mr. Plumtree's memory. I worked for him for a long time, and I respected him. I never believed he took his own life. I always thought he met with foul play so I'm thankful someone is looking into it. I worried that you weren't the right person for the task but after listening to your questions, I've come to the conclusion that you're competent."

"Thank you," I said, inserting a heavy dose of sarcasm into my voice.

He frowned, clearly not understanding the reason for it. "If there's anything I can do to help further, I will."

"There is one more question I have for you." I glanced up the staircase again. We were still alone. Even so, I lowered my voice. "Do you always have the key to Mr. Plumtree's study on your person?"

"I do."

"Could someone have got in there without your knowledge?"

"No. The maid has to ask my permission to clean the study, and I always watch over her when she's inside." That must have made the poor girl's work even harder. "Mrs. Plumtree didn't have access to the study, if that's what you're asking. She couldn't have known he took her letters."

"Do you think her capable of murdering her husband?"

He hesitated then shook his head. "No."

I stepped onto the porch but suddenly thought of one more question. "Did you know Mr. Plumtree before he made his fortune?"

"No. He employed me ten years ago, after he'd formed Gooding and Plumtree with Mr. Gooding."

I thanked him and trotted lightly down the stairs to the pavement, feeling as though I'd not learned a great deal, except for one important detail. I knew the date on which Mr. Plumtree became anxious about someone following him. If I could find out who he saw on that date, I could be well on the way to solving his murder.

* * *

Mr. Plumtree's assistant at the Moorgate office of Gooding and Plumtree Shipping Company wouldn't speak to me without checking with Mr. Gooding first. I thought he meant the owner of the business, but he returned to the waiting area with a young man. He was introduced as Jeremy Gooding.

This was the fellow Harry was investigating for Mr. Massie. I could see what attracted Hyacinthe Massie. Although not classically handsome, there was a quiet confidence about him. The glasses made him seem somewhat bookish, but the tall, broad-shouldered physique had the opposite effect. Overall, his appearance was intriguing.

He greeted me with a mixture of curiosity and caution in his wide-set eyes after I told him the reason for my visit. "I've never met a private detective before. I admit, you're not what I expected."

"I don't think I'm a typical representative of the profession," I said with a smile.

He smiled back, but his caution remained. He didn't invite me to his office so we stood somewhat awkwardly in the company's outer reception room with its wooden paneling, bookshelves filled with leather-bound books, and a long-case clock ticking loudly in the corner. The young man who'd initially greeted me returned to the polished desk situated in front of a wall of pigeonholes, each filled with documents or letters. Mr. Gooding indicated we should step away to have a more private con-versation.

"Is this about Tobias?" he asked.

"I've been tasked with looking into his death. It may not have been suicide."

He balked. "Well, it can't have been an accident considering how it happened. So…you're suggesting he was murdered?"

"Can you tell me about the altercation between Mr. Plumtree and the brother of the crewman who died when the *Elsie May* sank?"

He went very still. "I don't know what you're talking about."

"The irate brother of one of the deceased sailors called here and confronted Mr. Plumtree. I'm sure you're aware of it." When he didn't respond, I pressed on. "He also tried to see Mr. Plumtree at home but was turned away."

"How do you know about that?"

"I've just come from there. Mrs. Plumtree—"

"Leave Kitty alone." It came out a growl, taking me by surprise. I'd not anticipated the sudden change from amenable to annoyed. "She's got enough on her plate without having to speak to you."

The employee manning the front desk looked up. He seemed unsure whether to offer to escort me off the premises or pretend he hadn't overheard our exchange.

"Mrs. Plumtree was able to spare me a few moments of her time," I said. "She would like to find her husband's killer to prove he didn't take his own life. For her son's sake," I added.

Mr. Gooding's breathing had become more rapid as the moments ticked by, but his temper cooled as my words sank in. "Kitty is fragile. I'd appreciate it if you informed me before you questioned her in the future so that I can be there to support her." He was behaving like a relative. Or a lover.

"You two are close?" I asked.

He tugged on his cuff. "I consider her a friend."

I wondered if Hyacinthe Massie knew how close of a friend her paramour was to the newly widowed Mrs. Plumtree.

"What do you know about the altercation between Mr. Plumtree and the brother of the crewman?" I pressed.

"I wasn't here."

"That doesn't answer my question."

He blew out a breath. "I have nothing to say about it."

I was about to tell him that he still hadn't answered my question when we were joined by an older, balder version of Jeremy Gooding. He swept into the outer reception area with a welcoming smile and a ready handshake. He introduced himself as Mr. Gooding Senior. He seemed to know who I was and why I was there. When I saw the youth slip back behind the front desk, I realized how he'd become informed.

Mr. Gooding invited me to sit on one of the large armchairs. "It's a good thing that someone has taken an interest in Tobias's death. I never believed he killed himself. Murder, however…nasty business. Did Kitty Plumtree hire you?"

"I'm not at liberty to say."

He settled into the armchair with a deep sigh that strained his waistcoat buttons. He stroked his thick whiskers. "I hope Jeremy has been able to assist you with your inquiries."

"He was just about to tell me what transpired between Mr. Plumtree and the brother of one of the *Elsie May's* crew here in the office."

Jeremy glanced at his father. Mr. Gooding gave a barely perceptible nod.

Jeremy visibly relaxed now that his father was available to take command. "The man barged in here one day and demanded to see Tobias. He was upset. He shouted a great deal and refused to leave when asked. He pushed past Antony at the desk and went in search of Tobias. When he found him, he accused Tobias of being responsible for his brother's death."

"Why would he say that?"

"He was grieving and looking for someone to blame. The captain went down with the *Elsie May,* so the next people in the firing line were my father and Tobias." His tone was heavy, his face pained. Either the confrontation troubled him, or the sinking of the ship did, or both.

"And yet he demanded to see Mr. Plumtree, not your father."

Mr. Gooding took over from his son. "Tobias managed the *Elsie May*, not me"

"Was he to blame in any way? Did the brother have a point?"

"No," Jeremy said, somewhat defensively. "There was a terrible storm."

His father agreed. "After that confrontation here and then at Tobias's house, the brother must have come to his senses and realized we weren't to blame. He hasn't returned or caused any more trouble."

"So Mr. Plumtree's recent anxiety wasn't related to the grieving brother's accusation?"

"Anxiety?" Mr. Gooding stroked his beard again. "You are remarkably well informed, Miss Fox, although I think anxiety is overstating it. Tobias thought he was being followed, but he didn't believe it was that fellow."

"I think I saw him," Jeremy said, frowning in thought. "The man following him. He was outside the office here. Tobias said not to let him in, but the fellow didn't come closer. He stood across the road, just watching."

I removed my notebook from my bag and flipped to the page where I'd written the description Lowell had given me of the grieving brother. "What did he look like?"

"Average height, around my father's age, thin hair, gray beard."

I wrote it down, but it was not the grieving brother Lowell described.

"Any idea who it could be?" Jeremy asked.

I didn't want to give away how little I knew so I smiled secretively as I closed the notebook and returned it to my bag. "Mr. Plumtree's anxiety started last Thursday. Was that the day you saw the man across the road?"

Jeremy's gaze drifted to the ceiling before focusing on me again. "I think so, yes. It was also the day I first noticed Tobias acting oddly. I went into his office and he almost jumped out of his skin. He snapped at me and told me to knock in future."

"May I look in his office?"

Jeremy glanced at his father.

Mr. Gooding pushed himself to his feet and fastened his jacket button. "It's all right, Jerry. There's nothing sensitive in there that she can't see. Will you show her? I have a meeting."

Jeremy led me through to Mr. Plumtree's office and breathed a heavy sigh as he looked around. "It's largely as he left it, although anything he was working on has been redistributed to either my father or me."

The office was more workmanlike than Mr. Plumtree's study at home. There was a painting of a country hunting scene, the red coats of the riders providing the only color in a room that was mostly brown. A large map of the world took up an expanse on one wall and a bookshelf was filled with wooden boxes, and a variety of texts, all related to shipping, oceanography and trade.

I moved to the leather-inlaid desk. Aside from a heavy looking onyx inkstand, with brass ink pots positioned on either side of an onyx statuette of a horse, there was little on the desk surface. All the documents must have been cleared away. "What was he like?" I asked as I rifled through each of the drawers.

"Clever. Forthright. He didn't like weakness in others. He saw it as incompetence." His strained tone made me look up.

"I've heard he was a bully."

"Some would call him that."

"Did you ever witness him bully anyone?"

He shook his head.

"You're very protective of Mrs. Plumtree."

His jaw firmed. "What are you implying, Miss Fox?"

"Tell me what you thought of his treatment of her."

"Their marriage is—was—none of my affair."

I didn't press him further. He seemed to have taken it upon himself to protect Mrs. Plumtree and perhaps thought I was trying to pin the murder on her.

I was about to close the bottom desk drawer when a copy of *The Illustrated Courier* I'd initially discounted as being unimportant caught my eye. It had been folded over, showing page five on the top. One of the articles had been cut out. Indeed, not the entire article but a section of the accompanying photograph. The caption was also missing. The story was a report on the newly elected first mayor of Hampstead, the borough in which Mr. Plumtree lived. The newspaper was dated last Wednesday, the day before Mr. Plumtree became anxious and the fellow was seen lingering outside.

I showed it to Jeremy. "Do you know what was removed?"

He took the newspaper from me and read the article. "I'm afraid not." He handed it back.

"May I keep it?"

"I don't see why not. It's not relevant to the company."

I tucked the newspaper under my arm and announced that I'd completed my search. Jeremy held the door open for me. "I forgot to ask earlier," I said, "but do you know the name of the fellow who confronted Mr. Plumtree, or the name of his brother who went down on the *Elsie May*?"

"I'm afraid I don't. I wish I did, but the man didn't give his identity. He ranted a great deal. It was difficult to get through to him."

"Then I'll need a list of names and addresses of all the sailors who died."

"That's a good idea. The brother who confronted Tobias should be at the top of your suspect list."

Ten minutes later, I left the office with both the newspaper and the list of names and addresses for the deceased sailors. There were twelve, including the captain. I wasn't yet sure how I'd manage to visit them all, but I'd find a way. First, I wanted to call at the premises of *The Illustrated Courier*.

It was the same newspaper where the journalist who'd been following Floyd worked. As I waited in the reception area, the youth on the front desk greeted a man passing through as Mr. Paisley. It had to be the same man as Floyd's Mr. Paisley.

"Excuse me," I said, rushing to intercept him before he disappeared into the corridor. "Are you the journalist, Paisley?"

The man doubled back and regarded me. He was young, probably about my age, with a dark pencil-thin moustache and patchy whiskers. He gave me a pleasant smile. "I am he."

"I'm Cleopatra Fox, Floyd Bainbridge's cousin."

He regarded me again, this time more thoroughly. "Is that so?"

"Why have you been following him?"

He arched his brows as he gave me another thorough inspection. "Has he sent you to tell me to stop? If so, I must say you are the prettiest person to ever threaten me."

"I'm not threatening you, and he doesn't know I'm here. In fact, I'm here for something else and happened to overhear the clerk greet you by name. I'm not sure what I'm expecting to achieve from this exchange. I haven't thought it through."

He stroked his moustache with his thumb and forefinger as he once again studied me. Some men seem to think women dress to make themselves attractive to the opposite sex and therefore they have a right to look at you as if you were on display for their benefit. Mr. Paisley was one of those men. "Perhaps we can go to a teashop and you can think it through over a cup of tea and conversation."

"No."

He accepted my rejection with a rueful smile. "Then unless you have a point, I must be off."

"If I asked you to stop following Floyd, will you do it?"

"Not while he's in the presence of Miss Aldridge." Miss Aldridge was the mezzo soprano Floyd couldn't take his eyes off. "She's the one my readers are interested in, not him. Well, while she's with him, they are interested, naturally, but it's the hint of scandal that keeps them reading."

"What scandal?"

"I can't give up all my secrets, Miss Fox."

"You haven't given up any."

His smile turned sly. "Keep reading my column and all will be revealed in good time."

I took that to mean all would be revealed when he had enough evidence to back up whatever claim he was going to make about Miss Aldridge. I only hoped the scandal didn't tarnish Floyd's name along with hers.

"Does the scandal involve my cousin?" I pressed.

"Goodbye, Miss Fox. It was indeed a pleasure to meet you."

I watched as he rushed off, eager to get where he was going. Perhaps I should have agreed to accompany him to a teashop. If I had, he might have told me something about the scandal. I also hadn't eaten since breakfast, so it would be killing two birds with one stone.

But it wasn't worth it. Mr. Paisley seemed rather wormy to me, and five more minutes in his company would have been five minutes too long. I would warn Floyd about the impending scandal and leave it at that.

The clerk who'd gone searching for a copy of last Wednesday's edition of *The Illustrated Courier* returned with one in hand. I quickly skipped to page five.

The area cut out by Mr. Plumtree was part of the background of the photograph. The foreground focused on the new mayor as he addressed the public, while several gentlemen stood behind him. It wasn't until I read the caption that I realized one of the men was Mr. Plumtree. I'd not known what he looked like.

But why had he removed just that part of the photograph from his copy of the paper, and the caption, too? If he wanted to save it, he'd cut out all of it. Why just himself and the others?

I re-read the caption, but it merely listed all of the gentlemen in the picture as well as the firms they represented. The name of Gooding and Plumtree Shipping Company was in the middle. It occurred to me that the newspaper had made a mistake and attributed Mr. Plumtree's name to the wrong man. Since I didn't know what he looked like, I couldn't say for certain. He disliked incompetence so perhaps he'd come here to berate someone for the mistake.

"Have any of these men been here before?" I asked the clerk who'd returned to the front desk.

He studied the picture. "No, miss."

"Is this copy for sale?"

"It is."

I handed him sixpence and left with the paper. I

caught an omnibus from Fleet Street, intending to go directly home, but got off early and walked to Soho instead.

I was parched by the time I arrived at Broadwick Street so headed into the Roma Café. Harry was inside, perched on a stool beside the two elderly men who were always there. The proprietor, Luigi, leaned his crossed arms on the counter, a cloth slung over one shoulder. They were deep in conversation, but I wasn't sure what they could possibly all talk about. The two older men didn't speak much English.

Harry rose from the stool when he saw me. "Miss me already?"

"I miss your brain." A theory had begun to form on the journey home, but I didn't know if it was silly or not. I needed to talk it through with Harry.

He grinned. "It's my best feature." He indicated I should take a seat at our usual table near the window.

"Coffee, Miss Fox?" Luigi called from the counter.

"Tea please, Luigi."

He pulled a face. "One puddle of dirty water coming up."

"So?" Harry prompted. "How did your interrogation of Mrs. Plumtree go?"

I told him my impressions of the widow, and what I'd learned from her and the butler. "I then went to the office of Gooding and Plumtree. I met Jeremy Gooding and his father."

"What did you think of them?"

"It's hard to say. Both were helpful. I spent a little longer in Jeremy's company than his father's and should probably tell you that he's quite friendly with Kitty Plumtree."

"How friendly?"

"He didn't like that I'd spoken to her without him present. He called her fragile, and demanded I warn him next time I want to see her."

"From your description, she does seem fragile. Do you think there's something between them that I ought to report to Massie?"

I hesitated, not wanting to leap to the wrong conclusion. And yet I wanted Hyacinthe to know so she could make up her own mind. "Why else would he be so protective?"

"Men and women can be friends, Cleo. We are." He leveled his gaze with mine. "Aren't we?"

Luigi arrived with my tea, saving me from being sucked into the warm depths of Harry's eyes. A woman could drown in that gaze if she wasn't careful.

"I just thought you should know." I took a long sip of tea until I'd composed myself again then launched into what I'd learned at Gooding and Plumtree. "I bought a copy of last Wednesday's edition from *The Illustrated Courier* and found the photograph Mr. Plumtree cut out."

Harry studied the article and photograph for a long time. "All right, you win. I can't guess your theory."

"You've met him. Can you confirm if that's Tobias Plumtree?"

"It's him. You didn't know what the victim looked like?"

"No. I didn't take any notice of the pictures in the Plumtrees' drawing room, although I'm sure there must have been some."

"And you call yourself a good detective."

He may have been teasing, but he was right. I should have been more observant. "The thing is, I didn't know what he looked like, and that got me thinking that perhaps the middle-aged stranger Jeremy saw outside the office didn't know either. We know Mr. Plumtree became worried on Thursday and this newspaper is dated Wednesday. I think we can safely link his worry to this photograph."

"I agree."

"So, what if the stranger read the caption in the paper then married that to Mr. Plumtree's face because, like me, he didn't know what Mr. Plumtree looked like? What if he then went to the office of Gooding and Plumtree the following day, on Thursday? When Tobias saw him, he became worried for his life because he knew the man was a threat. But!"

Harry had been about to say something until I interjected. "But, then I realized that didn't make sense. If the stranger already knew Mr. Plumtree's name, he would have easily worked out where he worked. His name is in the company name. So that had me thinking that I had my theory the wrong way around. What if the stranger knew what Mr. Plumtree *looked* like, but not his *name*?"

"And he learned that, as well as where he worked, from the caption." He pointed to the company name in the newspaper. "It explains why he went to the office the very next day, not Plumtree's home."

I sat back, feeling somewhat exhausted after blurting out everything I'd learned, as well as my theory. It would have been easier if he'd stayed with me and we'd investigated together.

"I think you might be onto something," he said. "It's a good theory. Someone recognized Plumtree's face in this photograph, matched the name in the caption, then found out where the office of Gooding and Plumtree was located. But if the stranger didn't know his name or where he worked, then it's not someone linked to the sinking of the *Elsie May*."

"That's true."

He tapped his finger on the caption. "Who would know Plumtree's face but not his name?"

I smiled.

"You've thought of that too, haven't you?"

"It was you who told me Plumtree came from the slums. Perhaps someone from his past recognized him but didn't know his name."

I thought it was a good theory, but Harry looked bothered by it. His frown deepened when I mentioned Mr. Plumtree's slum origins. "What is it?" I asked gently, although I had an inkling.

He hesitated, but I didn't prompt him to go on. I wanted him to answer in his own time. Eventually, he did. "Plumtree managed to climb out of his miserable life and make something of himself. I don't like that we're dragging him back there, after his death."

"If his past is linked to his death, it's not our doing. We're just trying to get to the truth." I reached across the table and covered his hand with mine. "You may have come from a difficult childhood too, but from what I've learned about Plumtree today, I can assure you that you and he are not alike."

He stared down at our hands. "Neither of us managed to outrun our pasts."

"Your past is irrelevant. It's who you are now that matters."

He turned his hand over and lightly closed his fingers around mine. "It's relevant to some."

I caressed his thumb with mine then suddenly stopped as a thought struck me. "It bothers Miss Morris? Well, then she's—"

"Not her." He whipped his hand back. "I haven't told her."

Then he must be referring to my family, and how my uncle had unceremoniously dismissed him from the role of assistant manager when he discovered he'd been a convicted thief.

He suddenly stood. "I'll let you finish your tea in peace. May I make a suggestion about your investigation?"

I blinked rapidly at him, trying to re-orient myself. "Yes, of course."

"Telephone my father when you get back to the hotel, and ask him to have someone look into Plumtree's past. Find out where he came from and what he did before becoming co-founder of Gooding and Plumtree. No one becomes that successful from nothing. There are always steps that lead there."

I nodded and watched him leave the café. Where had our conversation gone so wrong? Was it something I'd said?

As usual, when we touched on personal matters, the conversation ended abruptly and awkwardness descended between us. I headed back to the hotel thinking about how I could return things to the way they were, when I should have been thinking about the investigation and my next steps.

CHAPTER 6

J managed to arrive back at the hotel in time to change clothes and join Aunt Lilian and Flossy in the hotel's large sitting room for afternoon tea with their friends. We whiled away a few pleasant hours before my aunt and cousin retired to their respective suites. I sought out Mr. Hobart instead and found him in his office, preparing to leave for the day.

"May I use your telephone to call your brother?" I asked.

"Of course," he said as he put on his coat. "Are there developments in your investigation?"

"A few. Harry suggested I ask his father to use his contacts at the Yard to find out more about the victim's past."

"It's marvelous that you're working together

again. You make a good team. I'm pleased the arrival of Miss Morris on the scene hasn't stopped your collaboration."

I touched the telephone receiver but didn't remove it from its hook. "So…"

He'd been about to open the door but stopped. "Go on."

"So…you don't think we should stop seeing one another? It's just that, I don't want to upset Miss Morris. I can see how it looks from her point of view."

He regarded me with those soulful blue eyes of his. "If Miss Morris is upset that you are in Harry's life then perhaps she's not the one for him. Anyway, it's early days in their relationship. I wouldn't leap to conclusions just yet."

He bade me goodnight then left, asking me to lock the door when I'd finished. I sat at the desk and put a call through to D.I. Hobart's house. I was glad he answered and not his wife. I didn't feel like hearing her frosty reception.

After we finished our conversation, I went in search of the staff I could confide in. Harmony had finished a few hours ago and was nowhere to be seen. Victor was on duty in the kitchen and couldn't get away. But Peter, Frank and Goliath were available and not overly busy. Under the guise of having a passing conversation in the foyer, I tasked them with calling at the addresses written on the list Jeremy Gooding had given me. We divided up the twelve names, taking three each.

"Find out if any of your three sailors has a brother aged in his early twenties who is stocky with a broad nose," I said.

"Is the brother a suspect?" Peter asked.

"Perhaps. He blamed Mr. Plumtree for the sinking of the *Elsie May*."

"Blimey," Frank muttered.

"Want us to question him if we come across him?" Goliath asked.

"No. I don't want him knowing why you're there at all. Make up an excuse about a report of a gas smell in the area and you're doing a check. At this point, I simply want the name and address of the fellow who confronted Mr. Plumtree."

"And you, Miss Fox?" Peter asked. "Are you sure you should visit your three alone at night?"

"I'll wait for the morning," I assured him.

The lift door opened and Floyd stepped out, a broad smile on his face. He gave John the lift operator a cheerful clap on the shoulder then approached me. My three companions scattered.

I smiled at Floyd. "You look dapper. Going out somewhere special?"

He fingered his white bow tie and stretched his neck. "I'm going to my club for a bite to eat then I'm off to the opera."

"Again? You must really like Miss Aldridge."

He shushed me then glanced around. "Don't let my parents hear you."

"Neither of them are here, and I'm quite sure they know about her. You've hardly been discreet. Speaking of Miss Aldridge..." This time I glanced around, too. We were alone, however. "I happened to bump into that journalist, Mr. Paisley, at the office of *The Illustrated Courier*."

"Cleo," he ground out through a tight jaw. "Did you have to interfere?"

"I didn't seek him out on purpose. I was there as part of my investigation. As to the rest," I sniffed. "I wanted to know why he was following you."

"And?"

"His response concerned me. Apparently there is a scandal involving Miss Aldridge that he'll expose when he can prove it. I thought you should know so you can...do what must be done."

"And what must be done?"

"Far be it from me to give advice. I'm not one to always do as I'm told. So I can't expect you to do as I say."

His lips tilted with his smirk. "But...?"

"I think you know what should be done, Floyd."

He removed his hat and dragged his hand through his hair. "Thanks for the warning."

"You looked very happy as you came out of the lift. Did John tell you a joke or is there another reason for your good mood?"

His smile returned, broader than ever. "I've been tasked with sending out new invitations and organizing publicity for the dinner."

"I'm so pleased for you. You'll do an excellent job of it. Your father must think so too."

"I don't know what made him change his mind."

I smiled to myself. "I'm sure he saw how well liked you are amongst the fashionable set. He knows how important it is to get them on board."

"Finally, all those parties paid off."

"Such a hardship it has been for you," I teased. "But seriously, congratulations."

"Don't congratulate me yet. It could well be a disaster. I plan on taking some risks with the guest list."

"Is that wise?"

He slapped his hat on his head and headed for the door, walking backwards. "Nobody could ever accuse me of being wise." He gave me a casual salute goodbye and left the hotel, whistling.

Floyd might no longer gamble with cards, but he still gambled in other ways. I just hoped the dinner had a different outcome than his card playing, because Harry couldn't help him if he failed.

* * *

I SPENT the morning traveling around the city, calling on the three addresses I'd assigned myself. I began with the captain's home. According to the housekeeper I engaged in idle chatter, he did not have a brother. The two other sailors on my list did, however one had tall brothers and the third fellow's brother was away at sea and had been for months, according to the grieving mother.

I returned to the hotel, hoping Peter, Goliath and Frank had some news for me about the families of the sailors on their lists, but unfortunately not everyone could be accounted for when they made their calls the previous evening. Nobody had been home at two of the addresses. In the homes where they managed to speak to someone, no brothers of the deceased matched the description given to me by Mr. Plumtree's butler.

I was about to leave again, to see if I could find someone home at those two remaining addresses this morning, when Miss Hessing emerged from the lift with her mother. She waved, and I waved back, as both women approached.

Mother and daughter were so alike with their height and elongated faces, but were quite different in every other way. Mrs. Hessing was as bold as her wide-brimmed hat with the fountain of black ostrich feathers on the crown fronted by a crimson and black bow. The real red rose pinned to the bow's center was beginning to wilt.

In contrast, her more demure daughter wore cream chiffon and lace with a pearl choker circling her throat. She made quite an elegant picture. She looked happy, too, and she didn't even bat an eye when her mother greeted me loudly when she was still several feet away. Heads turned. Some guests turned up their noses at the shrill voice.

I smiled warmly. "Are you heading out?"

"We're having luncheon at the Savoy with friends," Mrs. Hessing said.

I leaned forward, conspiratorially. "Don't mention the Savoy in my uncle's presence."

"Bah!" She flapped her hand as if swatting a fly. "Sir Ronald knows I'm a dedicated admirer of the Mayfair. The Savoy could never tempt me. But my friend insists. She prefers their restaurant."

"When our new restaurant opens, you must convince her to try it. I'm sure Mrs. Poole's menu will win her over."

"Will do, Miss Fox, will do. Ah. Mr. Hobart is there. I must have a word."

Miss Hessing and I watched her mother chart a course for the manager at full steam. The ostrich feathers rippled with every stride. "Is everything all right?" I asked.

"I'm not sure," Miss Hessing said, frowning. "Do you think they're discussing me?"

While Mrs. Hessing didn't glance at us, Mr. Hobart certainly did. "I think so. Do you know why?"

She sighed. "My mother is growing suspicious as to why I've been ill several times this week when she has met with friends in the afternoon. She thinks it's too much of a coincidence."

Miss Hessing didn't look ill. She looked flushed with contentment. "Is she right to be suspicious?"

She turned her back to her mother and Mr. Hobart and clasped my hand. She grinned. "He's marvelous, Miss Fox."

"I assume you're referring to Mr. Liddicoat." Mr. Liddicoat was a gentleman she'd danced with several times at various balls in recent weeks. When it became clear he was quite enamored with her, I'd helped broker their first meeting alone. Miss Hessing had mentioned him to me several times since, and always with a smile on her face.

"I am. We've been going for walks every time I can get away from Mother."

I squeezed her hand. "I'm pleased for you. But does the fact that you're lying to your mother mean she doesn't know about him yet?"

"I don't think she does, but she's suspicious about all these headaches I've been getting. She's probably asking Mr. Hobart if he has seen me leave the hotel when she's not here."

Knowing Mr. Hobart, he would be well aware that Miss Hessing had left the hotel in the afternoons. Even if he wasn't in the foyer to witness her departure himself, one of the front of house staff would have informed him. He knew everything that went on in the building.

"She could simply be asking him for the name of a good doctor for you," I said hopefully.

"Perhaps." She chewed her lip. "Will you find out for me?"

"I'll see what I can do, but Mr. Hobart prides himself on discretion. If your mother has asked for his silence on the matter, he won't tell anyone. Miss Hessing, may I make a suggestion that will negate the need to sneak around?"

"You want me to tell her," she said flatly. "I can't. Not yet. She won't approve of him. He's not the sort of man she wants me to marry. He's not wealthy enough or titled. She'll call him a gold digger and be quite awful about it. I know she will."

I placed a hand on her arm to calm her. "If you truly like him, you'll have to do it sooner or later."

"Clare!" Mrs. Hessing shrieked. "Clare, come along!"

Miss Hessing squeezed my hand, gave me a grim smile, and hurried towards her mother.

I joined Mr. Hobart and we watched them leave the hotel.

"What did Mrs. Hessing want?" I asked, not expecting an answer.

"I can't tell you."

"Then let me guess. She wants to know if her

daughter leaves the hotel when she's supposedly resting."

He didn't answer but his small smile told me I was right.

"I won't spy on Miss Hessing for you," I went on. "Anyway, I know where she goes, so I don't have to spy on her. She's—"

"Don't tell me!" Realizing how loud he'd been, he gave a self-conscious tug of his cuff. "If you don't tell me then I can report back to Mrs. Hessing that I don't know anything and it won't be a lie."

"Very wise, and diplomatic, too. It's unfair that she asked you to find out where Miss Hessing goes."

He smiled a greeting at a passing Prussian banker and his wife. Once they'd gone, he turned back to me. "I hope Miss Hessing's excursions don't place her in harm's way."

"They don't. Indeed, they make her very happy."

"I trust you, Miss Fox. I trust your judgement on this matter."

It was quite a responsibility he was giving me. I wasn't sure I wanted it.

He removed a folded piece of paper from his jacket pocket. "I'm glad I caught you before you went out again. My brother called and wanted me to pass on this information." He handed me the paper and waited while I read.

D.I. Hobart's former colleague had been busy this morning. He'd dug into Tobias Plumtree's past and discovered two interesting points. The first was that Mr. Plumtree used to go by another name. He was born Thomas Plum in Bermondsey. It wasn't clear when he changed his name to the more upper-class Plumtree but he was still known as Thomas Plum when he registered his first business.

The second point of interest was the second name that appeared on the company deeds of that first business. A woman by the name of Lady Marguerite Mannix had a financial stake in The Plum Trading Company. The business traded for nine years before it was dissolved. Sometime in the year after it closed and before Gooding and Plumtree opened its doors, Thomas Plum became Tobias Plumtree.

"I wonder if Mr. Gooding knew his partner used to go by another name," I said.

Mr. Hobart pointed to the other name on the page. "Lady Mannix often stayed here. She came from a good family and married well. She was popular, a favorite of the prince. Hostesses always included her on their guest list."

"Where is she now?"

"I don't know. She disappeared off the social scene some years ago and stopped coming here. Whether she stopped coming to London altogether, I couldn't say."

"Could she have died?"

He shook his head. "I'm sure I would have heard."

"What was she like?"

"Charming. Although she wasn't the most beautiful woman to grace this foyer, she was one of the most alluring, if you understand my meaning."

I think I did. He meant the men desired her.

"You should ask Harry. He knew her better than me."

"I will ask him. Thank you. One more thing. Did Mr. Plumtree and Lady Mannix stay here over the same period of time?"

"I don't think so. Lady Mannix had been staying here ever since she was a young bride and Mr. Plumtree was a more recent guest."

He wanted to check his records for precise dates, so I left him to his filing cabinet full of guest names, past and present, while I went in search of other people who might remember Lady Mannix. Staff who'd worked for the hotel for a number of years recalled a handsome woman with a good nature and a lot of charm. Frank even commented that she was rather witty "for a toff." I found the men remembered her better than the women, and their gazes turned fond when I mentioned her name.

The staff could only tell me so much, however. I needed to speak to someone who moved in the same circles. I knocked on my aunt's door in the hope she was there.

Her thin voice invited me inside. "How lovely to see you this morning, Cleo."

It was already the afternoon, but I didn't correct her. She sat in a darkened sitting room with the only light coming from the curtains that had been parted a mere inch. The strip of light sliced across the desk and cut through the middle of the room, avoiding Aunt Lilian's reclining form on the sofa.

She lifted a hand, inviting me to sit, then brushed her fingers over her forehead. It must ache, but she smiled through it, albeit wanly. I was pleased that she was fighting through her withdrawal and not taking more tonic to ease her pain and give her some energy.

"How are you, my dear?" she asked.

"Fine, thank you, Aunt. I'm working on an investigation, actually. The death of Mr. Plumtree is suspicious."

Aunt Lilian knew I investigated from time to time. She'd not been as overbearing as my uncle and even assisted me on occasion. Even so, she hoped I'd set it all aside one day and lead a more normal life. In her book, a normal life meant marrying well and having children.

She winced. "Spare me the horrible details. I can't cope with anything too gruesome this morning."

"I was hoping you could help me, Aunt. You see, I've discovered that Mr. Plumtree was in business many years ago with a woman known as Lady Mannix."

Her eyes widened. "Marguerite? How extraordinary. I didn't know she knew him."

That answered one question. "Are you surprised to hear she had a stake in his company?"

"Yes. She never mentioned it. And her late husband was the sort who wouldn't approve of going into business. He barely tolerated your uncle. He believed a gentleman shouldn't work."

"When did she become a widow?"

"She was quite young, around thirty, I think. They didn't have children and she never remarried."

"Why not?"

Aunt Lilian smiled. "She enjoyed being a widow. Some would call her notorious."

"In what way?"

"In the way young widows often are—she took lovers."

"Didn't the other ladies in society look down on her for that?"

"They would have, but she was one of the prince's lovers, before he moved on. They remained friends, however, and his favor meant she enjoyed a particular status."

"What happened? Why did she leave society suddenly?"

Aunt Lilian settled back down into the sofa and rested her head on the pillow. "The same thing that happens to all well-born ladies who've never been educated in financial matters. The thing about becoming a widow is that one loses a husband but gains freedom. It can be wonderful, for a time, until one realizes that bills must be paid. Gaining freedom means gaining financial independence, and few of us are equipped to manage money. Although it was never discussed, there were small signs that she was having financial difficulty. I think she lost everything. She managed for a time, relying on the generosity of friends, but eventually the friendships dried up too."

"Where is she now?"

"I have no idea. She simply disappeared from everyone's life. I never heard from her again, nor did anyone I know. She had close friends whom she may have remained in touch with, but she and I weren't *that* close."

I quickly calculated the date The Plum Trading Company had gone out of business based on the information from D.I. Hobart. "Was this in 1888?"

"Later. Around '90 or '91. She came to the hotel intermittently towards the end. She must have been having difficulty for some time before she completely stopped coming to the Mayfair."

That was at least two years after her business with Mr. Plumtree ended. Had she lost all her money when the company folded?

Aunt Lilian yawned and closed her eyes.

"Can I get you anything?" I asked.

"Close the curtains. It's too bright in here."

I closed the small gap between the curtains and left her to rest.

Harmony intercepted me the moment I closed the door. She signaled for me to join her at her cart and together we slowly walked along the corridor.

"One of the other maids saw you go into Lady Bainbridge's rooms," she said. "I've been waiting for you to come out again. I hear you've been asking around about a particular lady who used to stay here."

"Lady Mannix. She was Mr. Plumtree's business partner when he was still known as Thomas Plum." I filled her in on everything I'd learned about Mr. Plumtree's past as well as Lady Mannix. "My aunt says she was something of a merry widow." I quite liked the sound of that. I could see the appeal of being a widow, but it necessitated being married in the first place. It was that state, where a husband could control every aspect of his wife's life if he chose, that I wanted to avoid.

"Very merry, from what I heard." Harmony's wicked smile intrigued me.

I put a hand to the cart and stopped it. "You know who her lovers were, don't you?"

"Just one."

"Who?"

She bit her lip and pushed on.

I stopped the cart again. "It was my uncle, wasn't it?"

"No!"

"It couldn't have been Floyd. He was too young. So it must have been one of the staff. I can't see it being Mr. Hobart."

"Good lord, no. He's devoted to his wife."

"It definitely couldn't have been Mr. Chapman." I tried to think of other men who'd been on the staff long enough and might appeal to a celebrated society beauty, but drew a blank.

Except for one name.

"It was Harry, wasn't it?" I knew from the way Harmony wouldn't meet my gaze that I was right. "He must have been young when she stayed here." I did some quick calculations in my head. "Only eighteen."

"Old enough. And by all accounts, she was extremely flirtatious. She knew how to accentuate her best features too."

I let go of the cart and Harmony pushed it forward. When she realized I didn't follow, she stepped backwards, pulling it after her.

"Does it bother you?" she asked.

"Of course not."

"But you and he—"

"Are merely friends. Anyway, even if we were together, his relationship with Lady Mannix was long ago. He was barely a man."

She nudged me with her elbow and winked. "She was probably his first."

I resisted the urge to childishly cover my ears. "I don't want to hear what you have to say on the matter, Harmony."

She gave me a smug smile. "I thought it didn't bother you."

We parted ways at the top of the stairs. She continued on to take the service lift while I headed back down to the foyer. Mr. Hobart emerged from his office as I was about to leave the hotel and signaled for me to wait. He was momentarily waylaid by a guest before joining me.

He informed me that the records he kept about the guests showed that Lady Mannix and Mr. Plumtree didn't stay at the Mayfair at the same time. "Lord Mannix first brought his new bride here in the seventies. After he died she continued to come once or twice a year, right up until 1891."

That was a year or so after Harry started at the hotel, and three years after The Plum Trading Company dissolved.

"Plumtree's first stay here was in '92," Mr. Hobart went on. "He continued to come until '96."

"Which is when he married and bought a house," I finished for him.

He nodded.

It didn't make sense. Why did a Londoner need to stay at a hotel? "Did he move out of London between '92 and '96?"

Mr. Hobart handed me a scrap of paper. "This is the address he gave when he checked in."

It was in Northumberland. I tucked the paper into my bag and headed out, only to think of something. I doubled back, annoying Frank as he had to open the door twice for me.

I couldn't see Mr. Hobart so approached Peter instead. The assistant manager was looking over the day's reservations. Guests checking in today would do so from two o'clock and he wanted to be prepared to greet them by name. He'd taken a leaf out of Mr. Hobart and Harry's book to ensure he was well prepared with the personal touch the Mayfair Hotel prided itself on.

"Peter, can you do something for me when you have a chance? There's no hurry."

He closed the book and handed it back to the clerk behind the counter. We stepped away so we couldn't be overheard. "Is this about Plumtree?"

"It is." I handed him the piece of paper. "This is the address he gave when he checked into the Mayfair. I want you to telephone the closest post office and ask if Mr. Plumtree ever lived in the village."

"You think he lied? Why?"

"Appearances, Peter. Appearances are everything if one wishes to make a name for oneself."

He self-consciously straightened his tie.

I hurried off again, giving Frank a cheery wave as I passed. He couldn't scowl in return because another guest was entering the hotel at the same time.

I walked quickly to Harry's office. I was eager to talk to him about Mr. Plumtree and Lady Mannix. I'd got over my initial shock after learning of their relationship. Now I was curious; curious to see his reaction when he heard her name.

CHAPTER 7

I spotted Harry through the window of the
Roma Café at the same moment he saw
me. We both froze. His companion followed his
gaze. It was too late for me to turn and flee. I had to
brazen it out.

I entered and greeted Miss Morris with a smile.
Harry re-introduced us, although I hadn't forgotten
the beautiful brunette. It was impossible to tell
whether she remembered me. She kept her smile
bland and her features schooled.

"Enjoying lunch together?" I asked, rather stupidly considering they both had empty pasta bowls
in front of them.

"We've just finished," Harry said smoothly. That
was the thing about Harry. Very little fazed him.

Having the woman he was courting run into the woman he'd recently kissed would have sent most men into a spin, but Harry took it in his stride.

It would have been fun to mention Lady Mannix to him now, but I refrained.

"Would you like some pasta, Miss Fox?" Luigi asked from the counter.

"Not today, thank you, Luigi."

The two barnacles on the stools nodded a greeting. I nodded back.

Miss Morris watched the exchange with a slight tightening around her eyes. "You come here often, Miss Fox."

She didn't pose it as a question, but I answered it as if she had. "Only when I need Harry's assistance with a case. As I do today."

"Another investigation? How intriguing. I do envy you having interesting employment, but I don't think I could be as brave as you."

"I wouldn't call myself brave."

"Nonsense. You're extremely brave for asking difficult questions. I'd be too cowardly, afraid of what people must think of me. I like to be liked. It's a weakness of mine."

"Hardly a weakness," I found myself replying without thinking.

She stood and smiled. "I'd better leave you two to it. I have to get back to work anyway. Thank you for lunch, Harry." She gathered up her bag and gloves and slipped out of the café before Harry could open the door for her.

I watched her go, somewhat confused. Had she just insulted me? The more I thought about it, the more I was sure she had just informed me I wasn't very well liked. Not only had she couched the insult in subtlety, she'd made it appear as though she'd put herself down in the process. She was clever, I'd give her that.

Harry didn't seem to have noticed the barb, if that's what it was. Nor did he seem concerned that I'd interrupted his lunch. He seemed to take my presence in his stride as he invited me upstairs to his office.

"What can I do for you?" he asked as he sat behind the desk.

I sat too and placed my bag on my lap. I clutched it tightly between both hands. "Have you spoken to your father today?"

"No. Did his former colleague discover something about Plumtree?"

"He certainly did. Plumtree used to go by the name Thomas Plum. He was born and bred in Bermondsey. He started his first business venture under that name. It was financed by a woman. A lady, as it happens."

His brows rose. "Intriguing. Perhaps she was his mistress."

"She probably was, given her reputation."

His brows rose further. "If you've discovered that much, then you've asked around about her. That must mean your aunt knows her. Who is she?"

"My aunt knew her, but so did the hotel staff. She used to stay at the Mayfair sometimes. Her name is Lady Marguerite Mannix."

Never had I seen the cool, composed Harry Armitage squirm. But he did indeed squirm in his seat at the mention of Lady Mannix. He also blushed. He tried to hide it by dipping into his top drawer and making a great show of removing a notepad, even though there was one already out.

"I remember her," he finally said. "She was a guest many years ago, in my early days working there. I was just a porter then."

"You were more than just a porter to her."

He looked up sharply. "What's that supposed to mean?"

I set my bag on the desk and sat back with a smile. I couldn't help myself. "It means precisely what you think it means. Do you really want me to spell it out to you?"

"No!"

I grinned. "So the rumors are true."

He crossed his arms and thrust out his chiseled jaw. "It was a long time ago."

"Indeed. You were only eighteen. She was older but very alluring, so I hear. Were you smitten with her?"

He rolled his eyes. "You're enjoying this, aren't you?"

My smiled widened. "Or was she smitten with you? I'm sure an older woman would enjoy having a young, handsome man at her beck and call, day and night."

"Very amusing," he said wryly. "Now, if you stop teasing me, I'll tell you all about her."

As it turned out, he couldn't tell me much more than I already knew. Lady Mannix had somehow lost all of her husband's money after his death. She had no estate to go home to, as that had been left to a cousin who didn't want her there. Harry claimed her finances had been whittled down to almost nothing by the time he knew her.

"I got the impression she was lonely," he said. "Invitations had dried up. Her friends didn't visit. She wore out of date clothes and all her jewels were sold off. Then she just stopped coming to the hotel altogether."

"No one has heard from her since," I said quietly. "I wonder where she is."

He rubbed a finger over his top lip and his gaze shifted to his address book. "She wrote to me."

I blinked slowly. "She wrote to you?"

"A few years ago, care of the hotel."

"Of all the people she could have written to, why you?"

He regarded me with an arched brow and tilted head. "Can you not work it out, Detective Fox?"

Oh. Right. She'd hoped to renew their relationship. I cleared my throat and looked away. I couldn't look at him even though I dearly wanted to know if he'd taken her up on the offer.

He reached for the book and flipped through the pages. "I have the address where she was living at the time. She may have moved since, but it's a place to start." He found it and copied it to his notepad.

I held out my hand to accept the page, but he pocketed the notebook instead and stood. "It's best if I speak to her about this."

I stood, too. "Is it? Or do you just want to see your first love again?"

He picked up my bag and handed it to me with a smile. "Who said she was my first?"

* * *

LADY MANNIX LIVED in a grand townhouse overlooking Greenwich Park. She did not own it, however. Her late husband's aunt did, and Lady Mannix was her companion. The elderly aunt made this very clear when she gave us permission to speak to her niece-in-law. She grudgingly left the drawing room, leaning heavily on her walking stick. A footman closed the double doors behind her, but not before Lady Illingsworth shot Lady Mannix a glare of disapproval.

Once the doors clicked shut, Lady Mannix released a breath and visibly relaxed. "It is so good to see you, Harry. Even if it is under strange circumstances."

I'd explained the reason for our visit upon our arrival and pressed home the need for discretion. It was the only way that Lady Illingsworth would leave us alone with Lady Mannix.

"You look very well," she went on. "Very well, indeed."

"As do you," Harry said politely.

It was difficult to gauge Lady Mannix's age. She was extraordinarily pale, with some lines around her eyes and a soft jawline, but these hints did nothing to hide her strong features. Although Mr. Hobart had said she was no beauty in her day, I suspected she'd been striking with a curvaceous figure. When Harry walked in, she'd gasped at the sight of him then self-consciously touched her graying hair. She now angled herself to best advantage, sitting up straight and pushing out her considerable bosom. I may as well have not been in the room.

She touched her hair again. "You should have sent word that you were coming today. We could have received you properly."

"We're sorry for calling on you unannounced," he said. "It's fortunate that you were at home."

Lady Mannix's lips twisted. "She's a recluse and expects me to live as one, too. We do not go out. Not even for a walk around the park, and certainly not to anything that matters."

"You've lived here ever since writing to me?"

"After I last saw you at the Mayfair Hotel, things became…difficult. I had to take up her offer." She smoothed a hand down her black silk skirt. "My life is very different to how it used to be. Very different indeed." She spoke with candor, but I wasn't sure if that was because it wasn't in her nature to feel shame or because she felt comfortable with Harry.

It must be hard for a woman so used to living a life filled with parties and lovers to find herself contained within walls with only an elderly matron for company. It was no wonder her tone held more than a hint of bitterness.

"Do your friends call on you?" Harry asked.

"You mean my former friends? No. None know about my situation and that's the way I'd like to keep it." Her gaze flicked to me before shifting away again. "You understand, don't you, Harry?"

"Of course. No one needs to know we met you."

"You always were discreet." Her lips curved with her secretive smile.

Harry cleared his throat. "Miss Fox would like to ask her questions now."

"Ah, yes, about my former associate, Mr. Plum. Did you say you're looking for him? I'm afraid I can't help you."

"We're not looking for him," I clarified. "He passed away. We're investigating his death."

A number of emotions passed across her face, from disbelief to curiosity, but not sadness. "What do you mean 'investigating his death?'"

"The police say he killed himself, but others suspect he was murdered. I'm trying to get to the bottom of it."

She pressed a hand to her chest. "Good lord. I wish I could say I don't believe he would take his own life, but I haven't seen him in years. He could have changed in that time."

"When did you last see him?"

She thought for a few moments. "Our business concluded in '88 and we had nothing to do with one another after that."

"Why not?"

She shrugged. "We moved in different circles."

"You weren't friends?"

"No, Miss Fox. We were merely business partners. You obviously know that I financed his company or you wouldn't be here. We had an amicable arrangement for a number of years but decided to wind it up in '88. There was no animosity between us, no resentment or anything like that. If you've come here with the notion that I could be a suspect in his murder then I'm afraid you're mistaken. Not only did I not have a reason to kill him, but I never leave this house."

"Did you know he changed his name to Plumtree?"

"Did he? No, I didn't know. As I said, we lost touch. It happens."

"Was your company a success?"

The question caught her off guard. She took a moment to answer. "It turned a modest profit. Enough to launch his career and earn the trust of other investors, but not enough to live a comfortable life for the rest of my days once it wound up."

"Then why wind it up at all? Why not build upon that modest success?"

This time she answered smoothly. "I'm afraid he's the only one who could have answered that. I was merely a financial backer, Miss Fox. I didn't make any decisions."

"It seems odd that you wouldn't discuss that with him. As the majority stakeholder, surely he gave you an explanation for his decision."

She merely lifted a shoulder in a shrug. "Some men don't think women understand business so don't discuss it with us. I wish it weren't true, but that's their nature."

I didn't press her anymore. She wasn't going to deviate from her story, no matter how many times I asked. While I didn't understand why women allowed men to use their money in any way they saw fit and without question, I wasn't so naïve to think it didn't happen. It was conceivable that Lady Mannix handed over her money to a man she trusted and let him do what he wanted with it.

The real question was, why did she trust him in the first place?

"How did you two meet?"

"Why does that matter? It has nothing to do with his death, surely."

"It helps me get a rounder picture of him. I know a little of what Tobias Plumtree was like, but I know nothing about Thomas Plum. You did. It's interesting that a man from Bermondsey became business partners with the widow of a baron."

"We met on a steamship, as it happens. I was a guest of the captain's and he was a member of staff."

I waited but she offered no more. "And you decided to entrust him with your money after that? Forgive me, Lady Mannix, but it seems a great leap of faith on your part."

"Oh, it was. I don't deny that, Miss Fox. But he was a very smart man, and very articulate. He had excellent ideas that he was bursting to share with someone. I listened when no one else would. I could see he was driven to succeed and would put his heart and soul into whatever he chose to do. By the end of the two-week journey I decided to give him a chance and invest in him. It was a good decision."

"Was it? It seems to me that your life took a turn for the worse *after* the business dissolved."

She spread her fingers over her skirt. "That doesn't mean going into business with him in the first place wasn't a good idea. For nine years, everything was fine."

"Do you blame Mr. Plumtree for your change in circumstances?"

"Of course not. It's not his fault that I lived a life I could no longer afford. Miss Fox, is this really necessary? I didn't kill Thomas—Tobias. I didn't even know he changed his name."

"Do you read *The Illustrated Courier*?"

"What an odd question! No, I don't. We only read *The Times*."

I removed the newspaper article from my bag and showed her the picture. "Have you seen this?"

"No." She went to hand it back but spotted Mr. Plumtree in the background. She grunted. "He put on weight." She passed it to me. "No, Miss Fox, I didn't see that photograph and realize the man I knew as Thomas Plum was this fellow from Gooding and Plumtree, go to his place of business and kill him for whatever reason your perverted mind has thought up." She stood. "If you don't mind, it's time for Lady Illingsworth's tea and she doesn't like her routine to be upset." She pressed a button on the wall and the footman opened the door.

I tucked the article back into my bag and stood. "Thank you for your time. I appreciate it."

Her lips flattened. "Good day, Miss Fox."

She turned away from me and offered her hand to Harry. She smiled sadly. "You always were very good at indulging a woman's whims, but *you* ought to ask the questions. Your charm is your best feature."

Harry took her hand but shook it instead of kissing the back of it. "Cleo is the lead detective and had to ask those questions. Besides, sometimes charm doesn't get results."

Her smile slipped off. I wasn't sure if it was because he'd taken my side rather than hers, or because he'd used my first name, indicating that we were more than merely colleagues.

We passed the footman and followed the butler to the front door. There was no sign of Lady Illingsworth. He opened the door, but Harry didn't exit behind me.

"What newspapers do you have delivered?" he asked.

The butler's rapid blink was the only indication

he thought the question strange. "Lady Illingsworth reads *The Times*."

"And Lady Mannix?"

The butler hesitated.

"Does she have any newspapers that are delivered to the staff sent up to her room?"

"I'm afraid I'm not at liberty to say, sir. Good day."

Harry left and trotted down the steps to join me on the pavement. "She definitely reads something other than *The Times*." He glanced at the stairs behind the fence leading down to the basement service door. "Want me to check?"

"No. If the butler is any indication, the staff will be loyal. We won't get a straight answer from them."

It was a perfect late-spring day with the sun shining and only a light breeze. I suggested we walk through the park to discuss the case, but he declined.

"I need to return to the office. We can talk on the journey back."

His explanation made sense, but it didn't stop me wondering if he refused because the last time we walked through a park together, I kissed him and he liked it.

Speaking of kissing… "What do you make of Lady Mannix's answers? You know her better than me…do you think she lied?"

"I think she lied about the type of relationship she had with the victim. It wasn't merely a business partnership. I think she financed his company because she was in love with him."

"I agree. And if she loved him enough to give him money, how did she feel when he dissolved the company and went out on his own? He would have severed all ties with her, professional and personal. We only have her word that they parted amicably."

"Once he changed his name, she could no longer even find him," Harry went on. "Until she saw his picture in the paper and his new name and place of business in the caption."

"If she was resentful that he left her all those years ago, she could have lured him to the Crown and Anchor, slipped into his room unnoticed, confronted him and killed him."

"She would have needed help to get him into the noose, but she could have hired a local thug. Perhaps he was the one watching the Gooding and Plumtree office. It's a solid theory, Cleo. Well done."

"Thank you, but you were an enormous help. I'd never have found her without you. It was fortunate you kept her address. Why did you, by the way?"

He shrugged. "Habit. I was still working at the hotel at the time, and we always kept as much information as we could about each guest, no matter how small."

As convincing as he sounded, I didn't believe him. Information about guests, such as a new address, was kept in the hotel records in Mr. Hobart's filing cabinet. They weren't noted down in private address books.

He nudged me with his elbow. "You didn't spare her any quarter. I think she was shocked by how ruthless you were in pursuing answers."

"She didn't like it. She certainly didn't like *me* by the end of that meeting."

"Does that bother you?"

"No." I frowned, wondering why it seemed to concern him that it might bother me, then I recalled what Miss Morris said about liking to be liked.

He nudged me again. "Good. It would be a shame to waste your talent for interrogation because you preferred to make friends."

I laughed softly. "The day I want to be friends with the likes of Lady Mannix, you have my permission to tell me I've lost my mind. What did you see in her, anyway?"

He stared directly ahead. "She was different back then."

"Younger? Prettier? More flirtatious?"

"She wasn't a suspect in a murder investigation."

It was my turn to nudge him, and we both laughed.

* * *

ACCORDING TO PETER, the address Mr. Plumtree gave the hotel whenever he stayed was false. It didn't exist.

I sat with my investigative team in the staff parlor, sipping cups of tea and nibbling on cakes left over from the main afternoon tea held in the sitting room. It was the staff's favorite time of day, when the maids had finished cleaning, the kitchen staff hadn't yet begun the dinner shift, and the foyer was quiet. Guests were generally in their rooms, resting before they dressed for dinner. The hotel was at its most peaceful, or as peaceful as it could be at the busiest time of year. It was also the only time the staff could indulge in the best leftover cake and tarts to be found in London.

Goliath drew his long legs in as a maid passed. "Why would Plumtree lie about where he lived?" he asked once she was out of earshot.

Frank rolled his eyes. "Because he lived in a slum. He couldn't give the address of a squat in Bermondsey, could he?"

Before I could tell him he was wrong, Victor piped up. "He did it because he wanted people to think he was living outside London. He wanted folk to think he only came to the city for business."

"But why?" Goliath asked. "If he lived somewhere nice in London, why stay at the hotel at all? Why pretend to live in Northumberland?"

"To look like a country gent with a manor, land, horses, all of it. He wanted people to think him a success."

"Which in turn would attract investors," I added. "Or to keep the investors he already had. Mr. Gooding, for example."

"He spun a web of lies around himself," Peter muttered.

The more I thought about it, the more I suspected it was true. Thomas Plum changed his name, pretended to have a country estate, and stayed in a luxurious hotel from time to time, all for the sake of appearances. He tried his best to distance himself from his past, although he couldn't altogether wipe his slate clean. It wasn't a secret that he'd come from the slums.

Or perhaps that was part of the illusion, too. A wealthy businessman who'd built an empire from nothing would have a certain appeal. Investors might see that as proof he could help them become wealthier too.

What happened if that web started to untangle? What if someone saw through the illusion, and was upset at being lied to? Could they have murdered him in revenge?

Harmony voiced what I was thinking. "Maybe

his business partner, Mr. Gooding, discovered Mr. Plumtree wasn't as successful as he let on."

It was a good theory. I placed Mr. Gooding near the top of my suspect list, but below Lady Mannix. I wasn't prepared to topple her from prime position yet. In my opinion, a rejected lover could be as vengeful as a gullible business partner, and given she might be both, her motive was strong indeed.

CHAPTER 8

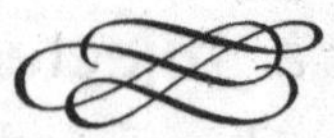

Sometimes the best part about going to dinner is the preparation beforehand with friends. I sat on the sofa in Flossy's room, mending the hem of a gown I wanted to wear, while Flossy soaked in the bath. She left the bathroom door open so we could talk. Harmony took in a selection of gowns for Flossy to choose from, but she rejected them all.

"I've got nothing to wear," she whined.

I rolled my eyes at Harmony as she passed me for the sixth time. "You have dozens of beautiful dresses."

"But I've already worn them all this season."

"You can wear them again."

She sighed. "You sound like Father. He called me spoiled, yesterday. He says I should consider myself fortunate to have so much."

"He's right."

"Then he told me to economize!"

I lowered my mending to my lap. "Is everything all right? Is the hotel in financial difficulty?"

"I don't know. Father never discusses such things with me. Do you think it is? Lord, Cleo, what will we do?"

"I'm sure everything's fine. The hotel is almost full and the restaurant will be a raging success. Don't worry." The restaurant *needed* to be a success. Uncle Ronald had spent a fortune renovating the properties next door to turn them into a dining venue fit for royalty. No doubt that was on his mind as he asked his daughter to rein in her spending.

Harmony carried the same pink and cream gown into the bathroom that she'd already showed Flossy. "What about this one, overlaid with lace at the bodice? I can remove three or four of the silk flowers from the hem of the rose ball gown and pin them at the décolletage here."

"That will work. It will look quite new. Harmony, you are my savior. Thank you." I heard the water slosh as Flossy got out of the bath.

Harmony set the gown down beside me then returned to the bedroom to fetch the ball gown with the flowers and the panel of lace. Flossy joined us a few minutes later and we all got to work, sewing.

Flossy chatted about our guests for the evening,

passing on the latest gossip she'd heard about them. None of it was particularly scandalous, but I enjoyed spending time with my bubbly cousin and Harmony. While she said very little, Harmony appeared to be listening intently.

Tonight, my aunt and uncle were hosting dinner with a close circle of friends in the hotel's dining room. It would be the last time they held a dinner there. In a few days hence, all dinners would be hosted in the new restaurant. This was a farewell, of sorts, a last hurrah in a venue that had seen thousands of courses served over the years to the wealthy and titled, dignitaries, international royalty and members of fashionable society. The room would still serve a purpose as a ballroom, but the new restaurant would become the jewel in the Mayfair Hotel's crown.

I was feeling a little more confident in the launch now that Floyd had been appointed to organize it. He knew the right people to invite.

As if thinking about him conjured him up, he joined us while we sewed. He threw himself onto a spare armchair and rested his feet on the low table opposite. Harmony glared at him and he removed them with an apology.

"You look a little harried," I said. "Is anything wrong?"

"It's this bloody launch dinner in the new restaurant. It's taking it out of me."

"I thought you were confident that everyone on your guest list would accept."

"The guests aren't the problem. Invitations have been sent and acceptances are rolling in. It's everything else. The painters are slow, the furniture company sent half the chairs we ordered and say the other half may not be ready on time, and apparently the amount of flowers we require needed to be ordered last week."

"What about the food? Is Mrs. Poole ready?"

"I don't know. I hope so. She's very experienced and efficient, so I'm sure everything's fine in that quarter."

"Floyd," I chided, "you must speak to her and ask if there's anything she needs. Your father tasked you with overseeing everything and that means following up with her and Mr. Chapman."

He sighed and rubbed his forehead. "I think I should make a list of things still to do."

Harmony sucked in a sharp breath. When we all looked at her, she bit her lip and lowered her head over her sewing.

Floyd narrowed his gaze at her. "Yes, yes, it's shocking that I haven't made a list before now. It's just that I'm not very good at note-taking. I tend to do things as they occur to me."

"That seems like a recipe for disaster," Flossy said.

"You could help, Floss. Come and be my assistant."

She pulled a face. "You already tell me what to do. If we made it official, you'd be unbearable."

I cleared my throat to get Floyd's attention then jerked my head in Harmony's direction.

"Harmony, do you know someone who'd be a good assistant?" he asked.

I rolled my eyes. Honestly, he was quite hopeless.

"I do," she said before I could get a word in. "Me."

I almost let out a small cheer, but held it in by biting my tongue.

"But you're a maid," Floyd said, somewhat stupidly.

"I know how to use a typewriter, I'm organized and efficient. I also know how the hotel operates, who to speak to in each department, where to find things and people, so I can get to work immediately. Someone from the outside would need to learn all of that before they could think about contacting suppliers."

Floyd grinned. "You're hired. Come to my suite tomorrow morning at ten and we'll begin."

"I'll be there at nine. I'll let Mrs. Short know, but I doubt she'll take my word for it. She'll require approval from either you or Sir Ronald."

He pushed to his feet. "Right you are."

As he turned to Flossy's writing desk, I gave Harmony a nod and a smile. I had a good feeling about this arrangement.

Flossy, however, did not. She'd looked more and more horrified during their exchange. "No!" she finally blurted. "You can't have her. Who'll do my hair and mend my dresses?"

"I'll still be available of an evening to help you prepare," Harmony said.

"You'll be too busy." Flossy flounced back into the sofa with a huff.

"There are other maids," I told her.

"But Harmony is the best at doing my hair. And would any of the other maids have thought about taking the flowers off one dress and adding them to another to turn it into something almost new? No, they would not. Harmony can't help you, Floyd. Find someone else."

Floyd sat at her desk to write. "I'm overruling you. Anyway, it's just until the dinner is finished. You can have her back then."

"I'll speak to Father about this."

Floyd kept writing, unconcerned about his sister's protest.

She needed to be told, however. "Flossy, this isn't your decision to make. It's Harmony's." I turned to her, brows arched in question.

Harmony looked trapped. She didn't want to displease either cousin. She knew the arrangement with Floyd was temporary and she'd have to return to her maid's duties after the restaurant opening. She didn't want to fracture the relationship she'd developed with Flossy.

A sharp knock on the door saved her from speaking. "Floyd!" came my uncle's deep baritone. "Are you in there?"

Floyd sighed as he rose. "He sounds angry. I wonder what I've done now."

Harmony opened the door and let in a bullish Uncle Ronald. He stormed past her without acknowledging her. He gave Flossy and me a cursory nod before shaking a piece of paper at his son.

"Are you mad?" he snapped. "Half the people on this guest list are artists, singers and dancers!"

"You agreed they'll garner the attention we need for the opening," Floyd snapped back. "Cleo, you were there. You must recall the conversation."

Fortunately my uncle continued to ignore my presence and glare at Floyd. I didn't want to be dragged into their argument.

"One or two is fine," he shouted, "but not this many! Did you not hear me when I said the dinner should be a genteel affair? The press will laugh at us. Not to mention the wives of the men who keep these women as mistresses won't come." He shook the paper in Floyd's face again.

Floyd snatched it off him. "You're exaggerating. Only three of the women on here are someone's mistress, and one of those is rumored to be with the prince. The others are famous in their own right. They're precisely who we need, Father. Once the press is aware of who is on our guest list, they'll be clamoring for more information about the dinner. Having pre-opening publicity is just as important as having the journalists there on the night itself."

Uncle Ronald wasn't used to Floyd standing up for himself. He certainly wasn't used to Floyd's explanations being valid. His temper cooled somewhat and he looked as though he might apologize.

Then he focused on something else that Floyd had done, or, rather, not done. "Mrs. Poole says you haven't checked in with her yet. Not only that, Mr. Chapman has concerns that the restaurant won't be ready on time. Have you spoken to the painters?"

"Not yet," Floyd mumbled.

"And what about the decorator?"

"I'll contact him tomorrow."

"Tomorrow is too late! It should have been done today!" Uncle Ronald squeezed the bridge of his nose. "I knew you weren't ready for the extra responsibility."

A thick silence fell, filling up the air and making it hard to breathe. I felt sorry for Floyd, but I knew speaking up in his defense would be a bandage rather than a cure. He needed to stand up for himself. But I changed my mind when my uncle spoke again.

"Cleopatra, you need to help him."

"I can't!" I blurted out.

His brow plunged. "Why not? What's more important than seeing that everything runs smoothly here?"

"Floyd already has an assistant." I gave Floyd an urgent nod to speak up. The last thing I wanted was to be saddled with helping him. The investigation would have to be put on hold.

He cleared his throat. "Harmony has agreed to take on the role."

"Who?"

Floyd indicated Harmony, sitting quietly on the sofa with her head held high.

Uncle Ronald shook his head. "You need a proper assistant. Find a suitable fellow. There must be hundreds capable of doing the job."

Every woman in the room bristled. I hoped Flossy would chastise her father for thinking a man needed to be appointed to the role, but she kept her mouth shut. She was probably too scared of him to speak her mind.

I wasn't, yet it was Floyd who spoke up first.

"I don't want someone capable of doing the job. I want someone capable of doing an *excellent* job. That's Harmony. Miss Cotton," he added, proving he knew her better than I realized. "She has the right attitude. She's efficient and organized. She knows the hotel inside and out. She's a good communicator and won't be satisfied until perfection is achieved."

Uncle Ronald pursed his lips as he regarded both Harmony and Floyd in turn. "And what say you, Miss Cotton? Do you want to work for my son? There's a lot to do and he won't be much help."

Floyd took the insult in his stride, more or less, and simply flattened his lips in response.

Harmony glanced at Flossy.

Flossy gave her a smile, proving she wasn't as selfish as her petulant outburst made her sound. "You will be very good at it, although not as good as you are at doing my hair. You should be Floyd's assistant, if you think you can put up with him."

Floyd huffed out a breath. "Cleo, would you like to insult me, too? It is your turn."

Harmony stood and addressed Uncle Ronald. "Yes, sir. I'd very much like to help Mr. Bainbridge make the restaurant opening successful. I already have some ideas on how to make the preparations run smoothly."

He put out his hand and she shook it. "Good luck, Miss Cotton. Now, someone needs to mention the new arrangement to Mrs. Short."

Floyd picked up the note he'd written. "I've already thought of that. I'll see that she's informed this evening."

Uncle Ronald grunted then saw himself out.

Floyd folded the piece of paper in half. "Not quite as hopeless as he thinks I am, am I?" He handed the paper to Harmony. "Your first task as my assistant is to take this down to Mrs. Short."

She accepted it and bobbed a curtsy. "Thank you for your faith in me, Mr. Bainbridge."

"Don't thank me yet. After this is over, you might never want to work for me again. I really am quite disorganized, you know."

"Oh, I know. But don't worry. I'm annoyingly efficient."

He laughed as he watched her go.

Flossy jumped to her feet and raced after her. "You will come back tonight, won't you? It's too late to organize someone else to do our hair, and you don't start your new role until tomorrow anyway."

"I'll return immediately, Miss Bainbridge." Harmony left, letter in hand.

Floyd sat with a sigh. "All in all, job well done. Now I can relax."

"You cannot," I told him. "Harmony will be an excellent assistant, but you still need to do some work, too. At least be awake and dressed at nine tomorrow morning for your first meeting."

He gave me a salute. "Yes, ma'am. I'm having an early night tonight, anyway. Mother wants me to attend this dinner with all of you."

"You won't go out afterwards?"

"All my friends seem to be occupied with family matters. It's the ball-and-chain season, and anyone with a title is expected to at least take a look at what's on offer this year."

Flossy made a sound of disgust in her throat. "It's not a banquet, Floyd."

"Agreed. It's more like a country market where it's every man for himself. The best girls are already taken. Luckily for me, I don't have to actively participate. I can watch from the sidelines as my friends make fools of themselves."

"Your turn will come."

"Until then, I shall enjoy my life."

"Is Jonathon looking for a wife?" Flossy asked. "I saw him in the Massies' box at the opera the other night."

"Why? You're not interested, are you?"

She pulled a face. "Lord, no. I just want to warn all my friends to avoid him if he's looking for a wife."

Jonathon was indeed someone to be avoided, in my opinion. He wasn't mature enough for marriage. That wouldn't stop his father from trying to marry him off to the richest heiress he could find, however. Hopefully Miss Massie wouldn't fall in love with him. He could be quite charming when he wanted to be.

"Jonathon wouldn't want to marry any of your friends anyway," Floyd said with a chuckle.

"What's wrong with my friends?"

"They're not rich enough. Old Lord Cremorne is putting enormous pressure on him to find an heiress. Not even Miss Hessing is rich enough for him, although Jonathon told me he would find a way to sabotage an arrangement if his old man made one with Mad Mrs. Hessing."

"He gets more and more horrid," Flossy muttered.

"There are one or two other American heiresses who could tempt him, but they haven't come over this season." He shook his head. "Perhaps the pressure he's under is why he's been so odd to me lately. Well, that and Cleo being cruel to him."

"Clearly it wouldn't have worked between us if his father wants an heiress," I pointed out.

"That isn't the only reason it wouldn't have worked, but you're right. Anyway, he's acting oddly of late. Hopefully he'll accept the invitation to the launch dinner."

"Speaking of the dinner, have you spoken to Miss Aldridge?" I asked. "Do you know what scandal the journalist is referring to?"

"What journalist?" Flossy asked. "And why does Floyd need to speak to the opera singer?"

"It's just about the dinner." Floyd got to his feet and headed for the door. "I'd best be off." Once his sister bowed her head to concentrate on her sewing, he put his finger to his lips to silence me.

I really didn't like keeping secrets, but it seemed I was always in possession of them. That was the problem with being a detective.

* * *

FORTUNATELY, Harmony's new position as assistant to Floyd didn't stop her from having breakfast with me before her meeting with him. I rarely saw her out of her maid's uniform, but she looked smart dressed in a navy skirt and jacket coupled with a white blouse embroidered at the collar. Although she wouldn't admit to being nervous about her new role, she didn't eat much.

Goliath arrived as we gathered up the dishes onto the tray. "Mr. Armitage is here to see you, Miss Fox. He says to dress for going out."

"Did he say where we're going?"

"No. Want me to go back down and ask?"

"It's all right. I'll be there in a moment."

"Right you are. One more thing." He removed a folded sheet of hotel letterhead from his pocket. "I found the brother of the sailor who went down on the *Elsie May*."

"Are you sure?"

"As sure as can be. He matched your description and lives at one of the addresses you gave me." He pointed to the name and address scrawled on the page.

"Thank you, Goliath. Excellent work."

"Any time, Miss Fox. Glad to help."

Harmony thrust the tray of dirty dishes at him. "Take this with you."

He backed away, hands in the air. "That's a footman's job."

"Then if you pass one on your way, you may hand it to him."

He accepted the tray with a sigh.

Harmony and I parted ways in the corridor after I assured her she'd be marvelous as Floyd's assistant. I headed downstairs and found Harry waiting outside, speaking to Frank. Considering Frank was a Bainbridge man, and my uncle didn't like Harry, it was a surprise to see them chatting amiably.

"What did you say to him to get him to be nice to you?" I asked as Harry and I walked off.

"We talked about football. His team Millwall have a new striker this year who looks good."

"I didn't know you liked football."

"I follow it. More importantly, Frank is a big Millwall fan."

"Nicely played. So where are we going and why?"

"We're going to the office of Gooding and Plumtree. There was a message waiting for me when I arrived at my office this morning from Jeremy Gooding. He claims a ledger from the *Elsie May* is missing and believes it was stolen. He wanted me to look into it. Apparently he got my name from Mr. Massie."

"That's a little awkward considering you're secretly investigating him on behalf of Mr. Massie. So why am I going?"

"You need to be involved in the investigation. The missing ledger could be linked to Plumtree's death."

When we got there, the situation played out a little differently to how I expected. For one thing, Harry didn't suggest that I be involved in the investigation. He told Jeremy and Mr. Gooding that I should be hired on my own account. He claimed he was too busy to take on another case, but was happy to give this one to me as he knew I'd already met the Goodings.

"But isn't Miss Fox too busy, too?" Jeremy asked. "She's investigating a murder, after all."

"The theft could be linked to the murder," Harry told him.

Mr. Gooding Senior had remained largely silent. He sat behind the desk, his solid frame filling the chair. It creaked as he leaned back and regarded us. When Harry again suggested they should hire me, Mr. Gooding finally spoke.

"I would prefer it if you were involved, Armitage. Perhaps you can advise Miss Fox."

"She requires no advising. She's capable of investigating on her own."

"That may be so, but that is my direction. Otherwise there are a dozen other private investigators we could hire if you don't agree."

"Mr. Armitage agrees," I said quickly. I didn't want to lose this fee-paying job altogether. "Let's begin, shall we? What was in the ledger that was stolen?" I removed a pencil and notepad from my bag and flipped to a blank page.

"It was a list of insurance claims for the *Elsie May*. Every piece of insured cargo, no matter how small, is listed along with the owner and their contact details."

"Why would someone want to steal it?"

"That's what we've been trying to work out," Jeremy said as he looked at his father. "We can't make any sense of it."

"Where was it stolen from?" I asked.

"Tobias's office," Mr. Gooding said. "Everything relating to the *Elsie May* is still stored in there."

"May we take a look?" Harry asked.

We headed along the corridor to Mr. Plumtree's office.

"Was the door locked?" I asked.

Jeremy nodded. "Only Father and I have a key."

Harry dropped to his haunches to inspect the lock. He pointed out some scratches around the metal. "Someone picked it, but not very cleanly. It probably took them a while to get in."

Jeremy unlocked the door with his key and we entered. He pointed out where the ledger was stored on the bookshelves along with several others. "It was clearly marked. Whoever stole it wouldn't need to look very hard to locate it."

Mr. Gooding opened the door of the cupboard under the bookshelves, revealing a metal strong box bolted to the floor inside. "What the thief didn't know is that there was a copy."

Jeremy's jaw dropped. "We keep a copy? Why?"

"The insurance company insisted." Mr. Gooding turned the dial back and forth a few times to unlock the door then removed several pages of loose paper. He sifted through them and returned some to the box while retaining others. He placed them on the desk and pored over them. "I still don't see why anyone would want to steal information about our clients' insurance claims."

I looked through the pages but didn't recognize any of the names associated with the claims.

Mr. Gooding sat on the chair and steepled his fingers. "The door's lock was picked, you say."

Harry nodded. "I'll check the front door before we leave, but I'm sure I'll find similar scratches on it."

Mr. Gooding addressed his son. "Who do we know who can pick a lock?"

Jeremy frowned. "No one."

"Precisely. That's the point, isn't it? People like us don't know people who can pick locks. Those sort are thieves. And where do you find thieves, Miss Fox?"

I gave him a blank look. "Prison?"

"The slums."

"Not necessarily."

"But usually. Indeed, I suspect if you canvas the thieves currently in prison, almost all are from the slums."

It was very difficult to argue with him when I didn't have access to the statistics. I also suspected he was right, even though I didn't want to admit it. "I'm afraid it'll take more time and resources than I have to interrogate every known thief in London's slums."

He wagged a finger in the air. "Perhaps I can help you narrow it down. You see, Tobias was originally from Bermondsey."

Once again, Jeremy stared at his father in surprise. "He was? Good lord. Extraordinary. And you knew?"

"It wasn't common knowledge, but he was always honest with me, right from the beginning."

That answered that question. "Are you suggesting I concentrate on thieves from the Bermondsey area?"

"Exactly, Miss Fox." He checked his watch then

pushed to his feet. "I'm afraid I have to go. The papers, if you please."

Harry handed back the loose pages and Mr. Gooding returned them to the strong box in the cupboard. He locked it and closed the cupboard door.

Jeremy scratched his head. "Does Kitty know? About Tobias coming from the slums, I mean."

"I don't know. That's none of our affair. Now, if you'll excuse me. Jeremy will discuss your fee then see you both out."

Jeremy agreed to the figure I stated for my fee without negotiation. He was too distracted to give it proper consideration. I pointed out as much to Harry after we left the office of Gooding and Plumtree behind.

"He seemed concerned for Mrs. Plumtree," he said. "Perhaps more than a mere friend should be."

"He also didn't know about the copy of the insurance claims stored in the strong box." My pace slowed and I eventually stopped. "Harry, I have a wild theory about the theft. What if Jeremy stole the ledger? He could have used his key to get in but scratched the metal to make it appear as though someone picked the lock."

Harry didn't like my theory as much as I did. "Why would he steal it?"

"I don't know. But I don't yet know why anyone would steal it. All I do know is that he is close to

Mrs. Plumtree and Mr. Plumtree's past is shrouded in secrecy."

"He didn't lie to Gooding about it. He may not have lied to his wife, either."

"I'll find out for certain but it's not just that—Jeremy is very involved in the company. Perhaps he's ambitious enough to want Plumtree removed. I'm not sure how the theft of the ledger would do that, but I'll keep an open mind."

Harry still wasn't convinced. "I think you're barking up the wrong tree with the son. The father, however, was very quick to point us in the direction of the slums for the thief. Why? Is it because he wanted to divert your investigation away from the true thief?"

"Which he might know was his son," I pointed out.

He spotted an omnibus lumbering towards us, horses snorting with the effort of pulling a vehicle that was so full, the seats on the roof were all occupied. "This will take me back to my office. Do I catch it? Or are you going to follow Gooding's suggestion of looking into thieves from Bermondsey, in which case I ought to accompany you?"

"No need. I'm going to continue to investigate the murder. I think you were right, and the murder and theft are linked. If I find one, I'll also find the other. I'm going to speak to the brother of the sailor."

"Do you want me to join you?"

"Thank you, but you have enough work of your own."

"It's tied to your case, in a way. I need to learn more about the Gooding family, and if they're linked to this murder, my client will not want his daughter to marry into it."

"True, but I think it's best if we part ways unless absolutely necessary."

He frowned. "Why?"

I didn't want to point out that Miss Morris probably wouldn't like him spending so much time with another woman. It felt as though I was elevating myself to a position of importance in his life. So I simply said, "It's more appropriate this way."

His frown deepened. "You've never been overly concerned about appearances before."

There was no good way to respond to that, so I simply waved and walked off. I felt his gaze on my back until I stepped into a hansom.

CHAPTER 9

Unfortunately, the man I wished to speak to was not at home. According to a neighbor, he was at work at the Royal Albert dockyard, where he was employed as a general dock hand. After a short omnibus ride, I alighted at the end of the dock. I was the only woman to get off.

Indeed, I was the only woman in the vicinity, which garnered some interest. I received stares from a few men dressed in sturdy clothes with shirtsleeves rolled to their elbows, revealing forearms covered with tattoos. A fellow whose bowler hat and jacket marked him out as a man in charge glanced up from the clipboard he'd been reading and inquired if I was lost.

I asked if he knew Mr. Bill Cripps, but he did not. He roundly told me there were a thousand men employed at the dockyard and that finding one would be a near impossible task. I thanked him and went on my way, following the railway track that ran the length of the dock.

On one side was the black hull of a ship that seemed to go on forever. Cranes plucked off its cargo, their gears grinding as they turned and lowered the crates onto the dock. Warehouse sheds lined the other side, their wide entrances open like hungry mouths waiting to be fed. A train whistle blew in the distance, and men shouted instructions to one another. Laborers pushing carts or rolling barrels stamped LONDON passed me, openly staring. I asked as many as I could if they knew Bill Cripps.

Finally one did. He called out to a colleague tying a rope as thick as his arm to a bollard. I knew without hearing his name that he was the man I sought. Mrs. Plumtree's butler, Lowell, had described him perfectly—early twenties, short hair, stocky build, a muscular face and broad nose. He straightened as I approached and looked me up and down.

I introduced myself and told him why I needed to speak to him.

The big man crossed his arms over his chest and settled his feet apart. "You think I killed him?" He leaned in and bared his teeth. "I never touched him!"

I swallowed. Perhaps honesty wasn't the wisest policy, but it was too late now. I had to brazen it out. "You must see how it looks, Mr. Cripps. After the *Elsie May* went down, you stormed into the office of Gooding and Plumtree, accusing the company's principals of causing your brother's death. You also went to Mr. Plumtree's home, although thankfully didn't cause a scene."

"I was upset."

"You were angry."

"I never hurt no one, and I haven't been back since that day."

"Why is that?"

He shifted his feet and lowered his gaze to the ground.

"Mr. Cripps, if you are indeed innocent then you need to prove it to me."

He rubbed the back of his neck. "It's s'posed to be confidential, but I ain't going down for murder. I never went back because Mr. Gooding paid me to stay away."

"Mr. Gooding Senior or Junior?"

"Senior. He weren't there that day I went to the office, but he must have been told about it later. He worked out who I was, same way you must have done, and paid me a visit. He told me I was mistaken about the reason for the *Elsie May* going down, that it wasn't his company's fault. I told him I didn't believe him. That's when he paid me and said I needed to stay quiet about it or he'd see me arrested for being threatening and causing a disturbance."

It seemed a little odd that Mr. Gooding was the one to approach Mr. Cripps when Mr. Plumtree was the focus of his attention. "When you went to the office of Gooding and Plumtree, you were angry at the company in general, not Mr. Plumtree specifically. But then you went to Mr. Plumtree's house. Why just his house and not Mr. Gooding's?"

"At the office, they told me Plumtree was the one in charge of the *Elsie May*. So I reckoned it was his fault it went down."

"Why do you blame him?"

"I don't anymore," he snapped.

"Come now, Mr. Cripps, you don't expect me to believe you changed your mind. Mr. Gooding's money may have bought your silence, but it can't buy your opinion. So why do you blame Mr. Plumtree for the sinking of the *Elsie May*? Why don't you believe it was the captain's fault, or the weather? Mr. Cripps?" I prompted when he avoided my gaze.

"All right, I admit I still reckon it's Plumtree's fault, but that doesn't mean I killed him."

"Go on."

"A ship like the *Elsie May* should have withstood a storm." He indicated the great hulking vessel behind him. It looked strong enough to withstand even the most violent weather. "Unless she strikes something, she should stay upright. Where she went down, there were no reefs or icebergs, nothing unexpected. And I knew the captain by reputation. He was experienced and competent. Rumor around here was that she went down because her owners didn't want to dry dock her after her last voyage. Some reckon she might have sustained damage to her hull but without putting her into dry dock, it was impossible to know for sure."

"I assume dry docking costs money."

"Aye, and puts the ship out of service for a time. The decision to keep her on the water would have been made by Plumtree."

"Did Mr. Gooding admit it was a mistake not to dry dock the *Elsie May* that night he paid you?"

He spluttered a laugh. "'Course not. But I reckon he knew it was his partner's fault. He apologized, and you don't do that unless you know you did something wrong."

A foreman shouted at Mr. Cripps to stop shirking and get back to work.

"Thank you for your honesty," I said, turning to go.

"It ain't the first time one of their ships didn't dry dock when it should have," Mr. Cripps said. "It's happened before, just not with the same consequence. Some folk here say Gooding and Plumtree have cut corners before to save money."

Now that was interesting. But were both company directors to blame for employing dangerous cost-cutting measures, or just Mr. Plumtree? It certainly looked as though Mr. Gooding was guilty. As Mr. Cripps pointed out, why pay a dissenter to keep quiet if you believe you're innocent?

* * *

THE ASSISTANT who showed me through to Jeremy Gooding's office was as shocked as me to see him crouching beside the seated Mrs. Plumtree, holding her hand. If he'd known his employer's son was being so intimate with the widow, he wouldn't have taken me through. He tried closing the door, blocking me out, but I wedged myself into the gap and forced my way in.

"How fortunate that you're both here," I said cheerfully. "It saves me an extra journey to see you, Mrs. Plumtree."

Jeremy stood and hastily backed away, bumping into the desk. The pen rolled off the stand and came to rest against a notebook. He dismissed the assistant with a jut of his jaw and invited me to take the spare chair. "This is not how it appears. I was comforting Kitty. She's had a nasty shock. I've just informed her that her husband was born and raised in Bermondsey."

"You didn't know?" I asked her.

Mrs. Plumtree dabbed her handkerchief into the corner of her eye. "No."

"There were no clues? His accent, for example?"

She teased the handkerchief between her fingers. "He did slip a few words of slang into his vocabulary, but only when he was particularly angry with me." Her chin wobbled. "I didn't think anything of it. I thought he picked it up off the sailors who worked on his ships."

Jeremy rubbed his hand over his mouth and jaw, his brow deeply furrowed.

"Did he become angry with you often?" I asked.

She shook her head.

"Why did he become angry?"

She pressed the handkerchief to her nose. "When I did or said something wrong."

"Such as?"

"Is this necessary, Miss Fox?" Jeremy snapped.

"It might be. Mrs. Plumtree? Can you answer the question, please?"

She offered Jeremy a weak, reassuring smile. "Such as when I said something stupid. I can be silly, at times. I tend to say things that enter my head without thinking them through first."

"And he didn't suffer fools," I said, repeating what a number of sources had told me.

"He was mean," Jeremy added, his tone calmer. "He expected everyone to be as clever as him and was cruel when they were not. He belittled Kitty, day in and day out. But she didn't kill him. Neither of us did."

"I think you need to clarify the nature of your relationship."

Mrs. Plumtree gasped into her handkerchief.

Jeremy bristled. "I've already told you, we're merely friends. What you saw just now was a friend comforting another friend. Kitty was upset after hearing about Tobias's past. He kept the truth from her for years. You must understand how shocking the news was for her."

"It's not unusual for a man not to be entirely honest with his wife."

"Yes, but her father should have discovered more about his background before the betrothal. In fact, he probably did know. That's the more shocking part here, Miss Fox. Kitty trusted her father."

It did seem as though he'd sold his daughter to the highest bidder. Again, amongst a particular set, it wasn't unusual. I didn't know whether an intended's background was something a gentleman usually kept from his daughter.

"Forgive me, but I have friends who are men," I said. "They do not treat me with quite so much affection as what I just witnessed." Harry sprang immediately to mind. If I were upset, he would probably crouch at my side and comfort me by holding my hand. But he was different, our relationship different.

Wasn't it?

"How dare you," Jeremy snarled. "Kitty is—was—a married woman, and I am courting a wonderful girl. Hyacinthe and I are very much in love."

"And yet affairs of the heart still happen." I almost blurted out that Hyacinthe Massie's father wasn't convinced that he was the right man for his daughter but refrained. Harry's investigation was a distraction that had nothing to do with the murder. "I can ask Mrs. Plumtree's servants if they have suspicions about your visits," I went on. "I'm sure not everyone is loyal."

"That's low, Miss Fox."

"It's all right, Jeremy." Mrs. Plumtree's quiet voice got his attention. "She needs to ask difficult questions if we are to get to the truth." To me, she added, "There is nothing between Jeremy and me except friendship. There never has been. He's just a kind man who saw a lonely, frightened woman in need of protection. I have so few friends, Miss Fox, and none who truly knew how dreadful my husband could be to me. Jeremy saw, and took it upon himself to provide a shoulder to lean on."

"Couldn't you have intervened before he bullied her?" I asked Jeremy. "Or confronted him afterwards?"

"A man doesn't interfere in another man's marriage."

"He should, if he sees him bullying her."

"It wasn't physical." His muttered excuse was a typical response. I didn't point out that there were other ways of bullying, not just physical. He seemed to already regret not stepping in on Mrs. Plumtree's behalf.

She rose, prompting Jeremy to stand too. "If I'm no longer required, I must go."

"I have work to do, too," he said.

"I have a few more questions for you," I said. "But Mrs. Plumtree's presence isn't required."

Jeremy huffed out a frustrated breath. "What is it now?"

I waited for him to close the door behind Mrs. Plumtree and return to the chair behind the desk. "I found the brother of the sailor who died on the *Elsie May*."

"The one who came in here raging like a bull? Good. Notify the police. My father will want to press charges."

"I wouldn't be so sure. You see, your father paid Mr. Cripps to keep quiet and not speak of his suspicions about the sinking of the ship."

"That's an outrageous lie!" But despite the vehement denial, I detected a hint of uncertainty in the flicker of his eyes. "You should talk to my father about this. He'll set you straight."

"I will, but he's not here, according to the clerk on the front desk."

He scrubbed a hand over his jaw again. "Then come back when he is here. Your questions are for him, not me."

"I'd like your opinion."

The door was thrust open and Mr. Gooding Senior strode in, all smiles and a cheerful greeting. "Ah, Miss Fox again! I was told you were in here. Have you discovered the thief already?"

I waited for him to sit down before I mentioned that I'd spoken to Mr. Cripps. The smile vanished and his face fell.

"Ah. I see how it looks." He glanced at his son. "You mentioned this to Jeremy?"

"I did."

"I didn't say anything in response," Jeremy said quickly.

"It's all right, Son. We have nothing to hide. Yes, I paid Mr. Cripps to keep quiet. The reasons are obvious. I didn't want any negative publicity. Not because Tobias did anything illegal. He took a risk by not dry docking the *Elsie May*, but it was a carefully considered risk. That was his nature. He didn't always play by everyone else's rules, but he never did anything illegal."

"Just unethical," I added.

"That's the way the public would see it, yes. If Mr. Cripps had continued with his accusations, eventually the press would have caught wind of it. We could have lost clients."

"Did you confront Mr. Plumtree after speaking to Mr. Cripps? Did you tell him you had to pay for the man's silence?"

"I did. And before you ask, he took it in his stride. There was no blame, no disagreement. You may find that hard to believe, but Tobias and I got along very well as business partners. Socially, we had little to do with one another, but here, we balanced each other." He spread his arms wide, indicating the office space of Gooding and Plumtree. "He was a risk-taker and I was more cautious. Sometimes he pushed me to take a leap of faith, and sometimes I had to rein in his wilder ideas. If I'd known that he'd skipped dry docking the *Elsie May*, I might have advised him to reconsider. Or he might have talked me around to his way of thinking. We'll never know."

Jeremy appeared to be listening to his father as intently as I was, watching for signs that he lied. The relationship between the two partners was something of a mystery to him, too.

"When you remember that Tobias came from nothing, you'll understand why he took risks," Mr. Gooding went on. "I think he felt that he wouldn't have come this far without taking a few. It's probably true. But I didn't know him before we started this company. He was already doing well by then."

He'd just given me the opening I needed. "Do you know where his money came from to begin this company?"

"Other businesses that he started then sold off for a profit."

"Can you be more specific?"

Mr. Gooding shifted his weight in the chair. "It was so long ago."

"But you would have done a thorough investigation before taking him on as a partner."

"Of course. That's how I knew his real name, where he'd come from, that sort of thing. His past was no secret to me, Miss Fox. I knew it and accepted it. Indeed, I even admired him for making a go of it and coming so far."

"There was only one business before this one," I told him. "The Plum Trading Company."

He waggled a finger. "That's it, yes. I'd forgotten. He was in business with a partner, but I can't recall the name. I do know Tobias was born and raised in Bermondsey as Thomas Plum."

"So you said earlier when you suggested we look there for a thief."

He stood and bade me to follow him to his office. He dug an address book out of his top desk drawer and leafed through it. "I wrote down his address here, years ago." He found the page and showed me. "There."

The entry could have been written years ago, or

it could have been recorded today. It was impossible to tell.

"May I copy that?" I asked.

"Certainly."

I wrote the address down in my notebook and thanked him for his time. Both he and Jeremy walked me to the front door. Mr. Gooding gave me the sort of lackluster smile one gives a friendly acquaintance. His son scowled. At least I knew Jeremy's response was genuine.

I didn't know what to make of his father. Was he truly unaware of Mr. Plumtree's risk-taking business practices? Surely no one in his position could be ignorant of his partner's methods. Nor was I convinced of Mr. Gooding's claim that he was completely aware of his partner's background.

Was he lying? Had he, in fact, not known about Tobias Plumtree's past until very recently?

Until right before he killed him out of anger for keeping that key information a secret?

* * *

THE LOCAL PHARMACY had a silence cabinet positioned in the corner, out of the way of customers. I stepped into the booth and telephoned D.I. Hobart to ask his opinion about the sinking of the *Elsie May*.

"Could there be a case for Gooding and

Plumtree to answer if they were found to be responsible for its demise and that of the crew?"

"Certainly." His booming voice crackled down the line. "Negligence that results in loss of life is a criminal offense. Avoiding dry docking a ship after it had sustained damage could be considered negligence. I may not know much about maritime safety, but I think it would be difficult to prove. I've seen expert witnesses disagree over key points in a case, causing them to fall apart. It's an expensive exercise to prosecute such cases, and the Crown is reluctant to take them on. It would have to be in the public's interest, and even then, the company directors could use their power and money to influence the verdict. Tricky business."

It was indeed. But Mr. Gooding could have been very worried that Mr. Cripps's agitation would lead to the public interest being stirred, and that in turn could encourage the police to look into it. A criminal investigation could bankrupt his company. No wonder he sought out Mr. Cripps and paid him to keep quiet.

D.I. Hobart asked for an update on my investigation, so I gave him a brief report, finishing with my next step—looking for anyone who might remember Thomas Plum from his Bermondsey days.

"Be sure to take Harry with you if you're going there," he said.

"I'm quite capable of asking a few questions of

some locals without requiring an escort." It was becoming irritating to always defend myself and my abilities. Besides, so far the slums of London had been quite harmless. While I wouldn't wander through them at night, they were safe during the day, as long as I stayed alert for pickpockets.

"I only meant you should take him because you don't know the area well. He does. You should also inform him about Gooding Junior comforting the widow. It pertains to his investigation."

That was true. Harry did need to know about the scene I'd walked into.

I headed to his office, only to find he wasn't there. I waited in the Roma Café for fifteen minutes and was about to leave when he arrived. He ordered a coffee from Luigi and joined me at the table in the window. He looked troubled.

"Is everything all right?" I asked.

"Of course." He turned on one of his smiles. I'd become familiar with them when he was assistant manager at the Mayfair, but had later realized that he used them whenever he wanted to pretend all was well. I wouldn't press him to confide in me, however. I'd also come to realize that pushing him too hard could sometimes push him away altogether. If he wanted to confide in me, he would in his own time.

I told him about seeing Jeremy comforting Mrs. Plumtree. He wasn't sure whether it meant anything, and asked me to report if I noticed any other signs of intimacy between them.

"I can't close my investigation into the Gooding family until I know they're not involved in the murder," he said. "I've stalled Mr. Massie but not told him why. He's not impressed with the delay."

"I'll work to solve it as fast as I can. Actually, perhaps you can help me. Two heads are better than one, and it seems you're at a loose end. Will you come to Bermondsey with me?" I checked my watch. It was almost two. "I don't have an afternoon engagement today but I do need to be back to prepare for a ball tonight."

"I thought you were worried that investigating together wouldn't be appropriate." He crossed his arms and regarded me levelly. "Even though your uncle has given his approval."

"I didn't want to test him yet." I gathered up my bag and stood. "As to being inappropriate, needs must. Shall we?"

We caught a hansom to take us directly to the address Mr. Gooding had given me. It stopped at the intersection with the short street as it wouldn't be able to turn around if it turned in. The brick buildings lining the street were narrow but sturdy, most likely housing more than one family each. A factory's chimney rose above the building at the end like an exclamation point. It spewed black smoke into the air and was probably responsible for the putrid smell that worsened as we entered the street.

A group of young children kicked a sack filled with rags. Harry handed out coins. Some ran inside, squealing in delight, but the older boys pocketed them, their fingers so quick and their movements so deft, it was as if they'd never even held them. Above us, clothes hung between the buildings. With no sunlight and very little breeze, they wouldn't be dry by sunset. Two women leaning on the sills of second floor windows, chatting across the street, looked down.

"What do you want?" one called out.

Harry tipped his head back, holding onto his hat to stop it falling off. "We're looking for the home where Thomas Plum used to live."

The women glanced at one another then disappeared inside. Moments later, they both appeared at their respective front doors. One was around my age, or a little older, but had the tired eyes of someone who'd experienced more hardship than I could ever imagine. She carried a toddler on her hip.

The other woman was older, her gray hair caught untidily in a bun at the back of her head. She had sharp cheekbones and even sharper eyes as she took us both in. "Why do you want to know where Thomas Plum lived?"

"We hoped to speak to someone here who remembers him," I said.

The younger woman hefted the child higher on her hip. "I remember his name, but not much about him. You knew him, didn't you, Lizzie? You've lived on this street forever."

"I may have." The older woman was careful, her gaze dropping to Harry's pocket.

He removed some more coins and handed her sixpence. "If your information is good, there'll be more."

She grunted. "Go on then. What do you want to know?"

"What was he like?" I asked.

The question took her by surprise but she quickly regained her composure. She lifted a shoulder in a shrug. "No different to most folk around here, except that he wasn't satisfied with his lot in life. He didn't want to stay a laborer. He reckoned he could get out and make something of himself. He used to talk about all the things he'd buy when he was rich." She huffed a humorless laugh. "No one believed he'd do it. Took us all by surprise when he moved away, money jangling in his pockets. Not that he ever shared his good fortune with any of us." She spat on the pavement at our feet.

"Did he come back after he moved away?"

"No. He didn't dare."

"Why? Was he afraid his success would make him a target for his former neighbors?"

She shook her head. "He had a friend. They were close, thick as thieves." She huffed another laugh. "They used to pick pockets at Borough Market. That was their patch. As they got older, what they picked weren't enough. They both got work as laborers, but Tommy wanted more. They were always plotting one scheme or another. Then all of a sudden the friend got caught and went to prison. It was around then that Tommy Plum left. Just moved out one day, never to be seen again."

"Why do you think that is?"

She shrugged again. "Some say he was scared he'd be caught next if he stayed. Others reckon he found himself on a good wicket and could afford to leave this place."

"Lucky bloke," the younger woman muttered.

"What happened to the friend?" Harry asked. "Is he still in prison?"

The older woman shook her head. "He's out now."

"What does he look like?"

"Gray beard, going bald, neither tall nor short."

That fit with the man Jeremy had seen watching the office of Gooding and Plumtree. His appearance coincided with the onset of Tobias Plumtree's anxiety.

"What's his name and where can we find him?" I asked.

The older woman inspected her dirty finger-nails. "Let me see if I can remember..."

Harry handed over another sixpence.

"I remember now," she said. "Baker. Ned Baker. You'll find him at The Duke Inn on Bermondsey Wall. He's an angry drunk, so watch yourself. Wouldn't want that nice face to get messed up." She looked at Harry as she said it.

"Where is the wall?" I asked.

"It's the name of a street," Harry said. "I know it."

We kept to the busier main roads on the way to the tavern. I never felt threatened, although I did feel conspicuous. Everyone stared at us.

Harry seemed to take it in his stride. "Finding the man who made Plumtree nervous is a stroke of luck."

"Good detective work, you mean. Luck has nothing to do with it."

He barked a laugh.

I smiled. "Very well, there was an element of luck involved. Considering no one from Plumtree's current life knows anything about his past life, we needed some luck. Otherwise we would have been searching for a needle in a haystack."

"It's incredible to think that Gooding didn't look further into his background and know about

Plumtree's jailed friend. For an important financial decision like entering into business with a new partner, I'd be thorough."

"Gooding not knowing is one thing, but what truly amazes me is that Kitty Plumtree hadn't a clue that he was from Bermondsey. If her father knew, he kept the information from her. Don't you find that extraordinary?"

He nodded.

I opened my mouth to say something but closed it again. Too late. Harry noticed.

"Go on," he urged. "Say it. You can speak openly to me."

"I was going to say that *you* would tell the woman you intended to marry about your past. You wouldn't hide it from Miss Morris, for example."

He grunted. "That was clumsily done, Cleo. If you want to ask me if I've told her yet, just ask me outright."

"Very well. Have you?"

"That's none of your business." His strides lengthened, a sure sign he was regretting encouraging me down this path.

"That's not fair. You led me to believe you'd answer me if I asked."

"I didn't. You assumed."

"Very well, then allow me to make another assumption. Two days ago, I asked you the same question and you said you hadn't told her so I assume you still haven't."

"A reasonable deduction. It may or may not be correct, but I would have made the same guess."

"So my next question is, *why* haven't you told her?"

I certainly wasn't expecting him to answer me and almost tripped over my own feet when he did. "I haven't found a way to tell her yet."

"If you're worried about how she'll react, you shouldn't be. She might be surprised, at first, but don't read anything into that. She'll be accepting and understanding, I'm sure of it. She seems like the sort of woman who'll take anything in her stride. I rather admire her for her even temper. I wish I could be as unruffled. It would save a lot of regret."

"Can we change the subject?"

I blinked at his hard profile, wondering what I'd said wrong.

We walked in silence the rest of the way to The Duke, an uninspiring tavern with a grim atmosphere thanks to the small windows, low ceiling, and dark woodwork throughout. It didn't help that the only patrons inside were clearly there because they had nowhere else to be in the middle of the afternoon. They sat slumped in booths or hunkered over tankards at the bar. The bar itself was nothing more than a plank of wood worn smooth by years of use rather than polish, and propped up by barrels.

The barman was the only one to look up when we entered. He didn't greet us, but simply spat into the cup he'd been drying with a towel. If that's what passed for cleaning the dishes in this tavern, I would refrain from ordering anything.

"Don't say a word and follow my lead," Harry whispered.

He approached the bar. I trailed behind, trying to ignore the sound of my shoes sticking to the floor.

"We're looking for Ned Baker," Harry said loudly.

One of the men sitting at the bar looked up from his tankard and squinted at us. He had a gray beard and his hair was thinning. It was difficult to tell his height while he sat on a stool, but I was quite sure he was the man we sought.

"Who're you and what to do you want?" he asked.

Harry held out his hand. "My name is Armitage and this is Miss Fox. We need to ask you questions about Thomas Plum, also known as Tobias—"

For a drunkard, he moved quickly. He launched himself off the stool and tackled Harry to the floor.

CHAPTER 10

$\mathcal{N}$ed Baker sat on Harry's chest and wound his arm back to take a swing. But he was drunker, smaller, and older than Harry and never stood a chance. Harry caught Baker's wrist and wrestled him off. He pinned him to the floor until he was sure he no longer posed a threat, then assisted him to his feet.

Not a single patron had lifted a finger to help. Some didn't even wake up. The barman peered over the bar to get a better look, only to sigh when he saw Harry get the upper hand.

Harry pushed Baker back onto the stool. While Baker wheezed as though he'd just run a mile, Harry hadn't broken a sweat. He tugged on his cuffs to realign them.

"Still want me to follow your lead?" I asked him.

He gave me a sharp glare before turning his attention back to Ned Baker. "As I was saying, Miss Fox and I are private detectives investigating the death of Thomas Plum, also known as Tobias Plumtree. We believe you knew him."

"Why should I answer your questions?" Baker snarled in a thick Cockney accent.

"Because there's reason to believe he was murdered, and you were seen loitering outside his office. After seeing you, witnesses say Plumtree became nervous. That makes you the number one suspect."

Each sentence increased the look of horror on Baker's face. "I didn't kill him! You can't prove anything! I ain't going back to prison because of that selfish dog. I ain't even seen him since before I went to prison, and I wish I'd never gone to his office after I got out."

"You don't look surprised to hear about his death."

"I read about it in the papers. He hanged himself at the Crown and Anchor. They didn't say it was murder."

"Do you read the newspapers often, Mr. Baker?" I asked.

He screwed up his face to peer at me. "Huh?"

"You saw a picture of him in last Wednesday's

edition of *The Illustrated Courier*. The caption mentioned his new name as well as his company name. You then went to the office of Gooding and Plumtree where you watched him come and go. He saw you and became scared."

One side of his mouth lifted. "He was scared, was he? Good."

"Why was he scared of you?"

"Because I'm not someone who should be meddled with."

"In what way did he meddle with you?"

He pressed his lips together.

"Was it his fault that you went to prison? Do you blame him for something he did years ago? Is that why you came looking for him when you got out? To get your revenge?"

"No!"

Harry took over the questioning. "It would be easy enough to obtain the court transcripts of your trial and find out why you went to prison. What won't be so easy for us to learn is what role Plum had in your conviction. This is your opportunity to tell us your side, without the police being involved. It's also your opportunity to convince us you had nothing to do with his death."

Ned Baker swiped up his tankard and took a long drink then wiped the back of his hand across his mouth. He swore under his breath. "All right. I'll tell you. Me and Tommy were good pals our whole lives. We were closer than brothers. I would have done anything for him, and I thought he would for me, too."

"You did some petty thieving together," Harry prompted.

"We got into scrapes, it's true, but we always got out of trouble. But what we earned from our…little enterprises weren't enough for him. He wanted more. He was smart, was Tommy. We'd read the newspapers together and he'd point to the businessmen who made their fortune, sometimes from nothing. He reckoned he could do it, too, if only someone would loan him the money to start. Then one day, we were looking through the house of a rich toff when the footman walks in. Tommy escaped through the window, but I got caught." He shook his head. "He should have come back for me. Together, we could have fought the footman off. But he just scarpered like a pathetic dog."

"So you went to prison for a number of years," Harry prompted. "For which you blame him."

Ned Baker's top lip curled with his sneer. "They pinned more than that burglary on me. I didn't deserve to get so much time, but there ain't no justice in this country." He spat on the floor.

"So that's why he was scared of you when he saw you last week," I said. "He thought you wanted revenge. But you say you didn't. So why did you go to his office?"

"I never spoke to him. The coward scarpered. Again."

"Just answer the question, Mr. Baker."

He ignored me and picked up his tankard. I took it off him and set it down.

"It seems you want me to guess," I said. "So I shall. You were going to blackmail him. You wanted him to pay you for your silence, to keep his past a secret."

"I just wanted what was mine," he growled through gritted teeth.

"Which was?"

He was on the verge of lashing out again, but I tried not to show my rising panic. Harry was here. He wouldn't let this man harm me. Even so, I kept alert, prepared to spring back out of his reach at any moment. We were too close to getting answers now to stop.

"Which was?" I pressed.

"Half."

"Half of what? His business?"

"It should have been mine, too. It was my idea to find a lonely rich lady. He wouldn't have considered it if it weren't for me saying he could do it."

I didn't dare glance at Harry. "What lady?"

"I don't know. It was my idea, but he found one while I was in prison. He visited me one day to tell me about it. He'd met her on a steamer. He told me she was a rich, lonely widow, just like I suggested

he should find. He made her fall in love with him."
He grunted a laugh. "That was the part where I thought our plan wouldn't work, but he reckons she thought he was smart and had potential. She wanted to invest in his business idea, a new trading company that would undercut the competitors but still turn a profit." He scratched his head. "I don't understand the partic'lars."

"Was the business a legitimate one?" Harry asked.

Ned Baker shrugged. "I reckon so."

"And how much money did the woman put in?"

Again, he shrugged.

"Do you know her name?" I asked. "Or can you describe her?"

"No. I do know they used to meet at the Crown and Anchor, the pub where he died."

This time I did glance at Harry. The coincidence was too great to ignore.

Harry placed some money on the bar and lifted his chin to get the barman's attention. "His next one's on us."

Ned Baker swiped up his tankard and drained it. He held the empty vessel out to the barman.

Harry asked me if I was ready to go, but I wasn't. Not yet. "One more thing," I said. "A ledger of insurance claims was stolen from Mr. Plumtree's office last night. Do you know anything about that?"

"No. I didn't take it. Why would I want to know about insurance claims? Unless the book was made of gold." He snorted a laugh.

"There was a copy anyway, so it doesn't matter."

Ned Baker accepted the full tankard from the barman and drank deeply.

I followed Harry out of the pub. We hadn't got far before I blurted out what was topmost on my mind. "The lonely widow must be Lady Mannix."

"It seems likely. But there's a problem with his story."

I frowned. "He seemed sincere to me."

"His story has a hole in it. At first he said he hadn't seen Thomas Plum since before he went to prison, then didn't see him again until that day he waited for him outside the office."

My heart sank. I'd forgotten that in my excitement. "If that's true then Plum *didn't* visit him in prison to tell him about the woman and his scheme." I stopped and glanced back at the pub door. "Should we confront him about the discrepancy?"

"Only if you want him thinking he's a main suspect. Right now, he believes we believe him. But that small change in his story, coupled with his presence at the office causing Plumtree anxiety, means he can't be dismissed easily."

It also meant we couldn't believe his story about the lonely widow. He might very well have known about Lady Mannix's connection to Plumtree and deliberately pointed us in her direction. Or he could have just guessed where his former friend's money came from.

Either way, we had to take his version of the story with a grain of salt until we could prove it was true—or not.

* * *

THAT EVENING'S ball was like all the rest I'd attended. Young women tried to catch the attention of the young men, who were scarcer in number. Wealthy eligible gentlemen vied to place their names on the dance cards of the prettiest girls. Impoverished gentlemen courted the heiresses. Chaperones gossiped while peering through their lorgnettes at their charges. Older gentlemen discussed politics or sporting pursuits while waiting for the refreshments to be served.

Even the decorations were the same. Lights blazed out the front, welcoming guests deposited by their gleaming black carriages. Floral garlands wrapped around the staircase railing and hung above the doors. More flowers spilled out of vases. Their color changed, depending on the hostess's preference, but otherwise they were the same at each ball. At some point in the night, I realized I'd stopped noticing the jewelry; when you saw rubies, sapphires and diamonds regularly, they ceased to become special.

The only difference was that I was no longer the new girl. My shine had dimmed. I was neither an heiress nor a beauty. In fact, I was that rare but undesirable species—an educated woman. The disinterest of my fellow guests suited me well. I was asked to dance enough times that I never felt entirely left out, but not too often that my feet became sore. I was able to stand with the wallflowers and observe proceedings.

There were always subtle goings-on at these events, and tonight was no different. Reputations had been ruined at the end of my last investigation and secrets revealed. This was the first time some had been able to revel in the salacious details with their acquaintances. It wasn't the gossip which intrigued me now, however. It was Hyacinthe Massie.

The Salt King's daughter had danced three times with Jonathon before the clock struck midnight. When she wasn't dancing, he sought her out and engaged her in conversation. At first, she seemed agreeable. But as the evening wore on, whenever she saw him approach, she walked off in the other direction or joined a group of friends. She was not in love with him.

Flossy and Miss Hessing both came off the dance floor at the same time and joined me. Flossy seemed to be in a flat mood, but Miss Hessing's steps were bouncy. She'd already danced four times with Mr. Liddicoat and even now, she couldn't keep her gaze off him.

"Will this night never end?" Flossy whined. "All the interesting gentlemen are dancing with other girls, and I'm left with the bucked teeth and two left feet brigade."

"Your dance partners have not been that bad," I told her.

"That's easy for you to say. You're not expected to choose a husband from amongst them." She sighed. "Perhaps Jonathon was right. Perhaps I'm too fat."

I rounded on her. "Don't listen to that cad. You're one of the prettiest girls here."

"I am on the larger side."

"Your figure is perfect the way it is. I wish I had your...attributes."

That produced a giggle from her.

Miss Hessing took her hand. "There is a gentleman out there for you, Miss Bainbridge. If someone as plain as me can find a wonderful man, then so can someone as pretty as you." Her gaze shifted to her mother, seated to one side with a group of her American friends. "If only she would understand how wonderful he is."

"She might," I said pointedly, "if you told her how much Mr. Liddicoat means to you."

As if she realized she was being discussed, Mrs. Hessing suddenly looked our way.

Miss Hessing opened her fan and held it to the side of her face to hide her mouth from her mother. "Unfortunately he has nothing to recommend him, in her eyes."

"The fact that he's kind?" I offered. "That he adores you and you him?"

"That's not enough for her."

"She might surprise you."

Flossy agreed. "You have to tell her at some point. The sooner you do it, the better. Otherwise, what will you do?"

"Elope." Miss Hessing said it with such conviction that I worried she might very well suggest it to Mr. Liddicoat.

That was one way to ensure he loved her, and not her fortune, I supposed. Elopement could put an end to her inheritance if her mother was angry enough. As much as I wanted to believe he truly cared for her, there was a part of me that thought Mr. Liddicoat might be a fortune hunter like the rest. That was the problem with having wealth. One could never be quite sure if friendships were genuine.

Aunt Lilian glided towards us with such smooth elegance that the hem of her gown barely ruffled. But as she got closer, I could detect the twitches in her facial muscles and her enlarged pupils, two signs that she was under the effects of her tonic. In another few hours, a headache would set in, she would grow restless then tired, and the vivacious woman standing before me would become the picture of misery.

None of that mattered to her now. She couldn't wait to impart some gossip. "Cleo, I have been asking around about Marguerite."

"Who?" Flossy asked.

"Lady Mannix. She was a popular figure, years ago, but disappeared from society."

"Why does Cleo want to know about her?"

Aunt Lilian flicked her fingers, waving off the question. "I've spoken to the ladies who were closest to her back then. None have heard from her in years. It's very odd."

Indeed, but I already knew Lady Mannix had cut herself off from everyone out of embarrassment.

"There is a rumor going about that she's living with her late husband's aunt, here in London. Nobody seems to know for certain, however. The aunt is a recluse."

"It must be false," Flossy declared. "If she were living in London, she would call on her former friends."

Aunt Lilian crooked her finger and we all leaned closer. The look she gave us was full of mischief and intrigue. "The odd thing is, both Mrs. Dysart and Lady Hookly are convinced they saw Marguerite, but on both occasions, Marguerite ignored them."

It would seem Lady Mannix wasn't quite as reclusive as she let on. Perhaps she went out when her companion had no need of her. I wondered if she went out of an evening to meet a former lover in a Canning Town inn...and then murdered him.

Aunt Lilian caught sight of a friend and moved away to join her only to see another friend and move on again. She was like a butterfly flitting from flower to flower, unable to make up her mind. Both Miss Hessing and Flossy watched her, somewhat stunned by the whirlwind my aunt could be when under the influence of her tonic.

"What was any of that about?" Flossy asked. "Cleo, do you know?"

"We were talking about Lady Mannix just the other day." I was saved from elaborating by my next partner coming to collect me for his allotted dance.

After an energetic two-step, I needed to go to the ladies' room to freshen up. I left the ballroom and headed in the direction I thought was the way, but when I found myself in an unoccupied sitting room, I realized I was lost. I retraced my steps until

I spotted a maid carrying a sewing basket. I hurried across the floor to her, but before I could inquire about the ladies' room, she opened a panel in the wall and slipped through the narrow door.

I'd not known it was there. A close inspection also revealed no door handle. How had she opened it?

With my curiosity piqued, I no longer had any interest in the ladies' room. I wanted to find out how to open the door. Indeed, I became obsessed with it, pressing several spots on the wallpaper. None opened the door.

I stood back, hands on hips and took in the entire area. Then I spotted it—the center of one of the pink roses on the wallpaper at waist height was darker than the others. I pressed it and the rose sank into the wall. Something clicked. With a little push, the door opened, revealing a flight of service stairs leading down.

I released the door and watched it slowly close on its own. What lay beyond it didn't interest me. It was merely a way for the servants to get around the house without being seen by the family or their guests. What interested me was the mechanism. I'd seen hidden doors before, but they usually had doorknobs or handles somewhere. This one was a patch in the wall that, when pressed, opened the hidden panel. The patch was darkened from regular use by staff with unclean hands.

I smiled to myself. The ball was proving to be worthwhile after all. It had given me an answer to a question that had stumped me. I now knew how the killer had got into Mr. Plumtree's room at the Crown and Anchor without being seen.

CHAPTER 11

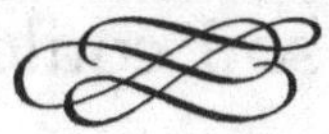

The brass king's head on the left side of the mantelpiece in the chamber of the Crown and Anchor was shiny beneath a layer of dust. The one on the right was dull by comparison, as if it had been touched frequently. I gave that one a tug.

It shifted forward like a lever. Something clicked and a panel in the wall beside the fireplace opened. Harry and I looked at one another and smiled.

Nancy elbowed us aside. "Blimey. I never knew that was there!" She watched as the door closed of its own volition, then tugged on the king's head as I had done. The door opened again. "Well, I'll be…" She peered through the gap. "I wonder how long that's been there."

"Centuries," Harry said with the certainty of

someone interested in architecture in all its forms. "Probably from Tudor times, when Catholics were persecuted. Priests would hide out in there."

"Where does it go?" I asked Nancy, who still blocked the entryway.

She stepped back so I could look in. "I can't see that far."

Harry unhooked a lantern from where it hung on the wall by the door. "Let's find out."

Nancy produced some matches from her apron pocket and lit the lantern. Harry went in first, lantern held in front of him. I stepped through behind Nancy, leaving behind the room in which Tobias Plumtree had been found hanging several days before.

The passage smelled musty, as though it hadn't been used in a long time. It wasn't as dark as I thought it would be. Cracks in the boards let in thin slices of light. That must be the external wall of the inn.

Nancy placed a hand on the opposite wall. "I reckon this is the neighboring room."

Up ahead, Harry stopped. He held the lantern high, revealing a door. "And where does this lead?"

"The next room, I reckon."

"Two doors down from the room in which Mr. Plumtree was found?"

"Aye." She tapped Harry's shoulder. "Open it.

Tonight, these rooms'll be occupied with customers who'll pay for a few hours with their favorite girl, but there ain't no one in them today."

Harry turned the door handle and pushed the door open with ease. The room on the other side was identical to the one in which Mr. Plumtree died. Even the right-hand king's head on the mantelpiece was duller than the other.

Now we knew how the murderer got into his room without being seen. We even had a good idea who the murderer might be. On the way to the Crown and Anchor this morning, I'd told Harry about Aunt Lilian's friends having seen Lady Mannix out and about. That contradicted her story of being a recluse. Ned Baker had also told us about a lady who was Thomas Plum's lover years ago and how they'd conducted their trysts at the Crown and Anchor. After meeting on a steamer, they'd also been business partners, but dissolving the business had been the start of her descent into poverty while Plum's star had risen. Ned Baker's story matched Lady Mannix's of how she'd met Plum. They must be one and the same person.

Perhaps she held a grudge against Thomas Plum for years, and when she saw him in the newspaper, it all boiled over. She asked him to meet her at the inn that held so many memories for them, then snuck into the downstairs bar, using a veil or hat to hide her face, and slipped into the room two doors along from Plumtree's. When Bull brought up the two bottles of wine, he'd seen Mr. Plumtree on his own and thought nothing more of it. But Plumtree had been waiting for his former lover, Lady Mannix. Perhaps she'd already joined him by then, which was why he didn't fully open the door to the innkeeper when he delivered the wine.

She'd come through the hidden passage, waited for Plumtree to get very drunk and pass out, killed him, then returned to her room the same way, before slipping out of the inn again.

"Nancy, who took this room on the night Mr. Plumtree died?" I asked.

She chewed on her lower lip. "I can't remember."

"Can you check the reservations book for us?"

She chuckled. "There ain't no reservations book here. If someone wants a room, they get a room if it's available. Ain't no one around here plans ahead. Bull might remember."

We retreated back along the passage to the room in which Plumtree died to find Bull the innkeeper standing there, scratching his beard.

"There you all are! Nancy, you left the bar unattended."

"I had to show these folk up here, didn't I? I knew you'd be back soon."

He nodded at the hidden door as it slid closed. "You think that's how the killer got in?"

"It seems likely," Harry said. "You knew about it? Why didn't you tell us about the passageway last time we were here?"

Bull shrugged. "I didn't think it was important. No one took that other room that night. It was empty."

"Someone still could have slipped inside unnoticed and used the passageway to get in here."

He rubbed the back of his neck. "S'pose you're right."

"Who else knew about it?"

"Just me and Nancy."

Nancy shook her head. "Not me. That's the first I seen it."

Bull indicated the king's head. "You never knocked that when you cleaned in here?"

"No."

"Does the name Lady Mannix mean anything to either of you?" Harry asked.

They both shook their heads. "Ain't no toffs come in here," Nancy said. "Except you two."

"She could have simply gone by the name Marguerite," I said. "She met Mr. Plumtree at this inn, years ago. Or Thomas Plum as he was known then."

Nancy and Bull glanced at each other and shook their heads again. "Describe her," Bull said.

"Medium height, dark hair," Harry said.

It was a dreadful description. "Large, er, bosom," I added. "She was alluring without being beautiful. These days, she has some gray through her hair and a fuller waistline."

Bull frowned in thought, but Nancy spoke up. "There was a woman downstairs like that the night he died." She looked up at the ceiling beam from which Mr. Plumtree had been found hanging. "She didn't come up here, though. No one did."

"But you said you were busy," Harry pointed out. "Perhaps she slipped upstairs while no one was looking."

"It's possible," Bull conceded.

"You didn't see the woman that night?" I asked him.

He shook his head. "Sorry. But her description is familiar. There was someone like that who used to come here years ago. Dark hair, curves."

"That could be anyone," Nancy pointed out with a roll of her eyes.

"She was a toff so I remember all right. I didn't know she was meeting Plum, though. I thought she just came here sometimes to get out of a bad situation at home." He indicated the hidden door. "She used to stay in that room, the one at the end of the secret passage."

We all followed his gaze.

It looked more and more likely that Lady

Mannix was our killer. But there were still some loose ends. I needed to talk it through with Harry, so I was glad when he asked Bull if he served coffee.

"Aye. You'd be surprised how many want coffee, especially sailors who've come from the continent. They reckon my blend's got a real unique flavor. It's prob'ly because I store it in the distillery out the back."

We returned downstairs and sat at a table away from the bar and the three other patrons. They were the same men we'd seen on our last visit to the Crown and Anchor, and they took no notice of us. Nancy lifted a crate filled with dirty tankards to carry into the scullery at the back while Bull made us coffee.

Despite the rough area in which it was located, I liked the Crown and Anchor. It had a comforting air about it. That might change in the evening, when dockers and sailors turned the venue from sleepy to rowdy, but for now, it was welcoming. The table was a little sticky, however. I kept my hands in my lap.

"Lady Mannix couldn't have done it alone," Harry said.

"Are you quite sure? By all accounts he wasn't a large man, and she's not a weakling. If he was incapacitated from drink, he would put up no resistance."

"It's not easy to move an unresponsive man, let alone lift him. Believe me, I had to lift more than one inebriated guest onto his bed after he fell asleep on the floor."

"I would have left them there."

"Some guests are too important to leave to their own destructive devices."

He really had been an asset to the hotel. My uncle was a fool to dismiss him.

"Assuming Lady Mannix had an ally," I said, "who would help her commit murder? They would have to be a very close friend, someone she could trust, and it seems she has none."

"Or someone who also had something to gain by eliminating Plumtree," Harry added. "Perhaps Kitty Plumtree, because he was a bully to her. Her son inherits and she's free to marry elsewhere, or to enjoy widowhood."

"That puts Jeremy Gooding squarely in the picture too."

"I don't think it does. I'm quite sure he's devoted to Hyacinthe Massie and still plans to marry her."

"Being quite sure is not the same as being absolutely sure," I pointed out. "Anyway, he can marry Hyacinthe but have an affair with Mrs. Plumtree."

"Do you really peg him as the sort to do that?"

"He's a wealthy man, Harry. He can do as he pleases."

"That's a very cynical view."

"I've seen a lot of wealthy and powerful men come through the hotel to know they aren't bound by the same moral code the rest of us follow."

"While I don't disagree that it happens, you can't lump every wealthy and powerful man together like that. Sir Ronald isn't unfaithful, and I've met other men like him."

I suspected my uncle was more devoted to the hotel than his wife, but I did agree that it was unlikely he'd strayed from the marriage bed. Harry would know better than me and I bowed to his opinion on the matter.

"Another thing I've noticed by investigating Jeremy Gooding is how involved he is in the business," he went on. "He'll step into Plumtree's role comfortably. That's more of a motive, in my opinion."

"He could also have easily stolen the insurance ledger, scratching the lock to make it look like a break-in. And he didn't know about the copy in Plumtree's office safe. He looked quite shocked when he heard about it."

Bull deposited two tin cups of coffee on the table. He crossed his arms and waited so Harry and I picked up our cups and sipped. It was the bitterest brew I'd ever tasted.

Harry coughed, his eyes watering. "Those sailors were right. It's very unique."

Bull puffed out his chest and sauntered off.

Harry put his cup down and cleared his throat. "The ledger may or may not have anything to do with this murder, although it's a remarkable coincidence if it doesn't. But I can't see why anyone would steal it."

I took another sip of coffee, determined to get through at least half so as not to offend Bull. "We can't discount Mr. Gooding Senior. While I don't know why he would want to steal his own ledger, his behavior is curious, to the say the least. Buying off Cripps so the press don't get wind of his suspicions is a dubious move. He's probably terrified of criminal negligence charges being laid against the company, but he can now place the blame on Plumtree, and Plumtree can't defend himself."

"It's certainly a compelling motive. He also gains complete control of the company until Plumtree's son comes of age."

"That could be why he pointed out that Plumtree was from the slum, even going so far as to give me his former address. He wanted to tarnish his reputation."

"Slum scum," Harry muttered with a bitter twist of his lips. "A man can never fully bury his roots."

"A man shouldn't need to," I said gently. "Not with those who matter."

Harry's lips twisted again, but this time it was

due to the taste of the coffee. "Do you think the filter is made from an old sock?"

"I appreciate Luigi's coffee even more." I picked up my cup and inspected its contents. "Come on. We'll brave it together."

I counted down from three then drank the remaining contents of my cup. Harry poured his into a bucket that Nancy must have been using to clean the floor but abandoned.

"Cheat," I said, once I recovered from my coughing fit.

"I value my health." He collected both cups and returned them to the counter.

With a wave for Nancy and Bull, we left the Crown and Anchor and took a hansom to Greenwich. We decided on the way that it would be necessary to speak to Lady Mannix alone, as we'd done last time. She wouldn't be honest if her patroness was present.

She might not be honest anyway.

Fortunately Lady Illingsworth agreed that Lady Mannix could go for a walk with us in Greenwich Park as long as she was back within the hour, took a parasol for the sun, and she remained close to Harry for protection. I wasn't sure what she needed protecting from on a weekday morning in a well-to-do area, but I didn't ask.

Lady Mannix couldn't get out of the house fast enough. She snatched a parasol from the stand in the hall and dismissed the butler when he offered to ask a maid to fetch her gloves and hat from her room. He looked horrified that she was leaving the house without them.

I had to walk quickly to keep up with Lady Mannix as she strode across the street and through the gate to Greenwich Park. It was not a park I was familiar with, but I recognized the Royal Observatory on the hill in the distance from a postcard I'd received from a friend once. The domes housing the telescopes were distinctive, particularly the large onion shaped one.

Lady Mannix lowered her parasol and breathed deeply, her eyelids fluttering closed. Harry and I glanced at one another but remained silent.

"Forgive me," she said, opening her eyes again. "We have a grand view of the park from the house, but simply opening the windows to allow in the air is not enough. I miss having the sun on my face. I miss being close to trees, and seeing the flowers." She reached up and brushed the bright green new leaves hanging from the lower branches of the trees lining the path.

"You truly don't go out at all?" I asked.

"Not unless she allows it, at times such as this. Such times are rare, however."

"Do you go out without Lady Illingsworth's knowledge?"

She looked sharply at me. "She finds out."

"That doesn't answer the question."

"I don't go out without her knowledge, Miss Fox. You may ask the staff if you don't believe me."

I didn't think asking the loyal servants for their opinions would get us anywhere. "Have you ever been to the Crown and Anchor?"

She huffed out a humorless laugh. "Don't be absurd. Lady Illingsworth doesn't let me go to the park, let alone to a tavern in Canning Town."

"I thought you knew nothing about Tobias Plumtree's death. How did you know the Crown and Anchor is located in Canning Town?"

"Because after you informed me of his death on our last visit, I searched through some old newspapers and found a reference to it. The article named the inn but reported his death as not suspicious." She took hold of Harry's arm as if they were a couple taking a leisurely stroll. "Will you let her speak to me as though I am a suspect, Dearest?"

Harry removed her hand from his arm. "You are a suspect."

She stopped and rounded on him. "Is this a joke? I told you, I haven't seen him in years. We had nothing to do with one another after the company was dissolved in '88. There was no animosity between us. It was an amicable business arrangement that came to a natural end."

"We spoke to a witness who claims you and

Plumtree were intimate when you began that business venture."

"Who said such a thing? What witness?"

"Is that why you gave him money? Because you wanted to help out your…particular friend?"

"That is quite enough. A lady never discusses such things."

"She does if she wants her name removed from the list of suspects."

Her lips pinched and she turned a frosty glare onto me. Clearly she blamed me for this line of questioning, not Harry. Well, I had nothing to lose. She already disliked me. I pressed her again. "Did you conduct your affair with Thomas Plum at the Crown and Anchor?"

She walked on, head held high. For a moment, I thought she wouldn't answer, but she was simply taking her time. Considering how best to respond perhaps, or think up a lie? "We met there, yes. He suggested it. I used to go in disguise, dressing plainly and removing all jewelry so I'd blend in."

Apparently her disguise wasn't good enough if Bull remembered her and identified her as a 'toff'. "Did you stay in a separate room to Plum?"

"Really, Miss Fox? Is this absolutely necessary?"

"Yes."

She appealed to Harry but he didn't come to her rescue.

She huffed out a frustrated sigh. "The first time

we met there, I took a different room to Thomas. I was a little nervous and I wanted somewhere to go to be alone, if necessary. The next times, I didn't bother."

"And on that first night, did you reach his room through the hidden passage?"

She hesitated for barely a moment, but it was a hesitation nonetheless. "I don't know what you mean."

"There is a secret passage between two chambers at the Crown and Anchor, and we believe you used it to reach Plumtree's room all those years ago without being seen."

She stopped again and this time rounded on me. "And you think I used it again last week to kill him? Miss Fox, no one knew me at the Crown and Anchor. Why would I need to go to his room in secret? Why would I care? I assure you, I did not know the passageway existed. This is the first I've heard of it." She'd been resting the open parasol on her shoulder, but she now raised it to block out the sun.

"I ought to go back to the house. I assure you both, I didn't kill Thomas Plum. I had no reason to. I hadn't seen him in years."

"Your current situation is his fault," Harry ventured. "Did he fleece you out of what you're owed? Did he not pay your fair share after The Plum Trading Company closed its doors?"

The muscles in her face tightened. Her nostrils flared. "Do stop with these cruel insults, Harry. It's unbecoming. You were always so agreeable, so sweet, but now...I don't even recognize you."

His jaw hardened. "Just answer the question, madam. Did he pay you a fair share when you were business partners?"

She blinked rapidly as tears filled her eyes. Then she drew in a deep breath, rallying. "My current situation, as you call it, is entirely my own fault. I spent more than I had. I don't blame Thomas Plum. I never have. Good day."

"We're not finished," I said. "Where were you two nights ago?"

She barked a laugh. "At the house, Miss Fox. Or are you suggesting I snuck out and killed someone else?"

"Tobias Plumtree's office was broken into that night and a ledger was stolen. Fortunately he kept a copy locked in his strong box, but even so, the theft could be linked to the murder."

"I was at home. Ask the servants. I never went anywhere." She thrust out her chin. "I never do."

"So your friends could not have seen you out and about?"

She looked me up and down, as if my question warranted a reassessment of my character. She must be wondering why I would mention her friends. "Who are your family, Miss Fox? Where are you from?"

"Cambridge."

"Perhaps things are different there than London, but I can assure you, people like me do not break into places. So no, I did not steal a ledger. The notion that I would is absurd." She turned to Harry. "You used to keep better company."

"You don't know the company I kept." He touched the brim of his hat. "Good day, Lady Mannix."

I had to hurry to catch up as he strode off in the other direction, heading further into the park rather than out of it. When he easily stepped over a puddle in our path, I hesitated, knowing my stride wasn't long enough.

He stopped. "Sorry," he muttered, returning to my side of the puddle.

"For what? It's not your fault she was rude."

"Perhaps it is my fault. I never answered her last letter. I think she hoped to punish me through you."

"That's an odd way to go about it."

His lips flattened. "Perhaps." He indicated we should follow her, out of the park. "I don't believe much of what she said, if anything."

"Me either. She continued to lie about being out of the house, so there's no reason to believe she told the truth about anything else. The problem is, how do we prove what's the truth and what's a lie?"

He shook his head, at a loss, too. "We've reached a dead end with her. There are no more routes to follow, no more witnesses to question. What do you think?"

I sighed. "I think you're right. Let's consider it overnight and discuss it again tomorrow."

"Is that your way of saying you want to talk it over with the hotel staff?"

"I might, although Harmony will be too busy. She's acting as Floyd's assistant while he organizes the restaurant opening."

"Good for her. She's perfect for the role. Perhaps she can take over from Sir Ronald's assistant one day. The fellow needs to retire."

My uncle's assistant was indeed getting on in years. He also did very little, but that was probably because Uncle Ronald preferred to do everything himself.

"How is Floyd handling the pressure of added responsibility?" he asked.

"All right, now that he has Harmony to help. He's keeping out of trouble."

"Let me know if you need my assistance with his…excesses again."

"That's kind, but I can't always rely on you. That's not fair to you, and if Miss Morris found out…well, it wouldn't be fair to her either."

His strides lengthened and he focused directly ahead.

"Harry, does she know you and I are spending even more time together lately?"

"I haven't had the opportunity to tell her."

"Find an opportunity. I don't want to be the cause of any awkwardness between you."

He flashed a grin that quite took my breath away with its suddenness and the way it lit up his face. "You think far too highly of yourself. You're not the cause of any awkwardness between Miss Morris and me."

"Oh. Of course not. I was joking."

"Thought so."

At least he was in a good humor about it. I, on the other hand, couldn't help the sinking feeling in the pit of my stomach. He'd put me in my place rather resoundingly—I wasn't important enough for him to bother mentioning me to the woman he was courting.

* * *

I was at a loose end in the two hours before it was time to dress for afternoon tea. I reported on the investigation's progress to the staff, including Harmony, who managed to spare a few minutes in her busy schedule to spend time with us in the parlor. Mr. Hobart also wanted to hear the latest news. He was particularly interested in hearing about Lady Mannix's current situation as well as confirmation that she'd had an affair with Tobias Plumtree when he was known as Thomas Plum. I swore him to secrecy, however. He couldn't even tell my aunt.

We parted ways in the foyer, Mr. Hobart turning to greet a new arrival to the hotel, while I headed for the lift. The doors opened and Mrs. and Miss Hessing stepped out. Miss Hessing pressed a handkerchief to her nose, her eyes red from crying.

I rushed towards her. "Miss Hessing, whatever's the matter?"

"Nothing," she murmured.

"Have you received bad news?"

She shook her head, but her eyes implored me. What they implored me to do or say, I couldn't fathom.

Her mother stamped the end of her walking stick into the floor. "Clare! Come!" She strode off.

Miss Hessing lowered her handkerchief as she passed me. "She found out about Mr. Liddicoat," she whispered, keeping her eyes on her mother's retreating back. "She's very upset that I've been meeting him without her knowledge. She's forbidden me to see him again. Oh, Miss Fox, what am I to do?"

Her mother swung around and thumped the end of the walking stick into the tiles again. "Clare!"

Miss Hessing dipped her head and rushed after her.

I watched them go with a sinking heart. Poor Miss Hessing. If she didn't stand up to her mother, she'd never be free of her. Even if her mother approved of Mr. Liddicoat, there would be something else. I wish I knew how to encourage her to be brave, but in truth, it was easier for me. I had no parent to please and no fortune to inherit or lose. It was a stark reminder that not everything was better with wealth.

At least the truth was out. Nothing could be solved by withholding it from her mother, but at least Miss Hessing could now try to find a solution to her problem.

I felt quite sure Harry would also come to the same conclusion. No matter how hard it would be for him to tell Miss Morris the truth about his past, she needed to know. Not telling her would be worse in the long run.

* * *

BEING WOKEN before sunrise by urgent knocking certainly gets the heart racing. I hurried to the door in my nightgown and threw it open to reveal Philip, the night porter, puffing after running up four flights of stairs.

"Sorry to wake you, Miss Fox." He put one

hand to the doorframe and another to his side. "I just got a telephone call from Detective Inspector Hobart."

My blood chilled. "What's happened?"

"There's been a fire."

CHAPTER 12

"*W*here?" I pressed. "Philip, where was the fire?"

"At an office."

Oh God. "Harry's office? I mean, Mr. Armitage's?"

He shook his head. "Plumtree and Gooding. Or Gooding and Plumtree. He says you should get there straight away, while the firemen are still on the scene, and ask them questions."

"What time is it?"

"Just gone five. The sun'll be up soon."

I thanked him and returned to my bedroom. I dressed quickly and was still doing up the buttons on my jacket when I reached the foyer.

Philip opened the front door for me. "Want me to tell anyone where you've gone?"

"Just Harmony Cotton if she's looking for me."

He gave a salute as I passed.

I walked quickly to Harry's flat, located only a few streets from his office behind a theater. The back door to the theater was closed, the theater lights off. Streetlamps still burned, providing the only light. If there weren't so many tall buildings in London, I probably could have seen the horizon glow with sunrise, but it remained dark in the heart of the city.

As I knocked on Harry's door, I had the awful thought that I could be interrupting an intimate moment with Miss Morris. He was alone when he answered the door, however, blinking at me somewhat stupidly. He wore only a pair of trousers, the suspenders dangling at his sides. I did not stare at his bare chest.

Well, I tried not to. I tried very hard. But in the end, I simply didn't have the willpower.

"Cleo?" The concern in his voice snapped my attention back to his face. He grasped my arms and dipped his head to study me properly. He was very much awake now. "Cleo, what is it? What's wrong?"

"There's been a fire at the office of Gooding and Plumtree. Your father called the hotel to tell me to go there now and speak to the firemen. He must have been informed by his former colleague. I thought I should bring you along."

"How magnanimous of you." He let me go, breathing a sigh of relief.

"Well, it is my investigation." I tried to peer past him, but he was blocking the view. "Can I wait inside while you dress or shall I stay out here? I wouldn't want to…be in the way."

He opened the door wider. "My flat is small but not that small."

It was indeed a cramped space, but at least the bedroom was separate to the sitting room.

"I know you're going to poke around while I get ready, so I only ask that you don't break anything." He pointed at a bookshelf. "There are some photographs from my childhood there, and you'll find some old school reports and things in the bottom desk drawer." He disappeared into the bedroom and closed the door.

"Do you really have no secrets?" I called out.

"From you? No. You discovered them all when you broke into the Dean Street orphanage and stole my file."

"I didn't steal it, I borrowed it. It's only stealing when you take something and don't give it back."

I looked through the box of photographs, smiling at the child version of Harry. Sometimes his beautiful mother was in the photograph too, but never his father. Harry had never known him, but that was the limit of my knowledge about the man who'd given Harry his name.

I was inspecting the titles of the books on the shelf when he returned, raking his hair with his hand, his jacket slung over his arm. He looked alert, despite the early hour. Alert but frowning.

I picked up a brown cushion and held it against the green-gray curtain for comparison. "Your taste in decorating leaves a lot to be desired. Miss Morris needs to furnish your flat for you."

"She hasn't been up here."

That answered that question, and he was none the wiser to my probing.

"I need to get a telephone installed," he said as we headed down the stairs.

"Even if you had one, your father would still have telephoned me. It is my investigation, after all."

"So you keep reminding me."

* * *

It was all over by the time we arrived on the scene. The fire was out and all but one of the Metropolitan Fire Brigade crew had left. The engine was parked directly in front of the office of Gooding and Plumtree, the two horses hitched to it patiently waiting. The driver extinguished the lamps while two broad-shouldered firemen dressed in blue uniforms looked up upon our arrival. Their brass helmets glinted in the first rays of sunshine.

Harry inquired after the lead fireman. They pointed to a man emerging from the building, then returned to the task of winding up their leather hose. We'd passed the vehicle with the ladder on our way. It appeared as though it hadn't been needed. The building was still standing and appeared relatively undamaged, although the smell of smoke hung in the air.

Harry and I approached the lead fireman and Harry introduced us, explaining why we were there and our connection to Scotland Yard. Officer Gannon handed his axe to a passing colleague.

"The fire doesn't appear to have done much damage," Harry said.

Officer Gannon removed his helmet and dabbed his sweaty brow with his handkerchief. "We managed to contain it before it spread too far, but there's considerable damage in one of the rooms. That's where the fire must have started."

The front door stood open and appeared unscathed, and it was difficult to see too far inside. If it wasn't for the strong smell of smoke, I'd never have known there'd been a fire.

"Any idea how it started?" Harry asked.

"Arson."

"How do you know?"

"There was no fireplace in that room. There was no explosion, so it wasn't a gas leak."

"They have electric lighting installed," Harry pointed out. "Could it have been faulty wiring?"

"While it's a common cause of fire, it wasn't the cause in this instance. The section of wall that sustained the most damage indicates where the fire began, but there are no electrical wires in it. The location is interesting, to say the least."

"How do you mean?"

"I'll show you."

"Is that allowed?" I asked.

"You're consultants for Scotland Yard, aren't you? This will become an arson investigation, so your lot will be involved. Might as well begin sooner rather than later."

Neither Harry nor I attempted to clarify our role.

The smoky smell grew stronger as we crossed the threshold, its miasma lingering, decreasing visibility. The front reception area was wet from the firemen's attempts to put out the fire, but otherwise unscathed. Officer Gannon held his hand to me. "The damage is minor here, but watch your step, Miss Fox. It'll be slippery."

I accepted his assistance as we entered the corridor and finally the office where the fire had begun. I wasn't surprised to find that it was Tobias Plumtree's office.

Everything was wet, and a coil of smoke still rose from one of the floorboards. The worst of the damage was to the bookshelves and the cupboard beneath. Ledgers, shelves, and the cupboard doors were nothing but a pile of damp ash. A heap of blackened and broken timbers collected where the desk had once stood, and the rug was completely destroyed. The rest of the office was scorched. I could see how Officer Gannon came to the conclusion that the fire started near the bookshelves. The only part of it left relatively undamaged was the metal strong box that had been housed in the cupboard underneath.

Harry bent to inspect it, but didn't touch. The metal could still be hot. "Someone tried to pick the lock. I can see scratches. There are scratches on the bolts in the floor, too."

"When they failed to pick the lock, they tried to remove the entire strong box," I said. "And when they failed to do that, they tried to destroy it in a fire."

Officer Gannon agreed. "He might have succeeded if the fire became hot enough to melt the metal, but we arrived before it got too fierce."

"How did you know there was a fire here at all?"

"A passerby alerted us. He was on his way to work and smelled smoke. Luckily for the owners of this place our station isn't far."

"Did you see anyone fleeing from the scene or lurking nearby?"

He shook his head.

We returned to the pavement where a small crowd gathered. We spoke to the witness who'd alerted the local fire brigade. He gave us his version of events then rode off on his bicycle. The bicycle explained why he'd been able to reach the fire station quickly.

Harry and I left to go in search of breakfast. Soon, Harmony would arrive at my suite to join me for our morning chat over eggs, pastries and coffee. I hoped my message reached her in time and that she took the tray back down to the kitchen before anyone noticed it outside my door and wondered why I hadn't collected it.

My usual delicious breakfast was merely a fond memory this morning. Harry and I walked to a more working class area and found a street seller setting up her cart. The old donkey looked as though it was still asleep with its head lowered. We purchased slices of buttered bread and coffee, which we ate with the laborers who were heading off to their work site for the day. The bread was rather delicious but I couldn't taste the butter. The coffee was surprisingly good, too, and wonderfully hot. The morning's chill hadn't yet been burned off by the sun, but it promised to be a nice spring day.

We'd spoken little to one another since leaving the office of Gooding and Plumtree, but once we finished our meal, we both had ideas we wanted to share. Harry allowed me to go first as we walked back to the shipping company's office.

"The arsonist and the thief are one and the same. He or she set fire to the office to destroy the copy of the insurance claim ledger after failing to open the strong box and remove it."

Harry agreed with my assessment but went one further. "They didn't know about the copy until after they stole the original, which means they learned about it in the last two days. We'll have to check with Gooding who he told, but I can think of a few suspects, beginning with Jeremy Gooding. He was surprised to see the copy on the morning we came to investigate the theft."

"We also mentioned it to Lady Mannix yesterday."

"Don't forget Ned Baker. We told him about the copy, too. I'd also add Mrs. Plumtree to our list. Jeremy could have told her, but if we ask, I expect he'd deny it to protect her. In fact, he'll deny he started the fire if we let him think he's a suspect. We should tread carefully."

That was four suspects. It was a manageable number.

"If only we knew why the ledger was so important," I said.

"If we'd known the copy was just as important as the original, we could have removed it from the office and taken it to a safe place."

I stopped and grabbed Harry's arm. "We're assuming they stole the original ledger because *they* needed to see what was inside. But the attempted destruction of the copy puts a different light on the theft. What if the point of the theft was to destroy it so *we* couldn't see what it contained?"

"Because it implicated them in the murder," Harry finished. "Unfortunately for the thief, the strong box the copy was stored in wasn't destroyed in the fire. Come on. Let's have another look and see if we can find whatever it is the thief doesn't want us to see."

It was a good plan. Perhaps the list of names associated with the insured cargo carried by the *Elsie May* when she sank would make more sense upon a second viewing.

We returned to Gooding and Plumtree to find the firemen gone and a distressed Mr. Gooding surveying the damage from the doorway. Jeremy stood further inside, amongst the rubble of Tobias Plumtree's office, hands on hips, as he studied the strong box. He seemed more interested in that than his father. Gooding Senior appeared to be simply trying to take it all in.

"You're here," he said, somewhat numbly.

"We came directly," Harry told him.

"The fireman said he'll put in a report to the police, but... I can't believe it. Who would do such a thing? Why?" He dragged a hand over his head. He was hatless, his jacket buttons undone, his tie crooked. He looked like he'd barely had time to dress before leaving the house.

Jeremy was little better. His shoes and the hem of his trousers were already covered in ash, and soot had settled onto his hair. His hands were still clean, however. He hadn't touched anything.

"You were both home when you heard?" Harry asked.

"Of course," Jeremy snapped. "It was six o'clock. Where else would we be?"

I sidled closer to Mr. Gooding and sniffed. He smelled smoky, but that didn't mean he'd been here earlier, setting the place on fire. I probably smelled, too.

Harry picked his way across the charred floor and crouched by the strong box. "Can you unlock it? We want to have another look at the copied pages of the stolen insurance ledger."

"Why?" Jeremy asked.

Mr. Gooding joined Harry and got to work on the dial mechanism. The door opened smoothly. It hadn't been damaged in the fire.

The contents, however, were another story. It wasn't fire that had got to the pages; it was water. The spray from the firemen's hose had been strong and water got inside through the minute gap between the strong box's door and its frame.

Mr. Gooding extracted the soaked pages and

held them away from his nice suit. Water dripped onto the floor. "Most of the ink has been washed away. I don't think we can salvage much of it."

Harry and I looked over the pages, too, but he was right. The ink was smeared and faded by the water. Very little of it was legible.

"Hang these out to dry," Harry said as he stood. "Can either of you recall if you told anyone about the copy of the ledger in the strong box?"

Both men shook their heads.

"That's company business," Jeremy said.

"Nobody? Not even Mrs. Plumtree? You two seem close."

Jeremy bristled. "I didn't tell her."

His father frowned. "You did see her yesterday. Are you sure you didn't tell her?"

"I didn't! Even if I did, she's not a suspect. Why would she care about the names in the insurance claim ledger?"

"That's what you employed me to find out," I said.

"Then I suggest you get on with it. In fact, Father, I think it's time we employ someone with more..." He looked me up and down. "...experience."

I waited for Mr. Gooding to disagree, but he stayed silent. He simply ran his hand over his head once more and sighed.

"Give me a little more time," I urged them. "Just

a few more days. I will find out who stole the ledger and tried to destroy the copy."

Mr. Gooding gave me a pained look. "I am sorry, Miss Fox. Jeremy's right. Now that events have escalated, it's time to find someone with the skills to solve this." He glanced at Harry.

Harry put up his hands. "Not me. I don't steal clients from colleagues."

"But he will do more to assist me," I said quickly. "I know we promised he'd help, but he's been busy. Until today, which is why he's here now. With both of us on the case, we'll solve this doubly fast, I assure you."

Harry raised his brows at me but kept quiet.

Both Jeremy and Mr. Gooding seemed to like the idea. At least, they didn't immediately disagree with it.

"We're not paying double," Jeremy said. "And we want Mr. Armitage to lead the investigation, and you to assist. He has the necessary expertise."

Harry opened his mouth, but I got in first. "Of course. You won't be disappointed. Now, if you think of anything relevant, telephone me at the Mayfair Hotel and leave a message. I'll pass everything on to Mr. Armitage."

"What sort of things?" Mr. Gooding asked.

"Why someone would want to destroy these pages would be a good start. Or if your employees noticed anyone acting suspiciously."

"We told you about someone who was," Jeremy growled. "The man who stood outside and watched the office last week, for one thing. And the fellow who came in here and demanded to speak to Tobias after the *Elsie May* sank. You should be speaking to them!"

"Jeremy," his father chided. "Let them do their jobs. This might have nothing to do with Tobias' death."

Jeremy's lips flattened. "So what will you do now, Armitage?"

Harry cleared his throat. "Well, uh, this fire has added another piece to the puzzle."

Jeremy's gaze narrowed. "What piece?"

"I'm afraid we can't discuss it at this stage of the investigation." Harry touched the brim of his hat. "We'll be in touch."

I led the way outside, Jeremy's scowl burning into my back.

"I'd better return to the hotel," I said as we headed for the omnibus stop. "Shall we meet up in an hour at your office to discuss our next move?"

Harry agreed that my appearance at the hotel was necessary to insure my family were none the wiser about me leaving before dawn. It was still early. I should be back before they ventured downstairs.

"Thank you for following my lead in there," I said.

"You gave in easily."

"I didn't give in. I compromised to save the investigation. If I hadn't, I would have lost it altogether. You're not the lead investigator, by the way, despite what I agreed to. You're my assistant."

"I never doubted it."

We walked on, but I could tell something about the new arrangement bothered him. I wondered if it was the extra time he would have to spend with me now, and how that would affect his relationship with Miss Morris. "What is it?" I prompted.

"The problem is, if we solve the case—"

"*When*, not if."

"*When* we solve the case, I'll get the glory, not you. If you want to begin your own agency, you need to develop a reputation, not as my assistant but as the lead. You should have fought harder."

"I know when to fight and when to compromise with men, and this was a situation that required the latter." My aunt once told me that negotiating with men was an art form. Like any artistic endeavor, the skill needed nurturing and practice.

But I'd be a fool to tell Harry that. I might need to use that skill on him one day, and it would be more successful if he didn't see it coming.

A girl shouldn't reveal all the tools in her toolbox.

* * *

Frank wasn't surprised to see me. He was surprised that I smelled smoky, however. "Have you been climbing down a chimney, Miss Fox?"

"There was a fire at the office of Gooding and Plumtree. Didn't Philip inform you?"

"Harmony told me you'd gone out and to sneak you back in when you returned without the Bainbridges seeing, but she didn't mention a fire. Wait here." He opened the door and disappeared into the foyer. A moment later, he returned. "It's all clear."

Philip must have informed Harmony, as I requested, and she informed the others. The night porter's shift had ended and the daytime staff were now on duty. It was only a little past eight, so most guests had not yet risen. Most of my family would still be tucked up in bed, although Uncle Ronald sometimes ventured down at this hour to speak to the senior staff before the hotel became busy. I spotted the housekeeper, Mrs. Short, locking her office door before heading to the service lift around the corner. Mr. Chapman and Mr. Hobart were nowhere to be seen.

Peter and Goliath lounged against the post desk, chatting to Terry the post clerk. When they saw me, they approached.

Goliath wrinkled his nose. "Have you taken up smoking, Miss Fox?"

I told them about the fire, all the while keeping

an eye out for my uncle. I repeated the explanation for Mr. Hobart when he joined us.

"That explains the smell." He handed me a piece of paper with a few lines written in his hand. It stated that Kitty Plumtree had telephoned and requested I call on her as soon as possible.

"Did she say why?"

"No."

Our little party beneath the chandelier in the middle of the foyer swelled by one when Harmony saw us and approached. Unlike the others, she already knew about the fire. She was more critical of me attending the scene, however. "You shouldn't have gone out so early."

"I didn't go alone. I collected Harry on the way."

"I'm not worried about you going about London at dawn on your own." She lowered her voice. "I'm worried about your uncle finding out."

Mr. Hobart nodded. "It was a risk."

"He has given his permission for me to investigate," I reminded them.

Harmony folded the clipboard she was carrying against her chest. "Only when it doesn't interfere with your life and when it doesn't put you in danger. If you trip up in any way, he'll revoke his permission. Besides, this morning I was more worried he'd think you were out the entire night."

"What do you mean?"

"The footman who brought the breakfast tray to your room left it outside the door when you didn't answer his knock. It was fortunate I arrived before anyone saw it sitting there and picked it up, but I was almost too late. Sir Ronald emerged from his rooms as I carried it off. He wanted to know why I was delivering breakfast to the guests on the fourth floor."

"What did you say?"

"That it was part of my role as assistant to Mr. Bainbridge to take him his breakfast."

"He believed you?"

"I'm not sure. He seemed skeptical that Mr. Bainbridge would be up at that hour."

Mr. Hobart, Peter and Goliath all agreed that it was a very unlikely event.

"You must be more careful in future," Harmony went on in her school mistress voice.

"I will. I'm sorry to put you through that." I clutched her arm. "Thank you, Harmony. You're a gem."

Mr. Hobart spotted Mr. Chapman and bade us good day, but not before he politely reminded Peter and Goliath that if they currently had nothing to do, to ensure they at least appeared to be busy. Peter immediately strode off in the direction of the check-in desk, but Goliath lingered with Harmony and me.

Harmony sniffed somewhat pointedly in my direction.

"I know I need to change," I said with a sigh.

"And spray some perfume on your hair."

The lift door opened and my uncle stepped out. Harmony and Goliath abandoned me to my fate.

"I'm not used to seeing you in the foyer," I heard Goliath tell her as they walked off. "It makes a nice change. You look smart in that outfit."

She peered up at him. "Are you flirting with me?"

Goliath blushed.

"Cleopatra!" Uncle Ronald barked. "A word, if you please."

I turned to him, smiling. "Yes, Uncle?"

He sniffed, then leaned closer and sniffed again. "Why do you smell smoky? Where have you been?"

"I, uh…"

Oh lord. If I didn't think of an excuse quickly, he might realize my smoky aroma and Harmony carrying a breakfast tray were connected. While I could probably convince him that leaving the hotel while it was still dark was necessary as part of my investigation, I didn't want Harmony to get into trouble for lying. As Harry could attest, my uncle didn't take kindly to liars.

"The smoking room. I've just come from there." I waved in the general direction of the billiards and smoking rooms. There would be no one in either at this time of day, but in the evening, they were usually occupied by several gentlemen. The reek of their cigars and pipes sometimes pervaded into the foyer itself.

His gaze narrowed. "Why were you in there?"

"Peter was busy so I offered to refill the decanters."

He glanced at Peter, perusing the register to see which guests were arriving and leaving today. He didn't look particularly busy.

Before my uncle questioned my explanation, I continued. "It's rather early. Are you on your way out, Uncle?"

"I'm looking for you. You weren't in your room."

I swallowed. "Oh? Is something the matter?"

"Yes," he said darkly. "Yes, it is. We need to talk."

CHAPTER 13

$\mathcal{M}$y one and only thought was to protect Harmony. She couldn't suffer because of my carelessness. But with the pressure on me to think of an excuse quickly, my mind went blank.

My temper, on the other hand, began to simmer. I was always worried about what my uncle thought of my actions. He made me worry about who I took into my confidence, where I ought to be at any given time of the day. Second guessing myself made me a less effective investigator. Not to mention, it was frustrating after being raised as a free bird.

"I had an unpleasant conversation with Mrs. Hessing last night," he said.

I blinked at him. That was not the way I expected the conversation to begin. "Oh?"

"She urged me to tell you to stop interfering."

I frowned. "Stop interfering in what?"

"Her daughter's life. She says you're giving her advice that runs contrary to her own wishes for Miss Hessing. She says you've been encouraging her to meet a man who is unworthy."

"He is not unworthy." I hoped.

He put up a finger. "And that you have helped her meet this man by lying to Mrs. Hessing's face."

"Mr. Liddicoat adores Miss Hessing and she him. Nothing untoward has occurred. They simply go for walks or meet at a teashop."

He stepped closer and lowered his voice. "That is not the point," he hissed. "I don't care if he's a prince. The point is that Mrs. Hessing is unhappy about it and she blames you for encouraging the relationship."

I stretched my fingers, reaching for some patience. It would not help to lose my temper now. "Miss Hessing is my friend. Friends help one another. They give advice. I've done nothing wrong. Perhaps if Mrs. Hessing spent some time with Mr. Liddicoat, she'd see he's a good man."

"Mrs. Hessing is a very valuable guest," he growled. "She stays here for weeks at a time, every year. She is paying a considerable sum to occupy one of our best rooms. *She* is paying, Cleopatra. Not her daughter. She is too important to this hotel, and therefore too important to ignore, no matter what we think of her requests."

There it was, in the baldest of words. Money was more important to my uncle than friendship, more important than doing the right thing. Whatever Mrs. Hessing wanted, Mrs. Hessing would get, and he would give it to her dancing a jig if she asked.

I shouldn't have been surprised. I always knew what he was, where his priorities lay. Yet my heart felt like a lump of wood in my chest.

My silence seemed to unnerve him. Perhaps he was expecting my temper to be stirred up and an argument to ensue. It's what usually happened when he gave a decree that I disagreed with. "Well, Cleopatra? Do you have anything to say?"

"Only that I am disappointed."

"Ah. Well." A look of relief washed over him. "I understand. But you can still be friends with Miss Hessing if you encourage her to give up Mr. Liddicoat. I'm sure that will go a long way to restoring you to Mrs. Hessing's favor."

I shook my head sadly. "That's not why I'm disappointed, and Mrs. Hessing isn't the one I'm disappointed in." I walked off, not caring that it was rude to do so.

Although I wanted to see his reaction, I didn't turn around. I wouldn't give him the satisfaction.

* * *

Kitty Plumtree stood in her husband's study, the fingertips of one hand resting on the desk. A few inches from her fingers was a letter addressed to her late husband. Mrs. Plumtree wouldn't even look at it when she told Harry and me about it.

"Lowell found it when he was cleaning out my husband's things yesterday," she said. "He thought you should see it. It may have a bearing on Tobias's…" She pressed her lips together and lowered her gaze.

Harry picked up the letter and we read it together. The name struck me first. It wasn't addressed to Tobias, but 'My Dear Tom.' Plumtree hadn't gone by that name in years. This was from someone who knew him from before he changed it. The rest of the brief letter was even more interesting.

My Dear Tom,

Imagine my surprise to find you are alive and well! It brings a smile to my face to know you achieved everything your heart desired.

I only wish that I were the fortunate one to share your life. Alas, you and I were not to be. I am not writing this to lay blame, but to ask that you merely give what you owe. So much has changed for me since we last spoke on that bitterest of winter days. I have suffered, and I suffer still. I am at my lowest.

We both know I would not be so low but for you.

For all that we once meant to one another, I hope you can quickly and without quarrel give me what I am due. That is all I ask. If you do not, I am terrified of what I shall be forced to do.

Yours always,

M.M.

Marguerite, Lady Mannix, had sent this.

We both know I would not be so low but for you.

It was as we'd always suspected. She blamed Tobias Plumtree for her poverty.

"Who is she?" Mrs. Plumtree's voice trembled. Her eyes were dry, however. "Who is this MM? Do you know?"

Harry held the letter between his middle and index fingers. "May we keep this for the time being?"

"Keep it for as long as you want," she bit off. "I have no need of it."

"You have no inkling who MM might be?" I asked.

She shook her head.

I wondered if Lowell knew about Lady Mannix,

but he'd left after showing us through to the study. "May we take a look around in here?"

She nodded but didn't leave. She watched on, her arms crossed over her chest, hugging herself.

I'd already looked through the study on my last visit, but I opened the top desk drawer again nevertheless. Harry went immediately to the stack of letterhead, personalized with a tree laden with plums. He ran his fingers over the topmost page, feeling the indents of the writing on the sheet that had once sat above it. The letter from Lady Mannix hadn't been dated. It could have been written months or years ago. Or it could have been recent. And Tobias Plumtree may have sent a reply.

Harry picked up a pencil and lightly colored in the page, slowly revealing the words that had been written on the sheet above like a reverse cloak.

> To Lady Mannix,
>   I owe you nothing. You have no rights to anything.
> Do not threaten me or you will find my bite is worse
> than my bark. Do not contact me again.
>   T.P

Harry folded the sheet and pocketed it before Mrs. Plumtree saw. "Thank you, madam. We can see ourselves out."

"Just a moment," I said. "Mrs. Plumtree, can you fetch Lowell, please? I'd like a word."

She left, still hugging herself. I made sure she was out of earshot before turning to Harry. "I looked through this study the first time I interviewed her. That letter wasn't here."

"You think she doctored it? That she knows who MM is and is trying to frame her for murder?"

"It's possible. I certainly don't believe the grieving widow act. She's glad he's dead. I don't blame her for that. He was horrible to her. But the fact she finds it necessary to act isn't helping me to assume she's innocent."

Lowell's light footsteps were preceded by Mrs. Plumtree's. She entered first, followed by the butler. He stood by the door, hands at his back, chin out-thrust. "You wished to see me, Miss?"

I held up the letter from Lady Mannix. "Where did you find this?"

"In the wall safe." He crossed the floor to a framed picture of a black stallion in a meadow. He removed it to show us the safe.

"Why didn't you tell me about that last time I was here?"

"I forgot."

Harry stepped up to the safe and opened the door. It was unlocked. It was also empty. "What else was in here?"

"Nothing, sir."

I didn't believe him for a moment. "You cannot

withhold evidence from us, Lowell. It's against the law."

"It's against the law to withhold evidence from the police in a criminal investigation, Miss Fox." His gaze met mine. "You are not the police and this is not a criminal investigation."

The man was infuriating. Unfortunately, he was also correct.

"I asked Lowell to go through this study thoroughly just yesterday," Mrs. Plumtree said. "Before, he only tidied up. But it's time to clear it out. This room can become a music room for George. I think he will have an excellent singing voice. Wouldn't you agree, Lowell?"

"He has a strong set of lungs, madam."

It seemed remarkably soon after Mr. Plumtree's demise to be turning his study into anything. His widow certainly wasn't sentimental.

"That letter must have been very distressing for you to read," Harry said to Mrs. Plumtree. "I'm sorry you had to see it." He was turning on his charms again, hoping that would get answers.

She removed her handkerchief from the inside of her sleeve and dabbed the corner of her dry eye. "It was very upsetting. Although I'm sure Tobias knew this MM from before he met me, I don't like the implication that he owes her and her threat that she'll be forced to do something she doesn't want to do. Do you think she meant..." She pressed the handkerchief to her chest. "Do you think she murdered him?"

"We'll get to the bottom of it, I assure you." He turned to Lowell. "Do you know who MM is?"

The butler stiffened even more, something I'd not thought possible. He was already ramrod straight. "I do not."

"Have you heard from Jeremy Gooding today?" I asked Mrs. Plumtree.

"No," she said. "Why? Is something the matter?"

"There was a fire early this morning at the office of Gooding and Plumtree."

She gasped. "Was anyone inside?"

"No one was harmed, but your husband's office was damaged. Someone wanted to destroy the strong box he kept there. Inside it was a copy of the insurance claims for the *Elsie May*."

"The original was stolen," she finished for me. "Yes, I recall you mentioning it. Why did someone want *both* copies of the insurance claims?"

"They didn't. They wanted to destroy them. Can you think why?"

She shook her head. "I'm afraid I know nothing about Tobias's business."

I addressed my next comment to both her and Lowell, since he'd been involved in identifying Mr. Cripps. "Did Jeremy Gooding inform you that we found the man who confronted your husband over the death of his brother, a sailor on the *Elsie May*?"

Mrs. Plumtree nodded. "It's good news. Have the police arrested him?"

"No, but he won't threaten you now. For one thing, your husband is gone. For another, Mr. Gooding paid him to keep quiet."

She frowned. "Oh. That is good of him, I suppose. It stopped the man returning, didn't it?"

"It did. It also stopped him going to the press or the police with his allegations. It stopped the police from making their own inquiries."

"With what aim?"

"With the aim of arresting your husband for criminal negligence."

Her lips formed an O. This time her eyes filled with real tears. "Was he negligent, Miss Fox? Was Tobias responsible for the deaths of the crew?" Her voice was thin, her lips pale. I was quite certain she was no longer acting. It upset her to think her husband might be responsible for the sinking of the *Elsie May*.

"We're not sure. We may never be sure. What we do know is, that man thought he was, and your husband's business partner was concerned enough that he paid the fellow to keep quiet."

"He wasn't." Lowell's voice cracked.

"Pardon?" Harry asked.

"Mr. Plumtree wasn't responsible for the *Elsie*

May going down. It was the weather. It was the captain's fault. It was…" He swallowed heavily. "It wasn't Mr. Plumtree's fault."

His vehemence took me by surprise. I'd never seen such loyalty from a servant before.

I made our excuses to leave, but Harry wasn't ready. He lightly touched Mrs. Plumtree's elbow to get her attention. "Are you sure you can trust the Goodings?"

She blinked back damp lashes and smiled wanly. "I can trust Jeremy. He has always been a true and loyal friend. His father…" She looked away. "He came here last night and asked me to sign a document."

"What document?"

"A legal one. Something to do with George's share of the company. He said it would make George a very rich boy. We would want for nothing."

A look of alarm flitted across Lowell's features.

"Did you sign it?" I asked.

She pressed the scrunched handkerchief to her forehead. "I wasn't in the right frame of mind. I asked him to come back another day."

"Don't sign anything without a lawyer present. Make sure it's a lawyer of your choosing, not Mr. Gooding's. Or Jeremy's."

"Jeremy only has my best interests at heart. And George's, too. He's not greedy, like his father. Ambitious to succeed, yes, but not at the expense of others."

"Please, Mrs. Plumtree. Listen to me. The only person who has your best interests at heart is you. You are your son's protector now. He needs you to advocate for him while he is still young. Don't let anyone talk you into any arrangement that doesn't benefit him. Do you understand?"

She nodded, but I remained unconvinced that my words had sunk in.

Lowell escorted Harry and me downstairs while Mrs. Plumtree retired to her room. I waited until we were at the front door before I spoke to him. "Don't let her sign anything without a lawyer looking it over first."

A flicker of surprise passed through his eyes—surprise that I'd guessed he had that much influence in this household. Mr. Plumtree's death had given Lowell an opportunity to step into the role of primary male. I was uncertain if that was a benefit to Mrs. Plumtree or not. "I will, Miss Fox. And thank you for that speech. She needed to hear it from someone she respects."

"Is her father still coming to London?"

"He wrote to say he'll be down next week."

"Doesn't he want to be here for his daughter now, in her time of need?"

"That is not for me to say."

I gave him a nod and he nodded back. It was a

shared moment of mutual understanding between us.

It didn't mean I trusted him.

As we crossed the road, Harry glanced over his shoulder back at the house. "So, Lead Detective Fox, where to next? Lady Mannix's house?"

"Of course. We need to confront her. We now have proof that she blamed Plumtree for her poverty, and proof that she threatened to get her revenge if he didn't help her."

We walked on for a few more minutes before he spoke again. "You're tense."

"I'm not."

"You're clenching your fists."

I unclenched my fists. "I'm not tense. I'm riled. Mr. Gooding is trying to take advantage of Kitty Plumtree. Her entire life, overbearing men have taken advantage of her, and now, when she is finally free of that horrid husband, another man comes along and tries to bend her to his will. It should have ended for her. She should be free to make her own decisions."

"I don't think she's equipped to make those decisions."

"Then she must learn."

"I agree. But she won't learn in a matter of days. It'll take time."

He was right. She couldn't learn to understand a legal document overnight, nor be ready to make the dozens of other decisions great and small that would now be thrust upon her. I shuddered to think what decisions someone like Mr. Gooding would force her to make before she was ready.

"Lowell was right," he said softly. "Your advice to Mrs. Plumtree was spot-on."

"Perhaps." I suddenly laughed, although my thoughts were far from light-hearted.

"What is it?"

"She could be the smartest of all our suspects. What if she has everyone believing she needs help when she's the most capable of them all, the most ruthless and manipulative?" It was difficult to imagine the timid Kitty Plumtree being any of those things, but I needed to keep an open mind and not be affected by how she behaved.

"What do you think of Mrs. Plumtree's reaction to the news about the fire?" Harry asked.

"She seemed unconcerned about the copy of the insurance claims being destroyed. She may have been acting, however." I threw my hands in the air. "I feel as though I can no longer tell when someone is acting and when they're not."

"Trust your instincts, Cleo. Most of the time, they're good."

"But not always," I added with a wry smile.

He returned it, proving he had come to terms with my role in his dismissal from the hotel. I'd never wanted to take his hand more than at that moment, and just hold it.

But I did not.

* * *

LADY ILLINGSWORTH WAS CONFINED to her room on doctor's orders. Apparently she suffered from melancholy and the doctor was a frequent visitor to the household.

"She is his favorite patient," Lady Mannix told us. "I believe her fees have paid for his recent move to a larger house. His wife must push him out of the door when our footman delivers a message to summon him."

The butler waited after showing us through to the drawing room, but Lady Mannix dismissed him without instructions. Considering our meeting the day before had not ended on friendly terms, it was understandable she didn't want us lingering. On the other hand, Harry had walked away from her after she'd insulted me, not the other way around.

Before we'd sighted the house, I'd asked him if he wanted to remain outside and avoid talking to her. He refused to be left out. I wasn't so sure it was a good idea for him to see her again, however. He needed a clear head for our interrogations. She'd rattled him yesterday, and Harry wasn't someone easily rattled.

I withdrew the letter from my bag and handed it to her. "This was found amongst Tobias Plumtree's possessions. It would suggest that you were unhappy with the way your relationship ended, and that you believed he owed you money."

She read the letter then started to laugh. "This isn't from me. I didn't write this." She stood and pressed the service button. The butler arrived and she asked him to fetch a diary from her desk. "I can prove I didn't write it." The look she gave me was positively righteous.

The next few minutes were excruciating on my nerves. Lady Mannix was so smug that she must be absolutely sure she could prove she didn't write the letter, and with every passing second, my confidence waned.

Finally, the butler returned and handed Lady Mannix the small leather-bound book. She passed it to me and I flipped through the pages. All entries mentioned the weather and the events of the day. Since she hardly left the house, they were short, sometimes merely a single line. Yesterday's entry described our visit and her delight at walking in the park.

"Now compare that to your letter," she said.

Harry peered over my shoulder as I positioned the letter beside the diary page with the most writing. There was a distinct difference in the way the T was crossed. The top of the capital A in the diary was rounded but was pointed in the letter. There were a number of other differences too.

I handed the diary back and stood. "Thank for your time, Lady Mannix."

"That's it? No apology, Miss Fox?"

"The investigation is ongoing."

She spluttered a laugh. "You think I wrote the letter in a different hand, don't you? You think I blamed Thomas Plum for my situation here, and that when I saw his picture in the newspaper, I lured him to the Crown and Anchor where I somehow strung him up all on my own. It's preposterous."

"Good day, Lady Mannix. We'll see ourselves out."

She followed us to the drawing room door. "You have no proof. Not a whisker. That letter is clearly a forgery, made up by someone who wants to blame me for the murder."

We headed down the stairs with her at our heels.

"Harry," she said. "Harry, slow down. Please."

He stopped on the landing. I continued to the base of the stairs to give them privacy, but I could still hear her.

She took his hand, but he immediately withdrew it. Her chin wobbled before she managed to regain her composure. "I know you don't want to be reminded of the…mutual affection we once held for one another, but I want you to think back and ask yourself, do you truly believe I am capable of murdering anyone?"

"As a detective, I cannot form an opinion based on character alone. I must look at the evidence."

She took a step back, as if pushed. Her lips silently formed his name.

Harry started down the stairs only to stop again. "One more thing."

Her face lifted. "Yes," she said, breathily.

"There was a fire early this morning at the office of Gooding and Plumtree. The only thing that was damaged was the copy of the stolen insurance claims."

Her jaw hardened and her eyes flashed. "You think I did that, too? I fail to see how you can blame me for it when I don't care about insurance claims, and I haven't left the house since I saw you two yesterday." She picked up her skirts and marched back up the stairs.

Harry trotted the rest of the way down the staircase to join me. The butler met us at the front door.

"Has anyone been in Lady Mannix's rooms today?" Harry asked him.

"Yes, sir, the maids."

"Did they notice anything unusual in there?"

A small dent appeared between the butler's brows. "Such as...?"

"Such as a smell that isn't ordinarily there?"

"No, sir. I don't believe anything like that has been reported by the maids." He opened the door and bowed.

We decided to head to Moorgate and see if the pages from the strong box had dried. Hopefully some of the list could be salvaged, and that those names meant something to us now.

"You asked about the smell in her room," I said to Harry as we settled into seats on the omnibus.

"I thought if she set the fire, the smell of smoke would have lingered on her clothes. Clothes which the maids then collected and washed."

"We would have smelled it on her hair."

"She could have washed it when she returned."

"True, but not dry it and arrange it before we arrived. Not thick hair like Lady Mannix's. Mrs. Plumtree is the same. I didn't think of either woman's hair smelling of smoke until I heard you question the butler just now, but I would have noticed if Mrs. Plumtree's had an aroma. It didn't."

Harry rubbed a hand over his jaw. "They also both seemed disinterested when they learned the fire destroyed the insurance claim copy. It could simply mean the guilty one is a good actress, or it could mean neither needed to destroy the strong box's contents."

Given that neither smelled smoky, it was probably the latter.

"You know Lady Mannix better than me," I said.

He arched his brow and gave me a withering glare.

"You do, Harry, and don't deny it. My question is, do you believe she wrote that letter?"

"I don't think she did, and it has nothing to do with how well I know her—or don't." Again, he pierced me with a pointed glare. "It's more to do with the diary. Even if she wrote the letter in a different hand to her diary, there would be some similarities. I spotted none. Besides, why would she bother to fake her handwriting at that point? She would have to know she'd need a reason to fake it, as well as assume Plumtree wouldn't destroy a letter from his former lover. Writing a fake as good as that would take time, skill and patience, too."

I was about to point out that she had an abundance of time, cloistered as she was in that house all day with no visitors, when something struck me. I clutched his arm in my excitement. "You're right, Harry. You're absolutely right."

"About...?"

"About Plumtree destroying the letter. Of course he would have destroyed it. He wouldn't want his wife discovering such an incriminating missive. He probably wouldn't want the servants seeing it either."

"So why didn't he destroy it?"

"You're missing the point. I think a letter never existed in the first place." I pulled it out of my bag.

"This was most likely written by Mrs. Plumtree to place the blame for the murder on Lady Mannix, her husband's former lover."

"You think she's framing Marguerite? You think she's that callous?"

I stared at the letter in my hands. The writing was not at all like that in Lady Mannix's diary. The writing in the letter was more jagged with straight lines, whereas her handwriting was more rounded, the letters smaller.

"This is written by a man," I said. "Mrs. Plumtree didn't write it. Lowell did."

"Or Jeremy Gooding."

Whoever wrote it, it explained why the letter was suddenly discovered. Kitty Plumtree's sudden desire to turn her late husband's study into a music room for her infant son was a ruse to get the fake letter into our hands.

"There's one thing we haven't considered," Harry said.

"What's that?"

"Two things, actually. Who knew about Marguerite's past with Plumtree? And who knew that Marguerite was aware of the secret passage between the rooms at the Crown and Anchor?"

"Neither Mrs. Plumtree, Lowell or Jeremy will admit anything if we simply ask," I pointed out.

"Not unless we present them with conclusive proof."

"Which is why we won't return to the Plumtree house yet. We'll continue on to Moorgate as planned. Perhaps those pages have dried and what's still visible makes more sense in light of what we've recently learned."

CHAPTER 14

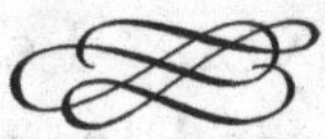

We alighted from the omnibus outside a stationer's shop in Moorgate and purchased a magnifying glass before walking the rest of the way to the Gooding and Plumtree Trading Company office. The front door and all the windows were open to flush out the smell of smoke with fresh air. There was still a way to go.

Aside from a young man at the front desk, there was no sign of other staff. He recognized us and directed us through to the corridor. We found Jeremy in the burnt-out office of Tobias Plumtree, sweeping up ash and dumping it in a wheelbarrow. His blue overalls were covered in ash and soot. Four other men ripped up damaged floorboards. Going by their expensive ties and spectacles, I'd wager manual labor wasn't their primary work. They were probably Gooding and Plumtree employees.

Jeremy visibly deflated upon seeing us. He enclosed the top of the broom in his hand and rested his forehead on it. "Go away."

"We won't bother you," I said. "We just want to look at the pages rescued from the strong box. Are they dry?"

He sighed heavily. "Check with Father. He's in his office."

I exited but Harry lingered. "You can find unskilled laborers at short notice through agencies. There's one near here."

"I know that." Jeremy pressed the heel of his gloved hand to his temple and squeezed his eyes shut. He looked exhausted. But he sounded bitter. "We can't afford to spend anything on cleaning this up."

"Why not?"

"Because we telephoned our insurance company office as soon as they opened, and they informed us that we're not insured."

"For fire?"

"For anything. We have no policy with them for this building or its contents."

Harry and I exchanged glances. My pulse quickened. "Who was supposed to organize the insurance?"

"Tobias." He grunted. "We don't even have the satisfaction of blaming him for the oversight."

I hurried out, Harry at my heels. I stepped into the corridor and turned to him. "Do you think—?"

"Yes, I do."

We found Mr. Gooding seated at his desk, his head in his hand as he pored over a document. He did not look up until we greeted him. He seemed as exhausted as his son, but his exhaustion wasn't caused by physical work.

"I'm afraid I'm very busy," he said, indicating the papers strewn across the desk. "Do you have news? Have you found the arsonist?"

I'd told Harry that he must take the lead when we spoke to the Goodings, but even so, he hesitated and waited for me. I glared at him until he capitulated.

"We came to have another look at the pages from the strong box," he said.

"They're outside in the courtyard, drying. You can look for yourselves."

"We will. But unfortunately they'll be too damaged to be of any use to us. You see, we need to see *every* name on that insurance claim list."

"Why?"

"We need to compare those names to the *Elsie May's* cargo manifest."

His already furrowed brow deepened further. "The manifest was preserved. It was moved to Jeremy's office after he took over Tobias's work so it wasn't destroyed in the fire. He'll fetch it for you."

"You don't understand. We need to see *every* name on the insurance claim or the exercise is pointless. Unfortunately, the copy is no longer legible in its entirety after the fire."

Mr. Gooding sat forward, his face clearing. "You're looking for a name that is on the manifest but *not* on the insurance claims list." A small smile tugged at the corner of his mouth. "You're looking for cargo that wasn't insured. No doubt our predicament here gave you the idea. But what makes you think our clients failed to take out insurance? No one's that foolish, and we don't encourage it."

"Don't you?"

"No! Absolutely not."

"What about Plumtree? He seems to be averse to insurance policies."

Mr. Gooding's gaze skimmed the floor, walls and ceiling. He sat back and closed his eyes with a sigh. "Yes, he does. I can see why he wouldn't take out insurance on this place. He tried to save us money. But why not for his clients? They pay the premium, not him. Did he pocket their money instead? Are you telling me my business partner committed fraud?"

"It seems likely."

Mr. Gooding gave an emphatic shake of his

head. "No. I don't believe it. Not taking out insurance here is one thing, but theft is quite another." He indicated the papers on his desk. "The money he would have spent on our insurance premium is all accounted for. Tobias didn't keep it for himself. He put it back into the business. If he didn't steal it from us, he wouldn't steal it from our clients."

"There is another explanation," I said, thinking it through.

Harry urged me to go on, but Mr. Gooding put up his finger, stopping me. "Please don't take offense, Miss Fox, but I don't think you know enough about how insurance works to understand the intricacies of this case. Have you ever taken out an insurance policy?"

I'd taken care of my grandmother's household affairs in the last few years before her death, including getting insurance. My gentle but indebted Grandpapa had failed to take out a policy. It was sheer luck that we'd never found that out the hard way, as Mr. Gooding had today.

I explained none of this to him, however. It was none of his business, and I didn't care what he thought of me as a person, only what he thought of me as a detective. "There was a long list of insured items in that claims book." I recalled enough of the copied pages to remember that much. "At first glance, it would seem every item of cargo was insured. If there were any missing, there were very few. I think what happened is that Mr. Plumtree thought he was doing his clients a favor by advising them how they could save money—don't insure their cargo. He wasn't stealing from them. There was no selfishness or malice in his intention. He probably never expected the *Elsie May* to founder."

Mr. Gooding rubbed his head and nodded. "I can see Tobias giving that advice out. He was a risk taker at heart, a gambler. He weighed up the odds and threw in his lot."

"That's one way of putting it."

Mr. Cripps, the brother of the sailor who'd died on the *Elsie May*, had said the company cut corners. Perhaps it wasn't the company, but just Mr. Plumtree. He'd also made the decision not to dry dock the ship before her final, fatal voyage. One person's calculated risk was another's negligence.

Harry took over the explanation. "That's why the killer didn't want us to see either the original insurance claim list or the copy. It's not to hide a name on it. It's to stop us finding the name that's *not* on it."

I nodded. "He or she was angry with Plumtree for advising them against insuring their cargo. Angry enough to kill him."

"We may not have the list of insurance claims anymore," Harry said. "But we do have a copy of the ship's manifest. Someone on the manifest won't have been insured. The insurance company should have a record of all correspondence and payouts."

He was right. Anyone they *didn't* contact was a suspect.

I led the way to Jeremy Gooding's office with Harry and Mr. Gooding following. Jeremy joined us and found the manifest. Glancing over it revealed another problem. Cargoes were listed under company names, not individuals. We would need to find the principals behind the uninsured companies to find the murderer.

At least we already knew the name of one client. The Massie Salt Company had cargo on board the *Elsie May*.

Harry closed the manifest ledger and tucked it under his arm.

Mr. Gooding telephoned the insurance company and informed them we were on our way and to give us whatever we required.

A mere ten minutes later we were walking through the door of the insurer of the *Elsie May's* cargo, or at least some of it. We spent the afternoon comparing the manifest against the insurer's payments and found only four listed on the manifest who did not receive a payout. The insurer had no record of them. Those four were now our main suspects.

As expected, they were companies, not individuals, so we returned to the office of Gooding and

Plumtree and checked the records of those four clients. We noted down the addresses and the point of contact for all four companies.

The painstaking process had been fruitful, but it had taken the entire afternoon. All four companies would have closed their doors for the day. I had to return to the hotel anyway. I was expected to attend the theater with my family tonight.

I told Harry about it as we caught the omnibus back to Piccadilly Circus. The sigh in my voice caused him to narrow his gaze.

"You don't want to go to the theater?"

"I do. I enjoy the theater. It's just that being in the company of my uncle is not my idea of an enjoyable evening. He gave me a thorough scolding this morning."

He turned to face me properly. "Because of the investigation? Or me?"

"Nothing like that."

He blew out a breath, relieved.

"He's upset that I took Miss Hessing's side against her mother."

"Miss Hessing stood up to her mother? That's a surprise. Over what?"

"Over a gentleman. And she hasn't stood up to her. She went behind her back. I encouraged her and have been roundly chastised for it, not by Mrs. Hessing but by my uncle. She couldn't face me herself."

"I know Miss Hessing is your friend, but do not get on Sir Ronald's bad side, Cleo. Not now when he's given his consent for you to investigate with me." The heavy dose of concern in his voice compelled me to quickly reassure him again.

"Don't worry. I won't do or say anything to make him change his mind." I rested my hand on his arm. "I know how to manage my uncle."

"How?"

"I can't give away all my secrets." I smiled, although in truth, I hadn't thought of a way yet.

Harry seemed satisfied with my answer. He smiled at me. Then he placed his hand over mine before letting go. He faced forward, a frown replacing his smile. He wore it all the way to the end of our journey.

* * *

THE PERFORMANCE at Her Majesty's Theatre on Haymarket was not to my taste and I was glad when it finally ended. As guests of the actor-manager and his wife, we enjoyed a lavish supper in the private banqueting hall of the massive central dome at the top of the building, along with a hundred other special guests who'd attended opening night.

Floyd's eyes lit up at the sight of the supper spread across the two long tables. "This will make up for Tree's performance. He can bore me to death any time as long as he feeds me afterwards." He forged a path through the crowd, only to suddenly divert his course towards Jonathon.

I craned my neck to see how the two friends greeted one another, but the crowd closed in and I was too short.

"Where did Mother go?" Flossy asked, also craning her neck. "I can't see her."

"To the ladies room, I expect."

"Do you think we should check on her? I don't want her taking more of her tonic."

I was about to point out that it would already be too late to stop her, but spotted Miss Hessing enter the banqueting hall with her mother. I grabbed Flossy's hand. "Let's find her."

We headed in the opposite direction to the Hessings, my heart sinking lower with every step. I was a coward for wanting to avoid my friend, but Harry's words kept ringing in my ears.

Do not get on Uncle Ronald's bad side.

I spotted him near one of the tables, his plate piled with various cuts of cold meat, chatting to a group of men which included Mr. Massie. I quickly scanned the room and found Hyacinthe Massie with friends. Jonathon wasn't with her.

He wasn't with Floyd, either, but was walking away from my cousin. Floyd stood alone, watching him, a confused frown on his face.

Flossy squeezed my hand. "There she is. How does she look to you?"

"Like she has just taken a dose of her tonic."

Aunt Lilian was the picture of a confident lady at the apex of the social order. She moved between groups of friends and acquaintances like a politician canvasing for votes, smiling the entire time.

But closer inspection revealed an uglier truth. Her hands shook. Her smiles were sometimes a result of muscular twitches, and she rarely stayed in one conversation long before flitting off to another. This energetic phase wouldn't last long. She knew she had to see everyone before the headache and nausea set in.

With a sigh of resignation, Flossy retraced her steps back to the refreshment tables. I began to follow her, but changed course when I spotted Jonathon. I'd sensed a mystery, and I was prepared to set aside my dislike of him to solve it.

After a cursory greeting, I asked him what was wrong between him and Floyd.

"Nothing." He looked over my head and tugged on his cuff.

"You've been avoiding him. Not just tonight, but ever since that night at Dutch's." I could add that it was ever since he'd told my uncle that I was conducting investigations with Harry, but I kept that to myself. He didn't know I knew, and that was the way I wanted to keep it.

"I've been busy," he said.

"Jonathon, stop this."

He lowered his gaze and looked at me through the curtain of blond hair. If he wasn't such a prick, he could skate through life on his boyish good looks. "Stop what?"

"Lying to me, for one thing; punishing Floyd for another. Your issue is with me, not him."

He scoffed. "Your ego knows no bounds. You think everything revolves around you, that you can do and say what you want and everyone else should simply go along."

"That's unfair, Jonathon."

I wasn't sure he even heard me. There was a gleam in his eyes, like a starving dog with the scent of prey in his nostrils. "You don't care who is affected by your selfishness."

I bristled. "Selfishness?"

"You show up in London, take your uncle's allowance and hospitality, and repay him by refusing to entertain a single eligible man who wants to court you. Not only that, you sneak about the city with undesirables while you play at being a female Sherlock Holmes. It's not only pathetic and immature, it's unfair to the family who took you in."

His words stung. They stung so much that tears pricked the backs of my eyes. Perhaps they wouldn't have wounded me if they weren't true, but I knew in my heart that there was an element of truth in what he said.

As much as I wanted to counter his argument, I found I couldn't. I was too disheartened—not for me, but for Floyd. It was in that moment I realized he'd lost his friend forever.

Jonathon went to walk off, but I stopped him with a hand to his arm. I needed to make a last-ditch effort to avoid the disaster looming on the horizon. The restaurant's inaugural dinner was tomorrow night, and Jonathon was one link in an important chain that could make it a success. Not only was he popular amongst the fashionable set, he was exactly the sort of fellow the press wanted to gossip about. A young, handsome, and titled gentleman who attended high society parties, courted women of questionable morals, and lived lavishly without a care for what the world thought. Gossip-mongering journalists like Mr. Paisley of *The Illustrated Courier* loved to write about his latest antics. With Jonathon attending the dinner, the press would clamor to write about what he and others like him thought of the event. If he was removed from the chain, it would be more difficult to interest them. If he pulled out, his friends might follow, and without the young and fashionable, the dinner would be a staid affair with just a few middle-aged friends of my uncle's and current guests of the hotel.

Up until now, I'd been sure Jonathon would attend and thought nothing more of it. I no longer assumed he'd be present tomorrow night.

"You will come to the dinner, won't you?" I asked. "Please. It means the world to Floyd and my aunt and uncle to have you there."

He looked down at my hand on his arm. "I know." It sounded arrogant, cock sure, everything I knew Jonathon to be. "I'll be there."

I let go. "Thank you. I appreciate it. We all do."

"I wouldn't miss it for the world." He smiled. It was an unpleasant stretch of his lips that worried me even more than his non-attendance at the dinner.

He walked off without another word. I was glad he was gone. Glad he was no longer Floyd's friend. Floyd deserved better. Unfortunately, neither he nor I would be rid of Jonathon forever. We would always have to endure his presence at functions such as these.

I wasn't sure if Uncle Ronald hailed me because he saw the exchange between Jonathon and me and knew I needed rescuing, or because he genuinely wanted me to meet his companions. I spent the next little while telling them why the hotel's new restaurant would be the best in London, making sure to praise Floyd's efforts in organizing its opening. They seemed interested, although I think their interest stemmed as much from the curiosity of having a young woman discuss business with middle-aged gentlemen as from a genuine desire to hear about the restaurant.

Uncle Ronald encouraged me at every turn, offering smiles, nods and leading questions that played to the strengths of my knowledge. He was the picture of a proud, doting uncle. He couldn't have been more different than when we spoke this morning.

This wasn't the first time he'd been kind to me after a scolding. It was as though he regretted it after his temper cooled but didn't want to apologize. In a way, this change in behavior *was* his apology. Saying sorry was too great a hurdle, but inviting me to discuss business with his friends was within his power. He was risking their disrespect and their ridicule by doing so. An educated woman with a head for business wasn't socially acceptable, but he'd judged his audience well tonight.

"Is she not clever for a young lady?" he asked them with a laugh.

His companions agreed, although some were simply being polite. Mr. Massie wasn't among them. He seemed genuinely interested in me and asked questions about my education and life in Cambridge. There were no airs about him, no sense that the world owed him. He was a self-made man who'd built his business from nothing to become one of the richest men in the country.

He would get along with Harry. There would be

mutual respect between them, I was certain. No wonder Harry wanted to make sure Hyacinthe married a good man in Jeremy. As far as the murder was concerned, I no longer thought Gooding Senior or Junior were suspects, but I was still unsure about Jeremy's relationship with Kitty Plumtree.

I followed Mr. Massie's gaze to his daughter, standing with her friends, their heads bent together as they exchanged whispers. "Is she not interested in the salt business?"

"No, but I have a son, so it's of no consequence."

And therein lay the root cause as to why women of the upper classes weren't educated. I wasn't sure why I expected a self-made businessman to be any different to a man born into wealth and privilege. Mr. Massie might find me interesting, but he didn't want his daughter to be like me. He wanted her to be just like the other girls in the society to which she'd been elevated.

As keenly as I wanted to walk away, I had a question to ask him. As one of the clients with insured cargo on board the *Elsie May*, there was something I wanted to know. With my uncle and the other gentlemen having moved the conversation on while Mr. Massie and I were talking, I could speak to him without being overheard.

"You must ship your salt all over the world."

He'd begun to look a little disinterested in our

conversation, but now that I'd turned it towards his business, he brightened. "To every corner of the earth. Massie salt adorns the tables as far away as New Zealand."

"Fascinating. There must be a risk of losing it in storms."

"Loss of cargo is not common these days. We have insurance, anyway, so the losses are kept to a minimum"

"But insurance costs money."

"Insurance companies aren't in business for amusement, Miss Fox." He laughed.

I smiled. "Of course. All I meant was, do people in business ever not get insurance when sending their goods around the world? To save money, I mean."

"Some would take the risk, I suppose. I don't recommend it. It could cost far more in the long run."

I wanted to ask him if Tobias Plumtree had ever suggested he not take out insurance, but I suspected it was a question too far. It would reveal too much about my investigation activities, something my uncle wouldn't want his friends to know.

"They would be foolish," Mr. Massie went on. "Foolish or inexperienced. Perhaps both."

So the killer was a foolish new businessman. I'd keep that in mind when we called on the four uninsured clients with cargo on the *Elsie May*.

* * *

I AWOKE to a pounding knock on the door. Not my door, this time, but further along the corridor. I threw my dressing gown around my shoulders and slipped my feet into slippers and prepared to ask whoever was making the noise to quieten down before they woke the guests.

I stopped when I spotted my uncle, standing outside Floyd's suite. I hurried towards him before he knocked again. His face was red, and the part of his neck that I could see over his stiff collar was mapped by bulging veins. "Uncle? What is it? What's wrong?" I gasped. "Is it Aunt Lilian?"

He thrust a newspaper he'd been holding at me and stabbed his finger on an article. "'Best friends court the same opera star,'" I read out loud.

I was interrupted by the door opening and Floyd blinking sleepily out at us. "Father? Cleo? What is it?"

Uncle Ronald snatched the newspaper off me and shoved it into Floyd's chest, pushing him backwards at the same time. He entered the suite. I followed and shut the door.

"Well?" Uncle Ronald's bellow came from the sitting room where he stood, hands on hips. With his red face, thick whiskers, and bulldog shape, he was the perfect candidate for a satirical cartoon of a steaming human teapot about to blow his top. "What do you have to say for yourself?"

Floyd's face was an entirely different color. He'd gone deathly pale. "I, I…"

I took the newspaper from him and read the article. The author, Mr. Paisley, claimed that Floyd was courting the opera singer, Miss Aldridge, but so was his best friend, Jonathon Hartly, son of Lord Cremorne. There was a photograph of Jonathon exiting the theater with Miss Aldridge, arm in arm and smiling at one another. Beside it was a photograph of Floyd, also with Miss Aldridge, wearing the same outfit and exiting the same theater. She had her hand to her face to shield her eyes from the sun glare while Floyd stared at the camera as if startled to see a photographer there.

I took his elbow, as much to steady him as remind him he was not alone. He seemed to have gone into a stupor. "Are you all right?"

"How did this fellow know?" he asked, numbly. Then it struck him, like a punch to the stomach that sent him reeling. "Jonathon."

It had to be he who'd told Mr. Paisley where and when Floyd would be with Miss Aldridge. He'd also informed the journalist to watch and wait for *him* and Miss Aldridge. It was his way of getting back at Floyd. And me. This was the scandal Mr. Paisley alluded to. It was the reason why Jonathon had given me that slick smile last night at supper.

He was looking forward to seeing the journalists feast on the carcass of Floyd's reputation once the story broke.

He knew that he could survive the scandal. He didn't care what his father thought. Indeed, the scandal would put off the parents of the marriageable candidates he'd been forced to entertain of late. It might even bolster his credibility with his friends. He *wanted* to be mired in scandal, at least for now, to get revenge on his father. Lord Cremorne would be livid.

Floyd's father would also be livid. Uncle Ronald loathed scandal that was attached to the family. He saw it as harmful to the Bainbridge reputation, and the Bainbridges were the name behind the Mayfair Hotel. A scandal for the family was a scandal for the business.

It was one it would survive. It was only a mild scandal, as far as the hotel was concerned. But my uncle didn't see it that way. He took it personally. He blamed Floyd, and Floyd would feel the lash of his anger. Jonathon had known he would.

It was cruel indeed.

"You fool!" Uncle Ronald grabbed the newspaper and shook it barely inches from Floyd's face. "How could you do this to me?"

"I—I'm sorry, Father." Floyd collapsed onto the sofa and buried his head in his hands. "I can't believe she would do this. I can't believe Jonathon…"

I sat on the sofa arm and rubbed his back. I opened my mouth to tell him not to trust a word in the article, but Uncle Ronald cut me off.

"I don't care if another ten men are seeing her! I only care that *you* have been caught. And on the very day of the restaurant opening, too! It's going to be a disaster, Floyd. An absolute disaster."

With my hand on his back, I felt rather than heard Floyd's groan. "I thought we were discreet. I didn't think the press knew about her."

Uncle Ronald threw the paper at him. It flopped to the floor where the pages came loose. "Clearly they did."

"I'll speak to the journalist. Ask for a retraction."

"What good will that do? For one thing, a retraction won't appear before tomorrow. And for another, who will care? The damage has been done. Not only does everyone know you're a cad who gets about with notorious women, but your best friend is your rival for her affections! It's pathetic."

"I'm sorry," Floyd muttered into his hands. "I'm sorry, Father. I'll fix it. I'll find a way."

"You can't," Uncle Ronald bit off. "The press won't care about the food, the other guests, the spectacle. All they'll care about is you, Hartly, and *that* woman. It'll be an embarrassing debacle that will take weeks for the restaurant to recover from, if it ever does." He stormed off and slammed the door behind him.

Floyd jumped, then he groaned. "Why would she do this to me, Cleo?"

"She? Don't you mean he? Jonathon?"

"I expect this from him nowadays. Things between us aren't friendly. It's just like him to create a rift by going after my girl. But why would Lily? I know we don't love one another, but I thought she cared enough not to be with another while she was with me." He sat back with a sigh. "I'll tell Jonathon not to come tonight. I'll beg if I have to."

"You'll do no such thing. Let him come. It may not be the disaster your father thinks it'll be. This article will interest other journalists. I'd wager the press will be there in bigger numbers than would have covered the opening otherwise."

"But they won't care about the restaurant. Father was right. They'll only care about the so-called love triangle." He kicked the newspaper across the floor.

I picked it up and looked over the article again. "Try not to worry. Just show up tonight looking dapper and sporting a dashing smile for the photographers. It'll be all right."

He sighed again. "I don't see how."

I kissed the top of his forehead, tucked the newspaper under my arm, and left to get ready. It was going to be a very long day.

CHAPTER 15

Floyd's problem occupied my mind all the way to Broadwick Street. The moment I stepped into the narrow lane, I set that issue aside, however, and focused on the investigation. We would find our killer today amongst the four uninsured clients of Gooding and Plumtree, I was sure of it.

The problem would be proving it. Even if we suspected one of the four, he or she wouldn't admit to being the killer. We'd have to find proof or force the murderer to confess. Hopefully the way to do that would present itself at the time.

I didn't stop in at the Roma Café before heading up the stairs to Harry's office. For one thing, I didn't want to linger over coffees this morning. I'd rather get on with our investigation. For another, the café wasn't all that enticing. Luigi had propped the door open and the smell of burnt milk wafted out.

I was about to knock on Harry's office door when I heard his deep voice. He had a visitor. I pressed my ear to the door and listened. Miss Morris's lighter voice responded to Harry, but I couldn't hear what she said. If she opened the door and found me standing on the landing, she would know that Harry was investigating with me. It might upset her and make her suspicious.

It could be that he was telling her right now that we were seeing a great deal of one another at the moment and that she shouldn't be jealous, but I couldn't be sure. Nor did I want to be the cause of any issues between them.

I headed back down the stairs and waited in the Roma Café. Luigi brought me coffee and apologized for the smell. Instead of returning to his position behind the counter, he sat with me.

"If I saw you pass by, I would have told you she was up there," he said, sheepishly scratching his sideburns.

"It's quite all right. I'm happy to wait here for a few minutes." Any longer than a few and I might be tempted to go without Harry.

"She calls on him most mornings before she goes to work."

"That's nice."

"It would be nicer if she took him coffee."

I smiled, thinking he was disappointed not to make a sale. But when he didn't return my smile, I wondered if it was because he was disappointed for Harry's sake that she lacked consideration for his needs.

I shook off the thought. It was neither fair nor my place.

I spent the next little while chatting to Luigi until one of the old men on the stools at the bar started speaking Italian to him. Luigi resumed his place behind the counter to make them another coffee.

With my cup finished, I checked the time on my pocket watch. I'd allow five more minutes before I abandoned Harry and continued on my own.

Four minutes later, he and Miss Morris passed the café. She walked closest to the window but faced Harry so didn't see me. If he saw me, he gave no sign. He stopped by the door, no doubt intending to come in. She stopped, too, and took both his hands in hers.

With the door still open for fresh air, I heard everything she said. "I don't want you to think I'm lecturing you. But you do understand my reasoning, don't you?"

"It's a very sensible reason. How can I fail to understand?" His voice was as even and placating as hers. "But *you* must understand that sometimes we have to be liberal with the truth to obtain information."

This was a conversation left over from our last investigation, when I'd not been honest with one of our suspects who also happened to work with Miss Morris. I hadn't been proud of my actions that day, but they had been necessary to obtain answers.

"It's the nature of our business," Harry went on.

"Our" business. He'd also said "we." He must have told her he was working with me again on this case.

"Of course," she said in the same agreeable tone. "But if you want to join the police force, you must be careful. Your reputation must be pristine, without blemish."

Join the police! So he hadn't told her about his criminal history yet.

Harry's throat moved with his heavy swallow. "As I said, I'm not interested in joining the police." Not interested? It wasn't the same as not able to.

"Not interested in a steady income and a stable profession? Harry," she gently chided, "I know you want to make a go of your agency, and I admire you for your entrepreneurial spirit, but if you could channel your intelligence and skills into the Metropolitan Police, you could go far. Indeed, you could reach the very top, one day. I have the utmost faith in you and your abilities."

"I don't want to join the police force."

She tilted her head to the side. "Come now, you must want it. It's your father's profession. It's a noble and respected one, nowadays. Isn't that what you want? The respect you deserve?"

It was true that most private detectives had a tarnished reputation, but some had risen above the rest and made a name for themselves. Harry was on his way to being one of them. If only she knew that, she might not push so hard for him to join the Metropolitan Police. If only she knew he *couldn't* join, she would drop the suggestion altogether.

He withdrew his hands from hers. "I don't wish to talk about it anymore."

"Oh. Of course, you should do as you wish." She stood on her toes and kissed his cheek. "I'll see you tonight?"

He smiled, but it lacked cheer.

She turned to go, catching sight of me through the window. Her lips parted with her silent gasp. Her gaze flicked to Harry then back to me as a groove formed between her brows. I smiled and waved. She gave a half-hearted wave in return then went on her way.

Harry joined me in the café. "How much of that did you hear?"

"All of it. Harry, have you still not told her about your past?"

"She knows that I was adopted as a teen after my mother died." He sighed as he sat. "But I haven't told her I never knew my father, or that I lived on the streets and thieved to stay alive." He gave me an expectant look. "Go on then. Tell me I should have told her everything."

"I'm sure you have your reasons for not mentioning it."

"Cowardice," he muttered.

I leaned forward, wanting to get my next point across very clearly. "That is never a word I'd use to describe you. It's not cowardice to want other people to think well of you, particularly when it comes to the woman you're courting."

He lowered his gaze to his hand, resting flat on the table.

"But you must tell her at some point," I went on. "And if she does have difficulty accepting it, then she's not the right woman for you, and it's better you find that out now."

The corner of his mouth kicked up with his half-smile. "You sound like my mother."

"That's because we're both wise."

He stood. "Come on. Let's interrogate our four suspects. I've thought of a way to trick the killer into revealing themselves."

"Are we going to be liberal with the truth again?"

He laughed, proving my teasing didn't bother him. "It's my favorite way of obtaining information."

* * *

OUR FIRST PORT of call was a warehouse fronting the docks. I'd been here mere days before to interview Mr. Cripps, the brother of one of the *Elsie May's* deceased sailors. I looked for him, but instead spotted someone I hadn't expected to see. Ned Baker, former friend of Thomas Plum's.

The last time we'd seen him had been at The Duke pub where he'd tackled Harry then reluctantly answered our questions.

As if he sensed me, he suddenly looked up from the barrel he was rolling. He straightened and put one foot on the barrel. He leaned an elbow on the knee and withdrew the cigarette dangling from his lips.

I nodded a greeting. He blew out a puff of smoke and continued rolling the barrel towards the cart. The other barrels on the cart were stamped W & G LONDON.

Harry indicated a warehouse. "This is it." Above the yawning entrance was painted the company name of WATERHOUSE AND GARVEY.

I turned back to Ned Baker, but he was no longer there and the cart laden with the barrels was being pulled our way by a stocky horse. We entered the warehouse ahead of it.

The foreman pointed us in the direction of a small office where a white-whiskered man sat at a desk. He did not look up when we entered but raised a finger while he copied numbers from a piece of paper into a ledger.

When he finished, he still did not look up, but he did acknowledge our presence. "Yes?"

Harry introduced us by name but didn't mention our profession. "We work for Gooding and Plumtree." It was the truth, albeit the liberal version.

The mention of the company earned him a scowl. "I'm very busy. What do you want?"

"We wish to talk to you about working with us again in the future. May we sit?"

The man hesitated then indicated the chairs. He introduced himself as Mr. Garvey. "If you're concerned about me moving my business to another shipping company after the disaster of the *Elsie May*, then allow me to reassure you that I have no interest in going elsewhere. Plumtree may have been my point of contact, but I can work just as well with his replacement."

"That is a relief," Harry said. "However, it isn't Plumtree's replacement that we want to discuss. It's the fact that you weren't insured."

Mr. Garvey's response was to thrust out his chin in a show of defiance.

"It has come to light that Plumtree encouraged you not to take out insurance in order to save you the cost of the premium. I wish to assure you, that is not company policy and his view did not represent the view of Gooding and Plumtree. We always recommend insurance."

Mr. Garvey put up both his hands in surrender. "Let me stop you there. It may have been Plumtree's idea, but it was entirely my own volition to agree to it. I don't hold the company to account. The storm was unfortunate, the loss of life and cargo a tragedy. I should have taken out insurance. I know better."

"Then why didn't you?" I asked.

"We didn't have a lot on board, and the insurance seemed disproportionate to the cargo's value." His whiskers flattened with his frown. "In hindsight, that was a foolish mistake. One I won't make again. Be assured, I don't blame Gooding and Plumtree."

"Mr. Plumtree didn't pressure you to disregard insurance?" Harry asked.

"He suggested it once; planting the seed, if you like. It was he who pointed out that the insurance premium was excessive for such a small value of goods. I should have given it more consideration before agreeing."

"It's good of you not to hold the company to account for your losses."

"Legally, I don't have a leg to stand on. I'm fortunate the loss can be easily absorbed. I only hope others who listened to Plumtree's suggestion could equally afford their loss. It's the smaller companies that would have suffered when the *Elsie May* went down, not the larger ones like us. I'm sure Plumtree didn't encourage *them* not to take out insurance, however. He would know which of his clients could absorb a loss and which could not."

His words circled around and around in my mind as we thanked him and left the warehouse.

Harry stopped to watch another cart laden with barrels stamped W & G LONDON enter the warehouse. They would be added to the other barrels piling up on the left side. The rest of the vast space was filled with crates and boxes with the company name stamped in bold black lettering.

"Waterhouse and Garvey are not in financial difficulty," he pointed out.

It would appear he was right. "But the murderer is, or soon will be, thanks to losing a great deal of cargo when the *Elsie May* sank. More than he or she could afford to lose. We're looking for a company that's smaller than Waterhouse and Garvey."

"One that's now in financial difficulty, with a desperate and angry owner, who believed Tobias Plumtree when he said the *Elsie May* was reliable and insurance wasn't necessary."

I looked over the list of four suspects. Of the three we were yet to speak to, one was a large company that manufactured railway parts, and another was located in a nearby warehouse. We discarded the large company altogether since they could absorb a loss, and called at the warehouse office. It was clear when we got there that they too were a significant size. The conversation with the manager went the same way as it had done with Mr. Garvey. He blamed himself for agreeing to Tobias Plumtree's suggestion and not taking out insurance. He didn't blame Plumtree, and the loss was small enough to provide a harsh lesson but not enough to make him want to murder the man who suggested it.

That left just one suspect, although I worried we'd receive the same outcome. Mr. Massie had told me to look for someone new to the business, and gullible or foolish enough not to take out insurance. After speaking to Mr. Garvey, we realized we were also looking for a small company where any loss was a financial blow.

But as we'd seen from the three companies we'd struck off our list, no one was foolish enough not to take out insurance if the loss of their cargo could ruin them. I was beginning to doubt every conclusion we'd made.

"What if we're wrong?" I said to Harry as we walked along the dock. "What if the murder has nothing to do with the insurance, or the lack of it? What if it has nothing to do with the *Elsie May's* sinking at all? The murderer might be Jeremy Gooding, attempting to get rid of his lover's rival."

"I finished my investigation, and I don't think he and Kitty Plumtree are lovers. Hyacinthe Massie knows all about their friendship."

"Lady Mannix then, out of anger at not receiving her fair share when their relationship ended and he shuttered their business." I stopped suddenly when I spotted a familiar figure up ahead, a cigarette dangling from his lips as he hauled on a rope. "Or Ned Baker, because he believes Plumtree should have gone to prison too, all those years ago."

Harry followed my gaze. "You want to confront him, don't you?"

"Do you have a better plan in mind?"

"Dozens, but I suspect you won't listen to any of them."

"I happen to think confronting him in front of witnesses is a better plan than doing it alone in a dark alley."

"I don't recall mentioning being alone or dark alleys," he said wryly.

I strode along the dock, not taking my gaze off Ned Baker. I didn't want him disappearing into the throng of dockworkers all dressed the same. "Follow my lead. I'm about to be very liberal with the truth."

"You mean you're going to lie outright."

"Exactly."

Ned Baker glanced around as we approached,

perhaps checking to see if his foreman was nearby, then removed the cigarette from his mouth with his thumb and forefinger. "You two again. What do you want?"

"We didn't know you worked here," I said.

"I pick up temporary jobs here sometimes." He puffed on the cigarette and blew smoke from the corner of his mouth. "You done?"

"Not quite. We've just learned that you were at the Crown and Anchor on the night of Mr. Plumtree's murder."

"That's a lie! Who told you that?" He looked at the faces of the men nearby, as if it might have been one of them.

"You knew about Lady Mannix," I pointed out. "You knew she was angry with Plumtree, too, albeit for a different reason than you. You knew she and he met at the Crown and Anchor all those years ago and used the hidden passage between rooms to see one another in secret. You devised a plan to set her up to take the blame for the murder, but first, you had to lure Plumtree to the pub, and to do that, you invited him to meet you there, for old times' sake."

"What are you talking about? I don't know about no passage between rooms. Whoever says they saw me leave there is lying. I never invited Tommy to the pub. *He* invited *me*."

I tried very hard to keep my features schooled and maintain a professional demeanor, but I suspected I failed. My gasp sounded loud, even amidst the noise of the dockhands' shouts and the grind of machinery. His initial denial had been so vehement that I'd begun to think my suspicion was wrong and he had nothing to do with the murder. After all, we had no evidence, merely a connection between Ned and Thomas Plum. But now I suspected Ned Baker held a vital piece of information that we'd been missing.

"So you *were* invited to the tavern that night," I clarified.

"Aye."

"By Tobias Plumtree."

"Tommy Plum, aye. I told him I wanted to see him. Next night, I get a message asking me to meet him at the Crown and Anchor. But I never went, so whoever reckons they saw me is lying. I didn't go anywhere near there because I didn't want to be seen with him. I'm known at that pub. We both are. I didn't want witnesses for what I was going to do."

"Murder him?" I had to ask.

"No! Bloody hell, Miss. No. I wanted to have it out with him. I wanted to tell him he was a coward, and a greedy one at that. But not there. If it got violent…"

"You didn't want witnesses," I finished.

He shrugged and sucked on the cigarette again.

"I waited for his response to my message about

finding another pub, but he never sent one. He must have died before he got the chance."

Harry and I exchanged glances. "You sent a message to him at the Crown and Anchor?" Harry asked.

Ned nodded. "I sent a boy and told him to ask around for Tommy Plum and tell him to name another place. The boy returned, said he delivered the message but there was no answer."

"Did the boy give the message to Plumtree in person?"

Ned shrugged.

"Where can we find him?" I asked.

"The boy?" He snorted. "Who knows?"

Ned's foreman shouted at him to get back to work and he made to move off.

"One more thing," I said. "The last time we spoke, you told us that Thomas Plum visited you once in prison. You claimed that's when you learned his lover financed his first business venture. But earlier, you told us you hadn't seen him since *before* you were jailed. Why the discrepancy?"

Ned Baker rubbed the back of his neck.

"Which version is the lie, Mr. Baker?"

"Answer her truthfully, or we'll report your lie to the police," Harry said.

Ned Baker's eyes widened with alarm. "Listen here. It was only a small lie. I *did* find out about the lady financing his business while I was in prison, but not from Tommy. I got a visit from a man, ten or eleven years ago. He didn't give me his name, but he wanted to know about Tommy's past. He asked me about Tommy's former business partner, a lady. But I knew nothing about her." He shrugged. "I lied to you because the man told me I wasn't to tell anyone about him visiting me. I reckon he didn't want Tommy to find out he was checking on him."

The visitor must have been Mr. Gooding. It had always seemed unlikely that a respectable businessman would go into business with someone he barely knew. He'd never claimed to be ignorant about Thomas Plumtree's past, and here was the proof that he'd told the truth. Ned Baker's story about Mr. Gooding visiting him in jail and asking questions about Lady Mannix made sense.

We thanked him and walked off.

"Whoever received that message in the Crown and Anchor is our killer," I said to Harry.

"It could be anyone. The pub is full of an evening with this lot." He indicated the hundreds of men working up and down the dock, on the ships, and in the warehouses.

"We can wait until tonight and see if the boy is lurking around the Crown and Anchor again. We can ask him to describe the person he gave the message to."

"He may have just been a lad passing by, a street

urchin in need of a coin. Finding him again will be impossible."

He was right, but I suggested we return to the inn anyway. Bull or Nancy might have noticed the boy and recognized the man he spoke to—a man who wasn't Plumtree, but his murderer.

I was still holding the piece of paper with the four company addresses on it. I'd been about to return it to my bag when I remembered the fourth name. The office address wasn't far. Indeed, it was in Canning Town, near the Crown and Anchor.

I pointed it out to Harry. "What if the owner of this company was at the Crown and Anchor that night and saw Plumtree enter? His office is close, so it's reasonable to assume he's a regular patron."

"And when he heard the boy asking after Plumtree, he paid the lad to give him the message instead. When he learned no one would be meeting Plumtree, he decided it was a good time to confront him."

"No witnesses."

Harry nodded along. "No witnesses."

* * *

THE DOUGLAS COMPANY'S office was located a mere two streets from the Crown and Anchor. I knew the moment I saw it that we were on the right path. The office was housed in a two-room flat within a run-down hovel in a dead-end court. We were looking for a company that could ill afford to lose any cargo, owned and managed by an inexperienced businessman. It was highly likely that the person who ran their company out of their Canning Town flat fit both criteria.

The company owner was not at home, however, so we retreated to the Crown and Anchor to wait awhile, and to ask Nancy and Bull if they knew him.

After a short walk, Harry held the door open for me. Inside, the same drunks sat in the same seats. Nancy stood in the same position, too, behind the counter as she dried a tankard. At the other end, Bull leaned his crossed arms on the bar. He was in deep conversation with two gentlemen but looked up as we entered. He greeted us with a nod and asked Nancy to serve us.

"Are you going to risk the coffee again?" Harry asked as we sat at a table.

I pulled a face. "I think I'll have tea."

We both ordered tea and Nancy returned to the bar to make it. I listened as Harry listed his reasons for believing we were on the right path to finding the murderer. After a while, I tuned out.

Bull had caught my eye. Or, rather, his right hand did. It was bandaged. When Nancy returned with teacups and a pot, I asked her what he'd done.

"He cut it," she said, glancing over her shoulder at him. "Fool. Almost sliced off his thumb, he says."

"You didn't see the injury?"

She shook her head.

I watched as Bull picked up a pencil in his left hand and tried to write with it. He couldn't manage it, and eventually gave up. "He's right-handed, isn't he?"

"Aye."

"So how did he almost cut off the thumb of his right hand? If he held the knife in his right, he should have sliced through the left hand."

She shrugged. "Maybe he tried to use the knife with his left hand."

Or perhaps he didn't cut himself at all. Perhaps he burned his right hand as he tried to open a strong box he'd failed to destroy in a fire.

One of the gentlemen put out his hand, only to retract it when he realized Bull couldn't shake it with his right. The three men simply gave each other awkward nods instead before the gentlemen left. "Who are they?" I asked Nancy.

"Something to do with his property down south, a banker or realtor, I reckon. It's sad, it is."

Harry and I glanced at each other. It was all beginning to make sense now. "Go on," I urged her.

"Bull bought himself a seaside cottage to retire to. I was going to manage this place for him, send him the profits for him to live off, but he's had to sell the cottage now."

"Why can he no longer afford to keep it?"

She shrugged a shoulder.

Harry asked another question before she moved off. "There's a distillery out the back, isn't there?"

"It's all legal! He's got a proper company set up and all. He sells the liquor to other pubs and has some contacts overseas. Good scotch whiskey it is, made the traditional way."

I suspected he'd already started trading with his international contacts. His first shipment was aboard the *Elsie May*. He'd invested a lot in that shipment. Indeed, he'd probably sent a sizeable portion of his whiskey off across the ocean. He may even have taken out a loan to fulfil a big order from a buyer. To save money, he'd not insured it on the suggestion of someone he trusted, a long-time patron of his pub.

When his entire shipment was lost, and his retirement plans with it, Bull blamed Tobias Plumtree. Then he murdered him.

CHAPTER 16

$\mathcal{I}$ watched Nancy return to the bar. My gaze slid to Bull, once again attempting to write with his injured hand. He must be confident we didn't suspect him of the murder or he would have tried to hide his bandages.

"Cleo," Harry said with quiet urgency. "Don't look at him. Don't let him know that you suspect him." He moved his chair closer to mine so we could talk.

"We should confront him here and now," I whispered. "You secure him and I'll fetch the police."

"The man is nicknamed Bull for a reason. Even with his injury, I don't think I can capture him and hold him. The drunks won't be any help, and we can't be sure Nancy won't take his side."

"Have faith in your own physical ability, Harry. I do."

"Your faith in me won't be a comfort when I'm searching for my teeth on the floor. Anyway, are we sure he's the right man? There are still some missing pieces of the puzzle."

I arched a brow at him. "Try not to get punched in the mouth. Your teeth are lovely, and this floor is sticky. That's why I'm very sure he's the murderer."

"Because the floor is sticky?"

"I'll explain later. I'll fetch the police while you stay here and keep an eye on him. You won't need to confront him unless he becomes suspicious, so look innocent and be friendly." I pushed my chair back and stood.

Harry stood, too. He looked like he was about to say something but changed his mind.

Looking innocent wasn't as easy as I thought. Bull saw right through my smiling act the moment he laid eyes on me.

He moved very quickly, for an older man. He emerged from behind the bar and blocked the exit. "Nance, stop her! If she gets the police, you'll be arrested for being an accessory to murder."

Nancy didn't move. She stood frozen to the spot, staring at Bull as he sized up Harry. Harry moved to stand in front of me to protect me, but I sidestepped out of his shadow.

I took advantage of Nancy's indecision. "Did you know he murdered Tobias Plumtree upstairs?"

She gasped. "No!"

"Then you're not an accessory, Nancy, you're merely a witness. The only reason to arrest you now would be if you interfered and tried to help him escape."

She pressed both hands to her stomach. Her bosom heaved with her ragged breaths. "I won't interfere. Go out the back door and fetch a constable."

This time, it was me who froze. I ought to go, but I couldn't leave Harry. Not if there was a chance he needed me. He was right. Bull was a large man. He might be older and sporting an injury, but if he charged at Harry, he would knock him over.

That was precisely what he did.

But Harry neatly stepped out of his way. Unable to stop himself, Bull tumbled into a table and chairs with an almighty crash. Wood splintered. Chair legs snapped off and rolled away.

"Nancy, fetch rope," Harry ordered.

The barmaid disappeared into the back room.

Bull staggered to his knees then pushed himself to his feet. "Let me go and no one gets hurt."

"We can't let you leave," I said. "You're a murderer. You hanged Tobias Plumtree after getting him so drunk he fell unconscious."

Bull bared his teeth. "He deserved it! He told me not to get insurance, and I lost everything!"

Nancy returned with a length of coiled rope. Harry went to retrieve it from her, but Bull intercepted him.

Metal flashed as he slashed the blade across Harry's shoulder.

Harry hissed in pain but remained alert enough to avoid the follow-up strike. Bull stepped closer and struck again, but Harry dodged it once more. He backed away with every forward step of Bull's, until he was up against the bar.

Trapped.

My heart thundered. Blood gushed through my veins. My mind suddenly went blank as Bull raised the knife. He aimed it at Harry's chest. Everything became blurry, sounds muffled, as if I'd been smothered with a blanket. I couldn't breathe, couldn't get free.

Yet there was a hole in the blanket, a bright light guiding me. I focused on it, and finally saw the way out.

I snatched up one of the chair legs from the floor and smashed it over Bull's head as he brought down the knife to strike Harry.

Bull staggered but didn't fall.

That momentary lapse gave Harry a small window of opportunity. He struck Bull's left hand, the one holding the knife, then struck again at his bandaged right. Bull pulled it into his body, snarling in pain.

Harry tried to get closer but every time, Bull lashed out with the knife. Harry only just managed to avoid getting cut across his middle.

"Harry!" I threw him the chair leg and he caught it.

Without a moment's hesitation, he slammed it into Bull's wrist, weakening his grip on the knife. With one more targeted blow, Bull dropped the weapon altogether.

It clattered to the floor. Harry kicked it towards me.

I picked it up, ready to strike Bull if he attacked Harry again.

But all the fight had left him. He kept his injured right hand close but his left dangled limply at his side. The wrist had already begun to swell and bruise.

Harry twisted Bull's arm behind his back and shoved him forward into the bar. He tied Bull's hands together with rope Nancy handed to him. He wasn't gentle, and Bull winced in pain.

"Nancy, go to the local police station and have them telephone Scotland Yard," Harry said. "Tell them we have Tobias Plumtree's murderer."

She hesitated. "But who will manage the bar?"

He shot her a glare. She hurried out of the pub.

Harry ordered Bull to sit on a chair then used the remaining length of rope to tie him to it.

Once he was secured, I leaned against the bar

for support. My legs felt a little weak, my stomach tied in knots.

Harry stepped back to regard his handiwork. Satisfied that Bull wasn't going anywhere, he joined me. The rush of blood that came with fighting still gripped him, however. I could see it in the glare he gave the three drunks, watching us silently from their stools, and the rigidity of his shoulders.

Then I noticed the blood discoloring his jacket sleeve. I removed a handkerchief from my bag and gently pressed it to the cut on his upper arm. He blinked, as if awoken from a stupor, and noticed the injury for the first time. The corners of his eyes tightened with his wince.

"It hurts?" I asked.

He placed his hand over mine and our gazes connected. There was heat in his eyes, but I couldn't be certain if it was caused by the fight or another, more tender, emotion. I knew precisely where the jolt within me came from, and why it reverberated through my body.

I also knew it was wrong.

As if we both came to that conclusion at the same time, his hand released mine and I slipped free. I gave him the handkerchief and he dabbed at the wound himself.

He eyed the knife where I'd set it down on the bar. "Thank you for hitting him on the head, but you shouldn't have got so close. I had the situation under control."

I scoffed. "How?"

"I would have ducked or moved to the side. The knife point would have become stuck in the bar, I would then tackle him to the floor. Or I could have leaped onto the bar and over it."

"What if you weren't fast enough to duck in time? Or strong enough to unbalance him?"

His eyes brightened with amusement. The earlier passion had vanished altogether. "I seem to recall you had no issue with my physical abilities a few minutes ago."

"I, er…" I cleared my throat. "I need a stiff drink. May we serve ourselves, Mr. Douglas?" I added in a louder voice.

Bull lifted his head. I took that as acknowledgement that he was indeed named Douglas and he was the owner of The Douglas Company. It would also do as agreement that we could help ourselves.

I rounded the bar and surveyed the bottles, tankards and cups arrayed behind it. "Your coffee is awful, by the way. Truly terrible. Let's see if your whiskey is better."

"You drink whiskey?" Harry asked from the other side of the bar.

"No, but you gentlemen all seem to like it so it must have a certain appeal." I poured a small amount from one of the bottles labeled with the

Douglas Company's label and sipped. The contents burned my throat as it went down. My eyes watered and I coughed.

Harry chuckled. "I don't think you're ready for a man's drink."

He knew how to get a rise out of me, and I knew he knew it. That didn't stop me from proving a point by drinking the remainder. This time I was ready for the burn and managed not to cough.

He grinned as I poured two fingers worth into another glass and handed it to him. He drank the contents without as much as a wrinkle of his nose at the strong taste.

Nancy returned fifteen minutes later and sometime afterwards, Detective Sargent Forrester from Scotland Yard arrived with two constables. I recognized him from a previous investigation where he'd accompanied D.I. Hobart. He greeted us both with enthusiasm and identified himself as the former colleague of Harry's father who'd suspected all along that Tobias Plumtree's death was murder.

He withdrew his notebook from his pocket and asked Harry to begin at the beginning.

Harry indicated me. "It's Cleo's investigation."

The detective raised his brows, his pencil hovering over his page. "Go on, if you please, Miss Fox. How and why did Mr. Douglas do it?"

The why was easy to explain, so I began with that first. The detective wrote it all down.

"So he was angry over losing a large cargo," he concluded as he wrote. "He blamed Plumtree for the poor advice and plotted to kill him in revenge."

"It wasn't planned ahead," I said. "It was a spur of the moment decision. He hadn't seen Mr. Plumtree for some time, perhaps not since the *Elsie May's* sinking. His anger had been brewing all that time and finally boiled over when Plumtree was suddenly in his pub again."

Bull kept his head down, his gaze unfocused, not offering a comment on my assessment.

I continued. "Plumtree thought he was meeting an old friend here, but a boy came with a message from that friend saying he wasn't coming. Bull intercepted the message and never relayed it. It was then that his plan formed. He sent Plumtree up to his regular room. Bull knew Plumtree didn't hold his liquor well and always fell into a deep sleep when he drank too much, so took up two bottles of wine. He probably stayed for a while and made sure Plumtree drank a considerable amount. Once Plumtree passed out, he tied the rope to the beam, formed a noose, and maneuvered his unconscious victim into it. You can see he's strong. Bull is, well, built like a bull, and Plumtree was relatively slight. With his superior size and height, Bull managed to loop the noose around the unconscious Plumtree's neck. He pushed over the stool to make it look like Plumtree had kicked it away himself."

"But the stool was too low for someone of Plumtree's stature to have used for such an endeavor," Detective Sergeant Forrester said as he wrote. "Hence my suspicion that he didn't take his own life."

"It was a very accurate assessment of the scene."

He looked up and smiled sheepishly at me. "Thank you, Miss Fox. Please go on. Your insights are invaluable."

Beside me, Harry shifted his feet and crossed his arms. The movement stretched his wound and he sucked in a breath between his teeth.

"Bull had been proprietor here for many years," I went on. "He knew Plumtree when he was Thomas Plum. He knew he used that room to meet his mistress, Lady Mannix, who'd once taken the room two doors down. She always arrived in simple clothes and pretended to be a local, but Bull knew what she looked like, what they were up to, and that Lady Mannix could have traveled through the secret passage between rooms to meet her lover in his room. He used that knowledge to frame her for the murder."

Nancy gasped. She placed a hand on her hip and glared at Bull. "You didn't use that passage to kill him. The hidden tunnel wasn't relevant to the murder at all."

"That's true," I answered for him. "He simply used his knowledge of it to form a case against

Lady Mannix. But, before that, he tried to blame you, Nancy."

She frowned. "He did?"

"Before we mentioned Lady Mannix to either of you, he said you knew about the passage."

"But I didn't!"

"He tried telling us that you must have known, implying that you were lying to us, planting the seed in our heads that you were the killer. He told us that you must have known about the hidden door and passage because you clean the rooms regularly. But I'd noticed how dusty the room was, and how dirty it is down here." I pressed my boot into the floorboard then lifted it. The sound of it sticking made Bull flinch. "You're probably an excellent barmaid, but cleaning is not your strength."

"Aye, true," she muttered.

"Finding that secret door and passage between rooms was probably the worst thing we could have done. I think it slowed down our investigation because we were convinced the killer used it. We never entertained the possibility that he simply walked through the regular door. But that's exactly what Bull did."

"Thank God I hate cleaning," Nancy muttered.

"At that point, we'd begun to suspect Lady Mannix, Plumtree's former lover and business partner. We knew she loathed him but had lost touch with him. We thought she'd seen his picture in the newspaper and discovered his new name and where he worked, but that article proved to be another false clue that led us down the wrong path. Although it *is* still relevant to the timing of the murder, and why it happened now and not after the *Elsie May* went down."

"Why?" Forrester asked.

"Plumtree's former friend, Ned Baker, saw it. Like Lady Mannix, it was the first he'd learned of Thomas Plum's new name and where he worked. Baker watched the office of Gooding and Plumtree after seeing the article then asked to meet him. Seeing Baker again after all this time made Plumtree nervous. He knew Baker was angry with him. But that anxiety was also irrelevant in the end. However, Ned Baker's message to Plumtree kicked off the chain of events that led us here."

"Back to Lady Mannix," the detective said. "You asked the perpetrator about her?"

"We did. We asked Bull and Nancy if Plumtree could have met her here on the night of his death. At first, both said he was alone. They saw no one. But Bull could see the opportunity to frame her and he took it, but he also kept Nancy as his back-up plan in case we ruled Lady Mannix out."

Nancy glared at her employer. "Is that so?"

"Bull had already planted the seed that you were lying to us, Nancy, by suggesting you must have known about the hidden passage, even though you denied it. He then described Lady Mannix, but in the vaguest of terms. Of course you had seen someone matching that description on the night of the murder. Dark-haired women with lush figures come in here all the time to service the men. Bull knew that if we discarded Lady Mannix as a suspect, it was logical that we'd think you were lying about seeing her here. There could be only one reason why you'd tell both lies—you were guilty. Or so he hoped we'd believe."

Nancy stepped up to Bull and slapped him across the cheek. "Bastard!"

Bull simply sat there, his shoulders stooped and his head lowered. He'd given up.

"Harry and I sat over there." I indicted the table where we'd had coffee. "We talked through the investigation together. When Bull brought us our coffees, he must have overheard us talking about the theft of the insurance list from Gooding and Plumtree. *He'd* been the thief."

The detective quickly scrawled that down.

"Realizing the absence of his name on the insurance claim list was a clue, he decided to get rid of it, thinking it would be harder for us to find a motive without it. But he didn't realize there was a copy in Plumtree's strong box. So after hearing us mention it, he tried to retrieve it from the strong box. When he couldn't, he tried to destroy the evidence in the fire. He succeeded. The copy was too damaged to read.

But it was his biggest mistake. It led us to the conclusion that the thief wasn't trying to steal the list to keep it for themselves, they were trying to *destroy* it. Once we realized that, it was easy to work out that the only reason to destroy an insurance claim list was to stop us discovering which names *weren't* on it, not which names *were*. We'd been looking at it backwards. Since the insurance company also kept records of claimants who received payment, we could compare their records to the *Elsie May's* cargo manifest. Any missing names meant they were uninsured and had suffered losses when the *Elsie May* went down."

I fished the piece of paper from my bag with the four company names noted on it and handed it to the detective. "These four were uninsured. The top three could absorb the loss, but Bull—Mr. Douglas —could not. He was new to international trading. If you scour his books, you'll probably find a large consignment of whiskey was on the *Elsie May*. Its loss proved so devastating that he couldn't see a way to recover. It ruined his plans to move to the seaside."

"You'll find the distillery out the back," Harry told the detective.

Forrester nodded at one of the constables who disappeared through the door behind the bar. He returned a few minutes later with a bottle of whiskey labeled with The Douglas Company label.

He tucked it under his arm. "Evidence."

Detective Sergeant Forrester closed his notebook. "Do you have anything to add, Mr. Douglas?"

Bull sat silently, sullenly.

With a shake of his head, Forrester pocketed his notebook and indicated to the constables to escort Bull from the pub.

Nancy was having none of it, however. She marched up to Bull and kicked him in the shin. "Answer him!"

He yelped in pain then swore at her.

She responded by stamping her hands on her hips. "What have you got to say for yourself? You killed an innocent man in cold blood—"

"He wasn't innocent!"

Forrester removed his notebook again.

"He wasn't innocent," Bull snarled. "I trusted him. I watched him rise from nothing to become the head of a profitable company. He started out no better than me, Nance. No better than us. But he made something of himself so I trusted him, trusted he'd do the right thing by folk like us. When he gave me advice, I listened. And it cost me everything! I was all set to move the distillery to the seaside and live a better life there, and now I look like a fool for not going." He spat on the floor near her feet. "He deserved what he got."

She shook her head sadly. "Take him away and lock him up."

The detective nodded at his two constables. Between them, they untied Bull and marched him outside.

Forrester thanked us. "Come to the Yard as soon as you can, and I'll take your statements. You too, please, Nancy."

"Can we do it now, here?" she asked. "I can't leave the place unattended."

Harry and I walked out of the pub together while Nancy and the detective settled on stools as she gave her statement. "I wonder what'll happen to the pub now," I heard her say before the door closed behind us.

Somewhere in the distance, a church bell struck midday. It had been quite an eventful morning. Luckily I had time to give my statement at the Yard and go home and get ready before the restaurant opening. Indeed, I had time to complete a few other tasks beforehand.

* * *

AFTER LEAVING SCOTLAND YARD, we stopped at a teashop for a bite to eat. It was the first opportunity we'd had to dissect the morning's events. I gave a deep sigh after my first sip of tea, satisfied that it was all over and relieved that no one had been seriously injured. Harry's cut had stopped bleeding and it didn't seem to bother him.

He'd refused to have a doctor check it, but he promised to call at the hospital. "After I go home and get a new jacket." He inspected the torn, bloodied fabric and clicked his tongue. "This was a new suit. I can't even repair it discreetly. The cut is nowhere near the seam."

"Next time, be sure to ask the villain to be more considerate."

He tilted his head to the side and regarded me with a small smile. "I don't plan on there being a next time."

I blinked at him as the burn of tears pricked the backs of my eyes. I lowered my gaze so he couldn't see. "Indeed. It was too dangerous today. I didn't know he had a knife, but even so, I should never have suggested you confront him."

"You didn't. You wanted me to fight him only if he started it. Which he did."

"Even so…"

He reached across the table and clasped my forearm. "Cleo, it's just a minor cut. It's fine." His thumb stroked my sleeve before he released me and sat back. "We should call at Gooding and Plumtree to collect your fee."

"*Our* fee. They appointed you to lead the investigation into the theft, remember."

We finished our teas and paid at the counter. Harry opened the door for me.

"Speaking of the Goodings," I said as we walked. "Have you given your report about Jeremy to Mr. Massie?"

"I have an appointment with him later today. I'll present my findings then."

"Which are…?"

"That Jeremy is a good man from a good family."

"What about his relationship with Kitty Plumtree?"

"I believe him when he says they're simply friends. He saw her being bullied by Plumtree and wanted to protect her. I can't give him a negative account for that. In fact, I applaud him for being supportive when she needed it most."

It was unlike Harry to simply accept someone's word. He must have other evidence. The only evidence I could think would sway him would be accounts from witnesses who'd seen the two of them together on more than one occasion.

"You questioned the servants, didn't you?" I turned to him. "No. You went right to the top. You questioned Lowell, the butler."

His smile was coy. "Nothing like that. Witness statements can't be believed."

Very true. If there was one thing I'd learned from our investigation into the death of Tobias

Plumtree, depending upon witness accounts was fraught with problems. "So how can you be so sure he's not in love with her?"

"Because I spied on Jeremy and Hyacinthe when they met in secret one evening. I may not have a great deal of personal experience of love, but I know it when I see it in others, and those two are very much in love. There's no room in his heart for another."

His statement stunned me. He'd never been in love? Poor Miss Morris.

"Oh, uh, I see. That's...wonderful. For them, I mean."

Talking about the widow and her butler reminded me I wanted to clear up one thing before I put the investigation to bed. But first, I wanted to collect our fee from Gooding and Plumtree.

* * *

THE DOOR to Tobias Plumtree's fire-ravaged office was closed. Jeremy informed us as we passed it that builders were due that afternoon to provide a quote for renovations. He must not have been in there today as he was clean, his hair and clothes free of ash and soot. The smell of smoke still lingered, however, both in the office and on him, and he looked a little tired from the exertions and shock of the day before.

Despite that, his face lifted when we informed him and his father that the murderer had been found. "He is also your thief," I said, and told them how we'd caught Bull. "He has been arrested. Detective Inspector Forrester will need to hear your version of events and will contact you soon."

Mr. Gooding scrubbed a hand over his beard. "Remarkable. Well done, Armitage. Send me an account and I'll see you're paid immediately for your work."

"I will," Harry said, "but only because Miss Fox doesn't have an agency yet. This was all her doing. She was the lead."

"We did it together," I clarified. "There is no lead in our partnership."

Mr. Gooding gave a wry smile. "Partners, eh? Be careful Armitage. Trusting someone who isn't family is a tricky business."

I would usually take offense over such a swipe at my character but considering the difficulty he'd just been through with Tobias Plumtree, I decided not to quibble. He was perhaps justified to feel a little bruised by his partner's business decisions.

Jeremy escorted us back to the front desk where a woman waited, her head down so that the wide brimmed hat obscured her face. She looked up upon our arrival and smiled at Jeremy. It was Hyacinthe Massie.

"Darling," he said taking her hands in his. He

frowned as he looked past her. "How did you get away from your maid?"

She grinned. "We were at the flower show together. I told her I was feeling unwell but insisted she stay as I knew she'd been looking forward to it for weeks. I asked the coachman to bring me here."

"He'll tell your father."

"I don't care." She stood on her toes and kissed his cheek. "You smell smoky. Is everything all right?"

He took her face in his hands and searched it with a dreamy gaze. "Perfect now that you're here. Absolutely perfect. I've decided to speak to your father tonight. Life is too short, and I can't wait any longer. I love you, Hyacinthe, and I want to marry you. If he refuses to give his permission, we'll elope."

"He won't refuse. I'm sure of it."

I was quite sure of it, too. I gave Harry a little shove in the arm when we set foot on the pavement outside the office. "Go and speak to Mr. Massie now. You were right. Those two are very much in love and should marry."

"Our appointment isn't for another two hours."

"Go!"

He laughed as he walked off, tossing me a wave. "And have that cut looked at!"

He saluted me without turning around.

* * *

Mrs. Plumtree paid me without me having to ask. She may have disliked her husband, but she didn't want her son growing up thinking his father killed himself. The verdict of murder was a satisfactory outcome. She paid me generously for my "tireless endeavors," as she put it.

"You are quite remarkable, Miss Fox," she said, ringing the bell for Lowell. "Will you stay for tea? I'd like to get to know you better."

"I would like that, too, but I'm afraid I can't. I see your father hasn't arrived to help you."

Lowell entered, and Mrs. Plumtree watched him stand straight as an arrow by the door, silently waiting for instructions. She turned to me. "I asked him not to come, after all. He's not needed now that I have engaged a good lawyer to take care of my interests. My father was…relieved."

I bade Mrs. Plumtree good day. With my purse feeling pleasingly heavy, I followed the butler to the front door. I didn't immediately leave when he opened it.

"Tell me, Lowell, did you write that letter from MM?"

He hesitated for so long that I thought he was thinking up a lie, but to his credit, he didn't try to deny it. "A letter arrived addressed to Mr. Plumtree from MM professing anger at his past betrayal. But you are correct, Miss Fox. It wasn't that particular letter."

"You manufactured it."

"I re-wrote it from what I could recall of the original. I saw it on his desk but he must have thrown it away later. After your first visit in which you informed us you were investigating whether a murder had taken place, I went looking for it. I couldn't find it, so I decided to recreate it. A letter from MM did exist, Miss Fox. I didn't make it up. I have an excellent memory so you can be assured my version was an accurate copy."

The fact it was the copy of a real letter explained the response Harry had uncovered, the indents of which were scored into a blank piece of letterhead underneath. The response was addressed to Lady Mannix, not MM, and I was sure the handwriting would match Tobias Plumtree's if we compared it to something known to be penned by him.

"If you don't mind me asking, how did you know it was me?" Lowell asked.

"We knew who MM was and compared the handwriting in that letter to her diary. It was completely different. And the handwriting in the letter seemed masculine. When I thought about it further, I realized Plumtree wouldn't keep such a damning letter. At first, I assumed it was a fake, not the copy of a real one, but then I realized it had to be a copy of a lost letter rather than an invention as you couldn't have known about MM. You didn't know Tobias Plumtree in his former life. To write it from MM meant you'd seen those initials somewhere before."

"Who is she?"

"That's irrelevant now. Why did you do it?"

"To protect Mr. Plumtree's memory. I didn't want anyone thinking he killed himself. Indeed, I knew he hadn't. He may not have been a good man to all, but he was good to me. I thought the person who wrote that letter was most likely the murderer, so I recreated it to present to you as evidence."

"Why not just tell me about it?"

"Isn't physical evidence better than verbal? You may not have believed my account, but you believed that letter."

"Until we discovered it wasn't real."

He pressed his lips together. I wasn't expecting an apology, but I hoped to see a sign of regret. I saw nothing but blank indifference. It would have to do.

I trotted down the front steps, bag in hand, and went in search of a hansom cab. It was four o'clock. Soon, I'd need to get ready for the dinner. But first, I had one more call to make. It was the most important stop I'd make this afternoon, and it had nothing to do with the investigation. I only hoped it proved fruitful.

CHAPTER 17

No important event runs smoothly, and the opening night dinner for the Mayfair Hotel's new restaurant was no exception. An electrical issue earlier in the day meant that half the lights didn't work. The doors and windows had been left open to allow the fresh paint smell to fade, but thanks to a sudden shower, the tablecloths closest to the windows got wet. The wrong center pieces had been sent by the florist, and Mrs. Poole had made a last-minute change to the menu after a particular ingredient couldn't be sourced in time.

But Harmony managed it all with her typical no-nonsense efficiency. She suggested the room's atmosphere was more intimate with only half the lights working, and the women would prefer it anyway as everyone looked better in low lighting.

When Floyd was still scolding the florist, she asked the assistant to fetch some pink roses to compliment what had already been delivered. She sent maids off to borrow dry tablecloths from other restaurants in the area and she saw that Mrs. Poole had everything she needed in the kitchen. She was magnificent.

The only one who was unhappy was Flossy, but she came around. Initially annoyed at having another maid arrange her hair, she brightened when she saw herself in the mirror. She declared the new girl Harmony had found a good replacement.

The family had to be ready early to speak to the journalists Floyd had invited to tour the restaurant before the guests arrived. Uncle Ronald walked into the restaurant anteroom with a scowl on his face but, after seeing the impressive turnout, had begun to smile. There were dozens of newspapermen. We answered their questions about the renovations, the menu, and the decorations, but they were more interested in the guests and kept asking when they'd arrive.

The wait only increased their anticipation. They exchanged whispers with one another. They craned their necks whenever someone entered the restaurant, only to sigh with disappointment when they saw it was only a member of staff. Mr. Paisley from *The Illustrated Courier* even boldly asked who Miss Aldridge would sit beside, Floyd or Jonathon.

Uncle Ronald rounded on the fellow, but Floyd quickly intercepted before his father could scold the journalist. "Tonight is about the food and the restaurant, Mr. Paisley," he said breezily. "The guests are simply here to marvel alongside you."

And marvel they did.

The anteroom was beautiful in its own right. The walls were papered in classic white and gold. Fireplaces bookended the room, although the fires in them tonight were small. The fronds of palm trees planted in large pots reached up to the ceiling, and comfortable armchairs gave weary journalists somewhere to sit and write up their notes.

But the anteroom was a mere hint of what lay through the doors in the restaurant itself.

Mr. Chapman and the decorator had chosen a spring garden theme for the night. There were over a dozen potted trees between the tables, and pink roses covering the walls on thin wire trellis. A stone fountain occupied the center of the restaurant. It too was covered with climbing roses. Goldfish swam in the pool at its base, their scales flashing as they darted about. Potted ferns encircled the pool, their leaves dipping into the water. Each table was decorated with flowers and more ferns piled into low, wide vases as though they'd haphazardly grown there. It all looked like a fantasy woodland from a child's picture book. The light music played by the ensemble in the corner completed the magical scene.

At ten minutes to eight o'clock, Harmony emerged from the wings where she'd been watching proceedings. She wore an elegant evening gown of coral silk, even though she would take no part in proceedings. It was a shame, but her job as Floyd's assistant was to make sure everything ran smoothly behind the scenes while he took care of the guests and journalists. He was the face, but she was the beating heart, vital yet invisible.

She spoke in his ear and he politely asked the journalists to leave and wait outside. He joked with them, teased them about feasting on the leftovers if they wrote favorable articles. They laughed with him, but none saw the nervous clenching of his fist, the hard swallow of his throat.

Harmony slipped outside with the journalists to see that everything ran smoothly for the guests' arrival. Mr. Chapman, dressed in his tailcoat and top hat, took up his position at the door connecting the restaurant and anteroom, ready to welcome the diners. Behind him ranged the sommelier and the head waiters in formal black tie, and at the back were the rest of the waiters wearing crisp white aprons.

My uncle and aunt stood inside the anteroom door with Floyd beside them, then Flossy and me beside him. From my position, I could see the carriages rolling up and the invited diners stepping out. The journalists clamored to the velvet rope separating them from the guests, while their photographers' cameras flashed. I smiled as I greeted each new arrival with all the grace my uncle and aunt expected. Alongside the hotel's most important guests were members of high society, among them Consuelo Montagu, the American-born Duchess of Manchester, and Lady de Grey, a renowned patroness of the arts. Their presence was entirely due to their friendship with Aunt Lilian.

The other half of the guests had come because Floyd invited them. They were the younger members of society, the next generation of gatekeepers who would one day rule over the balls and parties. Some were still finding their feet on society's ladder, but they were already making a name for themselves as arbiters of taste and fashion.

Then there was a handful of third tier guests—mostly dancers and singers. They were small in number but accounted for a disproportionally large amount of the public's—and therefore the press's—interest.

Journalists elbowed one another out of the way to get a better view of the ladies' outfits so they could describe them in minute detail to their readers. Photographers vied for the best position to set up their equipment, but they needn't have been so anxious. Whether Floyd had instructed them to wait for their photograph to be taken, or they'd posed of their own accord, the stars of the stage knew how to make a grand entrance.

None more so than Miss Aldridge. Every lady wore a beautiful gown, of course, but hers was extraordinary. The seed pearls on the bodice of her white silk dress gleamed in the flickering light of the torches lining the path to the door. She'd positioned the white cloak trimmed with white feathers in such a way that it didn't obscure the intricate details of the gown. She wore a feathered headpiece studded with pearls, a pearl and diamond necklace at her throat. She could never have afforded such exquisite jewelry. Nor could Jonathon or Floyd. One bold journalist asked her where it came from, but she gave him an enigmatic smile and a wink that turned the fellow's cheeks pink.

Miss Aldridge greeted my uncle and aunt, then continued to Floyd. She lingered to whisper something in his ear. He smiled at her and kissed the back of her hand. Camera bulbs flashed. Journalists scrawled in their notebooks.

Then Miss Aldridge moved on, greeting Flossy and then me. We exchanged pleasantries but nothing of consequence. Yet if the journalists had seen the way our gazes connected, with an understanding passing between us, they would have hastily made notes.

But no one saw, and Miss Aldridge moved on to Jonathon, waiting nearby. He offered her his arm in full view of everyone outside. She took it, her wide eyes turned lovingly towards him. It sent the journalists and photographers into a frenzy. The celebrated beauty had made her choice.

Everyone's attention turned to Floyd to see his reaction to the snub. But he didn't notice. His warm gaze was fixed on the pretty woman behind Miss Aldridge. Her understudy. Not only did he kiss her hand but her cheek, too. It was clear to anyone watching that she was the object of his desire.

He played his part superbly.

Until that moment, I'd not known if my earlier visit to the theater would bear fruit. I'd found both Miss Aldridge and her understudy rehearsing and put my proposition to them. Miss Aldridge wouldn't admit that Jonathon had recruited her into his scheme to humiliate Floyd, but I could see she regretted causing Floyd distress by being photographed with his best friend on the same day she'd been photographed with him.

Upon returning to the hotel, I'd warned Floyd that he was going to lose Miss Aldridge, at least for tonight. Out of the two photographs of Miss Aldridge in this morning's newspaper, her face had been visible only in the one with Jonathon. It was for that reason that I'd asked her to seek *him* out tonight, and for her understudy to cling to Floyd's arm. With dark hair and trim figures, they were similar enough that she could be mistaken as the woman in Floyd's photograph.

The journalists would need to eat their words after tonight's display. It was clear to anyone who watched on that the understudy had engaged Floyd's affections, not Miss Aldridge.

I doubted my cousin would return to Miss Aldridge's bed after learning of her involvement in Jonathon's deception. He was too proud to forgive such a betrayal, and he wasn't in love with her.

With the last of the guests now inside, a footman closed the front doors, locking out the journalists and photographers, and we filed into the restaurant behind them. Mr. Chapman escorted my uncle and aunt personally to the main table, but I took a small detour before I sat.

I touched Jonathon's elbow to gain his attention. "I wish you well," I whispered. "In all things, but in particular your endeavor to avoid marriage."

He looked down at Miss Aldridge, seated at the table. "Avoid?"

"You've gone to great lengths to immerse yourself in scandal to ruin all hopes of a quick betrothal to a suitable heiress. No one would be so cruel to his best friend if it wasn't to avoid something he utterly detested. Congratulations, Jonathon. No father would want you for his daughter now."

Instead of looking upset at the thought, his eyes gleamed as he held my gaze. "I never wanted to ruin my hopes of marriage until recently. And I only wanted to deter my father's choice of bride, not my own."

I walked away, my pulse racing from the fraught exchange. My one consolation was that after tonight, I didn't have to be polite to Jonathon. I didn't have to dance with him at balls or exchange pleasantries at parties. His friendship with our family was over.

I sat at my appointed table and marveled at the place setting along with the guests. Special silver cutlery engraved with the hotel's emblem of an M inside a circle had been made for the restaurant. The emblem was repeated in gold and burgundy in the center of each pristine white plate. Crystal glasses sparkled as waiters poured the wine.

My uncle made a hearty speech that resulted in polite applause. Applause became exclamations of "ooh" and "ahh" as the guests tasted the first of many dishes. Cantaloupe was followed by jellied consommé and cream of mushroom soup. Next came salmon poached in wine, with truffles and stuffed paupiettes, followed by saddle of mutton, green peas stewed with lettuce, and potato balls cooked in butter. More dishes arrived—poached chicken with asparagus tips in cream, quail with grape leaves, lobster and asparagus salad, artichoke hearts with marrow sauce, crayfish soufflé with truffle slices. And finally, a sorbet of champagne to cleanse the palate, before a dessert of poached peaches with strawberry mousse. Each course was accompanied with a wine chosen by the sommelier to complement the dishes. By the time the flower arrangements were removed from the center of the tables and replaced with fresh fruit, everyone was either on their way to being drunk or already there.

I'd refused some of the wines. My evening's tasks were not yet complete, and I wanted an advantage over my final adversary. With many guests no longer staying in their appointed places, no one cared when I abandoned my seat at the family table and asked Mrs. Hessing's nearest neighbor if I could swap with him. He looked thoroughly relieved to escape her tireless conversation. Miss Hessing saw me sit beside her mother but, seated at the other end of the table, could do nothing about it.

I signaled to the waiter carrying a tray of glasses filled with fiery amber liqueur. "Dear Mrs. Hessing," I began as I accepted two glasses and handed one to her. "I have been wanting to speak to you all night, and finally I have my opportunity."

Her lips pressed into a thin line. "Miss Fox."

I sipped the liqueur. "Delicious."

She sipped too. "Indeed."

"My uncle spoke to me about your concerns, and I wanted to assure you that I completely concur. I am concerned about Mr. Liddicoat's intentions, too."

She'd been about to take another sip but lowered the glass. "You are?"

"Oh yes. I've grown very fond of your daughter. She's so sweet and kind. It's her greatest virtue but also a weakness. That kindness, coupled with your fortune, makes her a target of unscrupulous men."

She grunted an agreement into her glass.

"I've taken it upon myself to warn her of certain gentlemen with reputations, but I admit that Mr. Liddicoat wasn't one of them. You see, I heard nothing against him. However," I interjected when she opened her mouth to speak, "that doesn't mean he is altogether good. It may simply mean he is subtler than the others, cleverer."

She grunted again. "He's a gold digger, Miss Fox. Believe me. I know one when I see one."

Her conviction intrigued me. "Oh? What is it about him that concerns you?"

"His affection for my daughter."

"I don't understand."

"Miss Fox, you are a smart and worldly woman, so I shouldn't have to point out that no man would be interested in a dull, plain girl like Clare."

I'd witnessed Mrs. Hessing's poor treatment of her daughter before. She either ignored her, belittled her, or ordered her hither and thither. But this declaration was a new low. It was cruel beyond words, coming from a mother's lips.

"Only a man who wants her fortune would court her," she went on.

I was struck dumb for several moments in which I could only stare. As she took another sip of her liqueur, I finally rallied. "I say with the utmost sincerity that I love Miss Hessing as a friend. Can a man not love her, too?"

She made a guttural scoffing sound in her throat. "They are entirely two different kinds of love."

My fingers tightened around the stem of the small liqueur glass. I'd not yet taken a sip, nor would I. My plan was to have the sweet liquid go to her head and make her more amenable to the ace I was yet to play in our game.

An ace I played now. "I have a proposal for you. Do you recall the former assistant manager of the hotel, Mr. Harry Armitage?"

A wistful smile softened her features. "Of course. Dear Mr. Armitage. Always so agreeable, and so handsome, too. He is missed." She pointed her finger at my uncle. "I told Sir Ronald he should never have let him go. He was the Mayfair's greatest asset."

"He's a private detective now."

"So I hear."

"He's very good. One of his specialties is the investigation of potential suitors on behalf of the parents of heiresses. Fathers all over London have come to rely on his assessment before they give their consent—or not. I suggest you don't take Miss Hessing's word about Mr. Liddicoat but employ the services of Armitage and Associates to investigate him. If there is anything unsavory to uncover, Mr. Armitage will find it."

She didn't dismiss the notion immediately, but neither did she agree. "He is very new to the investigation business. How could he have made such an impression already?"

I leaned forward and lowered my voice. "Just this week, a rather *salty* gentleman hired Mr. Armitage to investigate the suitability of a *maritime* heir for his daughter. Mr. Armitage found nothing amiss and there'll be an announcement very soon."

She might not have known who the heir was, but she certainly understood my hint about the salty gentleman. "The Massie girl," she said on a rush of breath. From the inspired look on her face, I suspected she was already planning on asking Mr. Massie if he recommended Harry.

"What I propose is this. Hire Mr. Armitage, if you can manage to secure his services. I hear he's very busy and isn't taking on new clients, but I suspect he will make an exception for you as he holds you in very high regard."

I worried my praise was a little too obvious, but she took it in her stride. Perhaps such flattery was heaped on her all the time.

I forced myself to continue. "If he finds something that points to Mr. Liddicoat being a gold digger, then I will explain to Miss Hessing. I'll be there to comfort her."

"She'll descend into hysterics."

"I'll help her overcome her sorrow because she's my friend."

Mrs. Hessing swirled the liquid around the glass, watching it intently as it stuck to the sides and slid slowly down. "And if Mr. Armitage should find Mr. Liddicoat is genuine? You will have me consent to their marriage based on the say-so of the hotel's former assistant manager?" So much for her fondness of Harry. In her mind, he was, and always would be, beneath her.

"If Mr. Armitage proves Mr. Liddicoat is from a good family, is hardworking, honest, and never shown a history of pursuing heiresses, then I only ask that you agree to let him court Miss Hessing. Then let nature take its course."

She continued to swirl the liqueur, her lips tightening again before a small smile stretched them. "I do so wish to see Mr. Armitage again."

"I'm sure he would like to see you, too."

A smattering of applause became louder as Mrs. Poole entered the restaurant on my uncle's arm. She wore an evening gown, not her chef's whites, and gave a curtsy as elegant as any debutante in front of the queen. The diners cheered, and called out their appreciation for her dishes, naming their favorites. Uncle Ronald beamed as he joined in the applause.

Then he turned that applause to Floyd. My cousin looked startled but quickly recovered. He bowed then put out his hand to the shadows near the back of the restaurant. When nothing happened, he strode across and steered Harmony out by the elbow. She'd never looked more embarrassed, but she managed to nod her thanks. My uncle's clapping was loudest of all, his smile the broadest.

After the applause died away and the diners resumed their chatter, I went in search of her. She was still directing staff with one eye on the clipboard. I crushed it against her when I hugged her.

"It all went off marvelously," I said. "You were fabulous, but of course I knew you would be."

She laughed quietly as she returned the embrace. "Thank you, Cleo. Now go back out there and enjoy yourself."

I plucked two liqueur glasses off a passing waiter's tray and handed one to Harmony. "I'd rather stay here with you and watch proceedings unobserved."

And stay there I did, finally enjoying a drink with a friend.

* * *

FLOYD AWOKE EARLY the next morning and made sure Flossy and I awoke early too by sending Harmony to knock on our doors. She apologized then invited us to have breakfast all together in Floyd's suite.

We found him reclining on the sofa wearing a brocade and velvet dressing gown. Spread across the table and floor were newspapers. Dozens of them, ranging from *The Times* to the somewhat salacious *Society Herald* and everything in between.

He leapt up and thrust a copy of the *Morning Advertiser* at me, and a page from the *Pall Mall Budget* at Flossy. "Look! Look at what they're saying!"

I read the review. "This is wonderful. They're calling it a triumph."

"This journalist raves about the food," Flossy said, grinning. "How does he even know what it tasted like? Ah, here it says his source was none other than Miss Aldridge herself. It then mentions her gown. Wasn't she the most beautiful creature in the room! Oh. Sorry, Floyd."

I searched my article for any mention of her. There was a description of her outfit followed by mention of her being escorted by Jonathon, but no mention of Floyd.

He handed me a copy of *Lighthouse* with a smile. "Third paragraph."

I read the relevant part. It described what Miss Aldridge wore, how she joined Jonathon, and how Floyd seemed besotted with her understudy. It went on to say that unfounded rumors printed in other newspapers of a rivalry between friends for the affections of the mezzo soprano proved unfounded.

I smiled tentatively at him. "Are you all right? I know it must hurt, but—"

He grasped my shoulders and kissed my forehead. "It doesn't hurt nearly as much as it would have if last night was a failure, and it would have been a failure if the press had focused on our so-called love triangle and not the restaurant. Thank you, Cleo. It was a brilliant move."

"Jonathon was completely outsmarted," Flossy said.

"No need to sound so smug," her brother told her. "He's been a friend to me all these years. His betrayal stings."

"Pish posh to him, I say. He called me fat, you know."

"That was years ago. You've slimmed down since then."

"That isn't the point!"

He held up his hands and backed away. "Anyway, all's well. I'll no longer be seeing Miss Aldridge. Her understudy, on the other hand, is quite the..." Realizing he wasn't chatting to his chums, he cleared his throat and muttered, "Never mind."

The four of us reminisced about the evening over breakfast then went our separate ways. Downstairs in the foyer, I nodded at Mr. Hobart and Peter, farewelling guests in the foyer. I walked out with Goliath as he wheeled a trolley full of luggage before thanking Frank for opening the door for me. I foolishly asked how he was this morning, and he recited a litany of complaints before I told him I was in a rush.

I was in no particular hurry, however I was keen to see Harry and warn him before Mrs. Hessing arrived to engage his services. Not that I expected her to be making calls before midday, but better to be safe than sorry.

Luigi asked me how the dinner went as he made coffee then sent me on my way with two cups balanced one on top of the other. I managed to get them upstairs without spilling a drop, but paused at the door to Armitage and Associates. Miss Morris had been here a few times of late and I was reluctant to walk in on them. I listened with my ear to the door, only to have it suddenly wrenched open from the other side.

"Eavesdropping again?" Harry clicked his tongue. "So unbecoming in a lady."

"Yet a virtue in a detective." I handed him a

coffee cup. "Anyway, I'm no lady. Just ask Jonathon."

His impish smile turned to a scowl. "What's he done now?"

"Fallen victim to my cunning plan to save Floyd's hide."

He stepped aside to allow me to pass. "Poor fellow never guessed that making an enemy of you would be such a grave mistake."

"Poor fellow? Jonathon's the last person anyone ought to feel sorry for, particularly you."

"Why me?"

I sat at the desk and sipped my coffee, keeping my gaze averted as he sat. "I've come to warn you to expect a visit from Mrs. Hessing. She's going to engage your services to investigate a fellow by the name of Liddicoat with a view to him courting her daughter. Or not. Although I'm quite sure he's a nice man and not after her fortune."

"Why do you say that?"

"I like him."

"You liked Bull, too."

I sighed. He was right. I wasn't the best judge of character. "Give Mr. Liddicoat a fair and honest assessment, that's all I ask."

He indicated the door. "Why not just knock, or walk right in as you usually do?"

"Miss Morris has been here a lot of late, and I

didn't want to intrude. If I heard her voice, I would have left and waited in the café."

"Ah."

I narrowed my gaze. It may have been only one word—barely a word, in fact, more of a noise—but the tone implied there was a story behind it. I didn't want to hazard a guess what that could be. Didn't dare. It might have been good news for them as a couple and I didn't want to hear it. I wasn't ready.

Even though I didn't encourage him, Harry gave me an explanation anyway. "Miss Morris and I have parted ways."

I slowly released my breath and my reservations along with it. Now I wanted to hear more. I wanted to hear everything. However, I merely said, "Oh? That is a shame. She seemed so..."

"Perfect?"

"Yes. But if you thought so, why did you end it?" I lowered my cup to the desk. "Oh. Sorry. She ended it, didn't she?"

"No, I did. As to her perfection, it's the very thing that bothered me about her after a while."

"That doesn't make sense."

He frowned then, as if he didn't quite understand it either, he simply shrugged. "Perhaps I don't like perfect women."

I spluttered a laugh. "A word of advice, Harry, do *not* tell the next woman in your life that she's imperfect."

"The next woman in my life will be perfect *for me*. That's all that matters."

It was such a sweet thing to say that it sent a little ripple through me. To hear such a man as Harry whisper it to me...

I shook my head to free it of that thought. No good could come of it.

"It's thanks to you that I realized she wasn't right for me," he went on.

I blinked stupidly at him.

"You said I should be able to tell her about my past," he went on. "That I should be able to tell her anything. But a part of me knew she wouldn't accept it, that she'd think less of me. Not that she would have admitted it. Anyway, I don't want to be with someone who can't accept my past." He saluted me with his teacup. "So thank you, Cleo. You saved me from making a mistake."

I smiled weakly. If I were a true friend, I'd tell him he hadn't given her a chance, that she may have surprised him by accepting his past if only he'd confided in her. But I couldn't bring myself to say it.

After a fortifying sip of coffee, I was able to speak about the thing that was utmost on my mind. "I am glad to hear that she didn't end it with you because of me. I mean, because of all the time we spend investigating together, that is. I would have felt guilty if that was the reason."

"It wasn't," he said lazily. "Now, tell me how last night went. Aside from making an enemy of Jonathon, and engorging yourself on rich food and expensive wine, did it go well?"

I indicated the newspapers on his desk. One was even open to an article about the restaurant. "You don't need to ask me. It's all in there."

He picked up the newspaper and skimmed the article. "If I want to hear how Miss Aldridge resembled a swan then yes, I can read these." He tossed the newspaper on top of the others. "But I suspect your observations are not only keener than the journalists' but more entertaining, too."

"Harry," I chided, "you know I don't like to gossip."

He crossed his arms on the desk and matched my teasing smile with one of his own. "You say that, but I believe you love it. You have an inquisitive mind, and what better way to find things out than listen to gossip. You wouldn't be a good detective if you didn't."

I set down the empty cup and picked up my bag. "And I wouldn't be a good businesswoman if I gave away all my secrets to my greatest rival." I stood. "Good day, Harry. Do let me know when you need assistance with a case."

"Who says I'll need your assistance? Perhaps you'll need mine."

"Perhaps I will."

One thing I was sure about—Harry and I would investigate together again. We made a good team. It was also becoming clear to me that neither of us wanted to work without the other.

Available 5th December 2023 :
MURDER AT THE POLO CLUB
The 7th Cleopatra Fox Mystery

A MESSAGE FROM THE AUTHOR

I hope you enjoyed reading MURDER AT THE CROWN AND ANCHOR as much as I enjoyed writing it. As an independent author, getting the word out about my book is vital to its success, so if you liked this book please consider telling your friends and writing a review at the store where you purchased it. If you would like to be contacted when I release a new book, subscribe to my newsletter at http://cjarcher.com/contact-cj/newsletter/. You will only be contacted when I have a new book out.

ALSO BY C.J. ARCHER

SERIES WITH 2 OR MORE BOOKS

The Glass Library

Cleopatra Fox Mysteries

After The Rift

Glass and Steele

The Ministry of Curiosities Series

The Emily Chambers Spirit Medium Trilogy

The 1st Freak House Trilogy

The 2nd Freak House Trilogy

The 3rd Freak House Trilogy

The Assassins Guild Series

Lord Hawkesbury's Players Series

Witch Born

SINGLE TITLES NOT IN A SERIES

Courting His Countess

Surrender

Redemption

The Mercenary's Price

ABOUT THE AUTHOR

C.J. Archer has loved history and books for as long as she can remember and feels fortunate that she found a way to combine the two. She spent her early childhood in the dramatic beauty of outback Queensland, Australia, but now lives in suburban Melbourne with her husband, two children and a mischievous black & white cat named Coco.

Subscribe to C.J.'s newsletter through her website to be notified when she releases a new book, as well as get access to exclusive content and subscriber-only giveaways. Her website also contains up to date details on all her books: http://

cjarcher.com She loves to hear from readers. You can contact her through email cj@cjarcher.com or follow her on social media to get the latest updates on her books:

facebook.com/CJArcherAuthorPage

twitter.com/cj_archer

instagram.com/authorcjarcher